The Great and The Small

Jan McCarthy

Rev. date: 05/16/2014

To order additional copies of this book, contact:
Xlibris LLC
0-800-056-3182
www.xlibrispublishing.co.uk
Orders@xlibrispublishing.co.uk
633267

CONTENTS

Chapter One: Percy Chills Out....................................... 11
Chapter Two: A Discovery... 18
Chapter Three: A Bacon Sandwich
                       and Briefing 23
Chapter Four: A Rather Appealing Tenant 28
Chapter Five: A Good Reputation.................................. 32
Chapter Six: Wellington 37
Chapter Seven: Greytown 43
Chapter Eight: Carol Pays a Visit 47
Chapter Nine: The Trouble With Carol........................... 52
Chapter Ten: Constitutional... 56
Chapter Eleven: Co-Opted 61
Chapter Twelve: Archie Unsettled...................................... 68
Chapter Thirteen: Affinity.. 75
Chapter Fourteen: New Arrivals 81
Chapter Fifteen: Topiaryphobia 85
Chapter Sixteen: Huruhuru 90
Chapter Seventeen: An Experimental Gardener....................... 95
Chapter Eighteen: Archie and Friends 100
Chapter Nineteen: A Moment 104
Chapter Twenty: Coffee and Biscuits............................... 108
Chapter Twenty-One: An Avid Student.................................. 111
Chapter Twenty-Two: Where is Roger? 116
Chapter Twenty-Three: Vegetables.. 121
Chapter Twenty-Four: House of Parrots................................... 125
Chapter Twenty-Five: A Significant Kiss 131
Chapter Twenty-Six: Ann-Marie Takes Stock 136

Chapter Twenty-Seven: A Fresh Start............................141

Chapter Twenty-Eight: Gladstone.................................146

Chapter Twenty-Nine: In the Meadow............................151

Chapter Thirty: Stopped in their Tracks..................156

Chapter Thirty-One: Archie Gets a Spring-Clean 161

Chapter Thirty-Two: Dinner and a Movie 167

Chapter Thirty-Three: A Garden Party 175

Chapter Thirty-Four: Native Wildlife........................181

Chapter Thirty-Five: Archie Receives Orders................189

Chapter Thirty-Six: Brandston..............................192

Chapter Thirty-Seven: Sister and Brother.....................197

Chapter Thirty-Eight: The Yew Band 204

Chapter Thirty-Nine: The Fate of Roger.....................210

Chapter Forty: Further Enlightenment.................215

Chapter Forty-One: Shopping Bags and Bathers 219

Chapter Forty-Two: Percy Gets a Fright 224

Chapter Forty-Three: Wedding Plans 228

Chapter Forty-Four: In Which there is
                        Overwhelming Provocation 232

Chapter Forty-Five: A Day of Love 239

Chapter Forty-Six: Bad News..............................246

Chapter Forty-Seven: Celebrations 252

Chapter Forty-Eight: Dinner and a Surprise 259

Chapter Forty-Nine: Gnome Sweet Gnome 262

"And I saw the dead, great and small, standing before the throne, and books were opened. Another book was opened, which is the book of life. The dead were judged according to what they had done as recorded in the books."

Revelation 20:12

There was a last great gathering of Gnomes in the Black Forest on Midsummer's Day 1820. All nine clans were present in force. The mood was grim. Everywhere forests were being felled to make space for humans: for their homes, for their factories, for their buying-and-selling places. The landscape, once so green and wild, was becoming fragmented as roads, canals and railway tracks were laid down. It was no longer safe to cross from one clan's territory into another for friendship gatherings, or for councils of war. The Elves, Pixies and Fairies were long gone. Only the Gnomes remained of the Little People. The last Leprechaun had thrown himself off a cliff into the Irish Sea in despair. As the moon rose, there was silence, marked only by a shuffling of small boots. At last, the Great Leader of all the clans spoke, pulling on his snowy beard, which fell to his knees: "Brothers," he said, his voice breaking with emotion, "Who can tell what the future holds for the Gnomish People? Not I. But Mother Earth sees, and the Sacred Trees see, and the Moon sees. Gnomes know the meaning of patience. Let us each find a place of safety, caring for one another as best we may. Humans are in love with technology, but one day, perhaps, they will awaken from their dream and seek the ancient paths once more. And, brothers, they will need our help, as they did long ago, when we first taught them how to live in harmony and in humility. We must be ready when they do. Taller they may be, but their heads are stupid with ideas of making their lives more comfortable. Go now, but be ready. Look for good men, for they will arise in time of need. When you find them, be gentle with them, for their own kind will not understand them. They will be alone, but for us. Farewell, my brothers, and may your minds and hearts be filled with courage." The Great Leader bowed to his brother Gnomes, and one by one they each returned his bow. Then, as silently as they had come, they turned and left the glade, one clan at a time, to wait—and to prepare . . .

Chapter One

PERCY CHILLS OUT

The Secretary of State for Work and Pensions awoke from a terrifying dream in which he was being chased by a small but determined army of tiny, fat men with beards and pointy hats. He often had such dreams but, having no belief in supernatural beings, or in prophecy, always dismissed them as soon as he became conscious. There was enough in the real world to terrify him.

The bedside alarm clock told him that it was 10.30 a.m. on Sunday 27th April. He had not long had his 60th birthday. He yawned, stretched, and put out a perfectly pedicured row of piglet-pink toes from under the bed covers whilst rubbing his eyes. The air of the bedroom was warm, which meant that the housekeeper, Mrs. Morrish, was already at work. Her first task every day was to switch on the central heating and turn it up full blast.

The Secretary of State was a person for whom the French would use the delightful adjective 'frileux'—that is, he was sensitive to the cold. He could never understand why so many of his colleagues and family members rushed off to the slopes as soon as winter brought the first snowfalls. His personal preference, had he been planning a holiday, would have been for warmer climes: a Tuscan villa, a tour of the Caribbean on a luxury yacht—but he hated travelling. The paparazzi were everywhere these days, not to mention the Common People with their eternal iPhones, and those damned cameras. You had only to smile at something you shouldn't be smiling at, and it would be all over Twitter within a few seconds. He wished government had the power to control social media. Having used the media themselves for centuries for propaganda purposes, they were alarmed to find their tame dragon was now turning round to bite them on the behind.

No, what he preferred, especially now that old age was creeping up on him, was the security and comfortable routine of home—that is, of his country house, Brandston Manor, with its acres of land surrounding the main buildings, its long approach lined with security cameras, and its high perimeter wall, patrolled by the private security company which was the current favourite of the government in office. Having recently come under attack from barrage after barrage of what he thought of (and sometimes referred to) as the Peasantry, protesting against the so-called 'austerity measures' imposed by the Cabinet, he relied completely on F5's ability to keep the rabble from his door, from his garden, from anywhere within half a mile of him.

His wife Marjory and two children: twenty-eight-year-old divorcée Elspeth and twenty-six-year-old bachelor Tim, had already voted with their feet several weeks ago, though the Press were as yet unaware of the fact, since it had all been dressed up as a lengthy visit to relatives in New Zealand. His wife had been unhappy with the machine-gun wielding security men who walked the grounds and went everywhere with the Secretary of State and his entourage. "But Percy, how do you know they're reliable?" she had asked, whilst seated at her dressing-table mirror, applying the same shade of coral pink lipstick she had used for three decades. "Reliable, dear?" he had echoed, in a voice that wobbled with barely-hidden panic. "I mean, what kind of scrutiny do they put them through when they recruit them?" she had insisted, turning to him with a frown. Marjory's frown, which Percy for some reason found rather sexy, was the nearest she ever got to a bad temper, so he took it—and what she was saying—seriously. "You know I'm not paranoid, Percy, but I have heard that some are ex-cons with histories of violence, fraud and all kinds of things. And it's not as if they have the morals . . . or standards . . . of the police . . . I mean to say, they don't have to be *transparent*, do they? You know what I mean. *Publicly accountable* and all that . . ."

He had been rather stumped for an answer, if the truth were told. It had never occurred to him to question the judgement of the Prime Minister when, one winter's morning, without warning, he had found himself flanked by his new bodyguards. He had responded to Marjory's question with a garbled sentence or two about "doing the best we can in the circumstances". Like his colleagues, he had accepted the advent of F5 with their immaculately-ironed black shirts and shiny, peaked caps as a necessity, for there was unrest all over the country, and his personal security was uppermost in his mind most of the time. It was easy to ignore the guns they carried most of the time: being black, they were camouflaged against the uniforms. You could almost fool yourself they weren't even there—at least, until they were shouldered and pointed at someone.

Part of the Government's austerity measures had involved making severe cuts to the police force, leaving them with no other option, when it had come to the London Olympics, but to hand over the security contract to F5. However, the resulting balls-up had left the Prime Minister with no other choice but to call in the military. Which was ironic, since the armed forces had also been the victim of cuts, with whole regiments, their history steeped in glory, disappearing as if overnight. Percy did not want to think too deeply about the whys and wherefores of the matter. One of his secretaries had passed on letters from war veterans in his own constituency that were full of expletives, and he had accidentally read a few before he had realised that they were withdrawing their votes from his party because they now considered him a traitor to the nation, and had quickly put them through the shredder, his face as red as the ministerial red box on his desk. He wondered if it would ever become possible to put Tweets through some kind of virtual shredder. He made a note to himself to ask one of the 'techies' about it when he got back to his office.

The Secretary of State eased himself slowly out of his cosy bed with its royal purple silk eiderdown, slipped into his leather slippers and tartan dressing-gown, and padded across to the huge picture window that afforded a view across the rose garden and the lake. He stretched himself and pressed the button that opened the curtains with a soft and satisfying swish. He was missing his wife: her cheerful good morning kiss, her reassuring smiles, but he was not going to think of her if it meant thinking about why she had gone off and left him in the lurch. Next to his wife, the thing that gave Percy the greatest pleasure was the sight of his estate, spread out before him on a Sunday morning. Especially when, having stayed up late the night before, he'd caught up on all his paperwork.

The flattish landscape that presented itself to view was turning greener by the day, but spring was—everyone agreed, even the cynics—over a month late this year. There were still small patches of frozen snow here and there, and the crocuses, which should have been in full bloom by now, were barely showing in the urns at the top of the steps that led down from the terrace to the gravel walk. He opened the window nearest to him just a crack, to smell the air. He found his stomach was churning. "All this crap about climate change!" he muttered, "Can't a man enjoy the view from his bedroom window without thinking about bloody greens and their bloody prophecies of doom?" He turned from the window too quickly, tripped over the edge of the Turkey carpet, and swore under his breath. He was always tripping up. His father had made him pick up his feet like a soldier in his boyhood, and he had rebelled against this command in his teens by deliberately dragging his feet. The habit had stuck. A journalist had once remarked that Percy walked as though he was 'skating on thin ice'. The irony of the comment had not escaped poor Percy.

He shook himself vigorously, like someone shaking a rag doll, and bent down to touch his toes, flopping from the waist, allowing his hands to swing, and remembering not to lock his knees. This was a stress-busting technique his therapist had taught him, and he had found it extremely useful, though a little risky to try in a confined space—for example, in the loo at the House of Commons. He stood up, feeling rather dizzy. His face, in the dressing-table mirror, looked like a tomato. "Shoo! Shoo! Out with the negative! In with the positive!" he said, waving his hands in front of him and pulling up his mouth into a smile. He spent five minutes doing some tai chi exercises: 'painting the rainbow', 'the dragon waves its tail' and 'carrying the sun', which made him feel much more powerful and confident.

Once he could breathe normally, he turned back to the window which, because he was a few feet away from it, now afforded him only a view of the sky. Just then he remembered that it was Sunday—his favourite day of the week, for obvious reasons—and so, slapping his bald, pink head with both hands, he did a little skip and, taking a short detour to the bathroom, he proceeded to the morning-room, where breakfast was already laid before a blazing log fire. Percy sat down in his favourite green leather armchair and lifted each dish cover in turn: bacon with scrambled eggs lay under the first, blueberry muffins (home-made) under the second, kippers under the third. Percy had a somewhat sensitive stomach (especially just after doing the ragdoll flop), and never knew in advance what would tempt his appetite, so his cook was under instructions to 'do the works' every day. He opted for kippers. They were juicy and delicious. He helped himself to three.

"I think I may go for a stroll with Roger after breakfast," he said out loud to the empty room. The family portraits in their ornate frames looked silently down at him, but as he surveyed their unmoving faces, he imagined he felt their unspoken approval. The Manor had stood for five hundred years, and the financial investment it had cost successive generations of Brandstons had been worth it. It was a beautifully-designed, solidly-built, tastefully modernised, handsomely furnished testament to canny investment. In the olden days, those investments had been in anything from horses to slaves. Nowadays, Percy's stockbroker handled his portfolio, but the bulk of his income came from rental properties, oil (extraction and refinery), and a payday loan company that was proving to be a delightful little money-spinner. It had ever been the custom of the Lord of the Manor to 'beat the bounds' on Sunday mornings, whilst his wife and children went to the village church to do the religious side of the family duties. It would not have occurred to this latest Lord of the Manor to attend church in his wife's absence. He subscribed, in his heart and sometimes out loud, to the maxim 'Children—Church—Kitchen' when it came to the role of women. He loved his wife dearly, for the simple reason that she had always fulfilled her traditional duties perfectly, and without question.

Percy had been careful to choose a wife who had been raised in the traditional way, but knew of some alarming cases of well-bred politicians' wives breaking away and rebelling, and was grateful that his Marjory had remained true to her vocation as his spare rib. They had been brought together by their respective parents as soon as Percy had been sent down prematurely from Cambridge University (for a misdemeanour involving a college servant known to be a left-wing activist and a pot of red paint). Her family had money; his had land, a name, and even more money. It had been—the society columnists had agreed—a match made in heaven. Marjory was the sensible eldest of five sisters with a doting uncle of whom she was the favourite, for she spoke little and appeared to listen and Uncle Morty liked to hold forth.

Uncle Morty Bland had been an art collector during the Second World War. He had bequeathed his niece enough *objets d'art* to fill two Brandston Manors, and had taught her to take a rational approach to life. Reality, said Uncle Morty, could never equal the beauty and glory of a fine painting or beautifully-crafted sculpture, so why upset oneself? When life takes a downturn, distance yourself from the world and have a therapeutic rummage through your china cabinets, and you will soon be feeling fine. Fortunately for Marjory Brandston née Bland, there were several dozen cabinets containing fine china and antiques in Brandston Manor, and at least one in every room, including the upstairs bedrooms, the nursery and Marjory's *boudoir*. It didn't matter what was going on, or where she was: she could flop into a chair, contemplate a teapot, a clock or a figurine, and pull herself together again.

Percy Brandston poured himself a cup of coffee from the pot, and began with kippers and toast, before moving on to the preserves. "Yes, after all," he said to his silent audience, "Here at home a man may safely enjoy the fruits of his labours." He breathed a contented sigh as he tasted the delicious coffee, specially imported from the higher slopes of Macchu Picchu, and proceeded to spread butter lavishly over his kippers. Later on, after his walk, he would ring his wife and speak to his children, and then he could look forward to the wireless, the papers and his dinner of roast beef and apple pie . . .

Chapter Two

A DISCOVERY

It was just after midnight on that fateful day when two of F5's finest, Damien Grey and Harry Posnic, stopping to smoke a cigarette and call in to HQ to render their hourly report, found the corpse of Percy Brandston lying in a ditch under an ash tree at the far end of the water meadow. It was their favourite spot for a smoke, for the ash tree had large roots that spread wide and were perfect for lounging on, and the huge trunk afforded a screen so that one's red end could not be seen through the Manor House observatory's telescope, or by the boss if he happened to look through his binoculars.

Damien and Harry were both respectable members of their profession and, as it happened, they had been work colleagues for the past fifteen years. The previous summer, they had been made redundant from an electrical goods factory that was in the process of going to the wall. They had received news of their redundancy on the same day and gone to a pub in the East End to drown their sorrows and discuss other employment options, together with a handful of other colleagues who had all lost their jobs on the production line. While thus occupied, they had bumped into a group of F5 employees who were enjoying a pint or two after a shift. One of the F5 men had overheard part of their conversation and suggested they apply for jobs with their company, which they referred to as 'The Firm'. Damien had a pregnant wife and two young children to support. Harry had a live-in partner and an ex-wife to whom he paid maintenance. Neither could afford the luxury of a career break. They, and two others, had jumped at the chance, and had been taken on straight away.

Nine months into the job, they were enjoying themselves. The work was seldom irksome, for they had been assigned almost immediately to protect the Secretary of State, which meant, for the most part, patrolling the grounds of Brandston Manor, or forming a cordon around Percy Brandston when his car entered or left the gates. Another team took over when he was travelling. The most trouble they had yet encountered was when, occasionally, a group of protesters gathered outside the gates to take Mr. Brandston to task over the effect his government's austerity measures were having on the more vulnerable in society: the disabled, the long-term sick, the jobless, the homeless, the elderly—those who were on a low income and/or dependent on benefits. Those who, if they had tightened their belts any more, were apt to cut themselves in two. Not the most dangerous people, certainly not difficult to control. While they felt bad to be waving guns in the faces of people who one could hardly class as a real threat—especially those in wheelchairs and those who were clearly emaciated and ragged ("Like something from Dickens," as Damien had said more than once)—they were only too grateful for the regular income they received. And, as yet, nobody had managed to do more than flick a few spots of yellow paint over Percy Brandston's bespoke clothing.

Colleagues from the factory (which had now closed down) who had not taken up the opportunity with F5 were still signing on at the local Job Centre and having a hard time of it, especially the older ones. The first time they had been to sign on, they had been asked "So, what have you done to find work?" which was ironic. Some had started at the factory as sixteen-year-old apprentices, and had taken pay cuts when orders had fallen, in order to help keep the business going for everyone. Some had gained promotion to supervisory roles because of their excellence at the job. Some had been training new workers for years. Each had invested in the factory in one way or another and, in spite of the rather repetitive nature of the work, they had been happy to think of working there until retirement. Now, a few months into joblessness, they were being told to 'get skilled up', to learn how to make job applications online, or that their CVs weren't good enough, or that their 'interview skills' needed improvement, and they were feeling deeply angry.

The cigarette break had turned into a two-cigarette break. One of their former colleagues, Dan McCree, had just committed suicide after a session at a so-called 'return to work agency'. He had been assigned to this agency by the Job Centre to improve his employment prospects, and had just completed a refresher course in forklift truck driving, as his Job Advisor had dropped strong hints about work opportunities coming up shortly at a car works some twenty miles away. He had worked out that, on the minimum wage, he would just about be able to do the commute if he spent the week nights away from his family and stayed with his sister, whose home was near the car works.

His wife was unhappy at the prospect of seeing him only at weekends, but had accepted the idea when she had seen the hopeful smile on her husband's face: the first smile she had seen in weeks. They would manage somehow. The Government were promising every day that their austerity measures were working, and that the economy was recovering. The old factory might even be bought up and reopened. The thing was to look on the bright side. Keep your spirits up. Nobody would give a job to someone who looked defeated and miserable.

At the end of the refresher course, he had been told that the car works had already recruited workers from an employment agency a fortnight earlier, and that they had their full complement: he was not needed after all. Dan McCree had gone straight from the agency to the Thames and thrown himself in, after wrapping his head in duct tape to ensure he would be unable to breathe, if the instinct to survive betrayed him.

Damien and Harry sat with their backs to the solid, somehow comforting trunk of the ash tree and puffed away for a while in silence. "My God," said Harry after a minute or two, "When you think of what state of mind he must have been in . . . It doesn't bear thinking about, does it?" "No," agreed Damien, "To have been so far gone he forgot he was leaving his family in the lurch. He loved them a lot. Always with the photos out at lunch break, showing us how much the kids had grown, and how beautiful his wife was . . ." Harry nodded. "I hear she's gone back up north to her folks in Liverpool. Poor woman. What will she tell the kids when they start asking?" Damien frowned, "Christ knows!" he said angrily, "How about, *Daddy got tired of trying as hard as he could and being told he wasn't trying hard enough by some git in a suit?*" Harry passed him an extra strong mint, and they sat for a while, sucking on their mints in silence.

It was then that a small movement in the patch of weeds on the downward slope that lay between them and the ditch caught their attention. They both stiffened, and their hands went to their hip holsters. They switched on their powerful head torches and directed the light towards the ditch. It was about three feet deep. There was a ploughed field on the other side. Whatever had been moving had disappeared. "What the . . . ?" breathed Harry. Damien joined the beam of his head torch to his colleague's and caught his breath. The two men stood up slowly, keeping one hand on their holsters while the other went to their breast pocket radios. They waited in silence for any further sign of movement, but all was still and silent. It was then that the combined beams from their torches picked up the body lying face up in the muddy ditch. The stream, which flowed along on the far side of the corpse, bubbled along regardless.

Percy Brandston's face was as pale as the moon which hung in the sky above. It was immediately obvious that he was dead, for his eyes were staring and his mouth open, caught in mid-scream. Surprising that no-one had heard cries. The assault must have been sudden and swift. Perhaps his scream had been cut short by a hand, or some other object placed over his mouth. Harry and Damien moved closer and hunkered down. On closer inspection, the poor unfortunate seemed to have bled out. Even his socks and shoes were soaked in blood. "My God! What the hell happened here?" exclaimed Harry. He looked at his colleague in horror. There was silence for a long minute. They didn't dare to utter what was on their minds: that somehow, someone had got past the patrols and killed the Secretary of State, right under their noses. Damien was as white as a sheet. "Let's call this in," he said, in a voice that was cracking with terror. "Be careful what you say," whispered Harry, "This could be bad for us . . ."

Percy Brandston's dog Roger was nowhere to be found when a complete sweep of the estate, including all the buildings, had been conducted. He was presumed to have escaped through a hole in the perimeter wall, though the detectives who were eventually invited to attend could not find one large enough that showed signs of recent disturbance. The entire force of twenty F5 security men assigned to protect Percy Brandston was immediately stood down and replaced with armed police and MI5.

The F5 employees, and their area manager, were corralled in the barn and kept under proper guard. Mobile phones and tablets were confiscated, but not before three or four of the security men had phoned home with the news that the Secretary of State for Work and Pensions was dead.

The disappearance of Roger the Labrador was not the only unfathomable mystery that presented itself: Mr. Brandston had clearly been bitten to death. And by very small teeth. Lots of sets of very small teeth. The dog seemed somehow to have slipped his lead, or he would probably have been considered the prime suspect, in spite of the fact that his bite was far bigger than those found on the body. The biggest mystery of all was that there was subsequently found to be no DNA anywhere on the body, or on the dog-lead, or at the scene, apart from that of Percy and his canine companion. Swabs were taken with cotton wool and saline from around every single bite mark—of which there were thousands—and not one of them yielded a single clue. The only immediately evident fact was they appeared to be in very organised arrowhead-shaped patterns . . .

Chapter Three

A BACON SANDWICH AND BRIEFING

"I've never seen the like," pronounced Inspector Masters of the local police, over a cup of tea and a bacon sandwich in the canteen the following lunch-time. He was making the most of a spare half hour to catch up, having had nothing to eat for twelve hours. His team had just come on shift, but he had been called in by the Detective Chief Inspector in the middle of the night, to be briefed at the scene of the crime. Not that he had been allowed more than a quick tour. The big boys were all over this one. He'd never in the whole of his forty-five year career seen so many officers, uniform, plain clothes and forensics people wearing all-in-ones—or men in expensive overcoats trying to keep their shoes out of the mud and talking into state-of-the-art mobile phones—in one place.

It had crossed his mind immediately that there were too many of them there, trampling around in the dark, and that some of them might even be there expressly to contaminate the crime scene, rather than to gather evidence. If that were the case, it wouldn't be the first cover-up in human history.

The team had gathered around Masters, some of them greedily eyeing his sandwich. He didn't have much to say to them. So far, he had not been told what level of involvement was expected of him and his colleagues. Probably policing the road outside the Secretary of State's mansion and nearby junctions, where the press and members of the public were likely to gather. Possibly patrolling the perimeter of

Brandston Manor, but from the outside of the boundary, to prevent incursions. He was due to see the DI in twenty minutes.

"If he'd been in the stream a few yards further on, I'd have suspected piranhas had got loose from an aquarium. Even his earlobes had been bitten through in places. They've already called in a team of top forensic pathologists to see if they can find any DNA. Drawn a blank so far. My wife thinks it was aliens." Most of the officers who had gathered round to listen risked a chuckle at this, but one or two turned pale themselves, especially those who regularly watched the Sci Fi Channel on TV. It was a sign of the times that no-one risked contradicting the idea that aliens might have killed a government minister. The world was growing weirder and less predictable by the minute.

"Sir," asked a detective, full of enthusiasm to do his duty for Queen and Country, "Has anyone been out with the dogs yet, to see if they can pick up the trail of Roger the Lab? I'd like to volunteer, if not, Sir. There have been cases of dogs picking out the perpetrator, haven't there, Sir?" Detective Inspector Masters looked at him wearily over the top of his glasses. Detective Sergeant Jim Jackson, whom everyone good-naturedly called Brillo, because his short, fuzzy, steel-grey head of hair looked exactly like a popular brand of scouring pad, was a valued member of his team. He had been on the force for ten years, and he had good instincts and a thorough approach to his work. His excitability never got in the way of his police work—it just gave him extra energy. When the rest of the team were relying on coffee and pinching themselves to stay awake, Brillo was the one who kept them all focused by his constant questions, insistence on reviewing evidence and looking for new angles, punching away at his computer keyboard, and pacing up and down.

"All in good time, Jim, all in good time," Masters answered, his mouth full of bread, brown sauce and bacon, "You'd be well advised to get some food inside you while you can. I think we're in for the long haul with this investigation. That's if we get a look in." He managed a tired smile, for Jackson reminded him of himself years ago:

all bright-eyed, bushy-tailed and in a rush to solve and sew up a case. In his experience, it didn't last. The least he could do was give the lad a bit of gentle advice and encouragement. Jackson beamed back and elbowed past his colleagues to join the queue for food. "And the same goes for all of you who are on my squad," Masters added, "See you back in the office on the hour. The rest of you, no spreading gossip and rumours. You know the score. The media will be all over this, and if I find out anyone's been tattling, I will personally be all over you! Until I receive further orders, we carry on as normal. Cases and tasks already assigned, in other words."

There were disappointed looks, and a chorus of "Yessir!" as Masters' team, one by one, picked up plastic lunch trays from the pile and joined their colleague in the queue. They all chose to sit close together, though not at Masters' table, seeing he was in a hurry and they didn't want to disturb his thoughts. They munched their egg and chips, salads, lasagne and macaroni cheese, and the conversation was all about football results, reality TV programmes, and where to get the best deal on a summer holiday abroad. It wasn't just a matter of loyalty to Masters, and obeying his instructions. They were all well-trained professionals who knew what was expected of them, and that taking a ghoulish interest in a case that would probably not come their way, especially when there were other cases of equal importance—though not involving famous people—sitting on their desks, was not the done thing. As they chatted away, each of them was reviewing his or her caseload, deciding priorities, making mental notes of phone calls to make, or people to interview, or reports to write.

Masters wiped the bacon grease from his fingers, brushed the crumbs off his jacket and stood up. Before he left the canteen, he scanned the scene, feeling a rush of pride, trust and satisfaction. It had taken him years to put together this team, and every one of them had excellent qualities which, when combined, amounted to a lot more than the sum of their parts. Two had received bravery awards. One had an eidetic memory. Another was the most emotionally-intelligent individual he had ever met, and was the one to whom he preferred to assign the unpopular task of communicating bad news to next of kin. Another was a wizard with the office computers: whenever they were misbehaving, which they all seemed to do at once, all he had to do was walk up and down the rows of desks, and the machines would suddenly sort themselves out, as if they were mabinogi: apprentices in the presence of the Chief Druid.

Now for his meeting with Detective Chief Inspector Lionel Baird. Masters took the stairs two at a time, knowing that Baird would have his coffee percolator on, and the offer of a cup was a given. Baird and Masters went back a long way, and the mutual respect they enjoyed served to strengthen every aspect of their work. They also ran half marathons together, to raise funds for the Police Benevolent Fund, their diet of coffee and bacon sandwiches notwithstanding.

Phil Masters knocked on Baird's office door at the end of the corridor and went in. He was greeted by the aroma of fresh coffee, and a friendly smile. Half an hour later, feeling slightly awash from three cups of Baird's delicious brew, he went to look for Jim 'Brillo' Jackson, to give him the good news that the disappearance of Roger the Lab was his mystery to solve. "Just keep clear of the big boys, Brillo," advised Masters, "and you're not to go onto the Brandston Estate, other than to pick up one of Roger's old collars for the dogs this afternoon at three. Don't ask any questions, and don't talk to any F5 staff. That's an order, come from the top. Report back to me if you get lucky." Yes, sir!" said Jackson, already halfway to the coat stand, "Leave it to me, sir! Thank you, sir!" Masters smiled once more, and headed for his own office, where twenty-five open cases sat in their buff folders, demanding his immediate attention.

In the Great Diaspora of Gnomes that followed the final gathering, many Gnomes stowed away on ships and spread across the globe, seeking places of sanctuary. From the icy wastes of the Poles to the great burnt deserts of the world, they set up camps, dug their burrows and made a new life, keeping to their traditions of honouring Mother Nature, of working when it was light and sleeping when it was dark, of taking care of one another and of any wounded creature that needed their care. From humans they kept well away. The time had not yet come for a Reconciliation. The madness of humans grew to excess: there was pollution, pillaging and decades of toxic warfare that poisoned the land, the water and the air. Humans forgot that grass is better than concrete or tarmac, that an apple is better than a meal produced in a factory and wrapped up in plastic, that a slow ride on a bicycle is better than tearing down a motorway so fast that you, and others around you, are in mortal danger, that a real person is better than a screen image of a fantasy one . . . Gnomes sat in their burrows, stirring their mushroom soup, and shook their heads in near despair. When would the Awakening of Humans come? How long, O Great Mother, how long? But in a suburb in the Heart of England, there was one man who was to change the course of history: a blue-eyed man with a love of gardening . . .

Chapter Four

A RATHER APPEALING TENANT

Mr. Archie Prescott awoke, most reluctantly, from an extremely pleasant dream in which he was sitting by the side of a slow-flowing river, on a grassy bank, with his hand on the warm knee of an unseen woman. They were laughing, and he felt contented and free . . .

It was cold in the bedroom, in spite of the thick ex-army blankets he had hung at the windows in lieu of curtains. It always took an hour or so to get the place warm. He had been sleeping in his dressing-gown and a pair of thick socks, as he always did from mid-October till the end of April. He often dreamt he was side by side with a woman, which was fine by his standards. Archie had been single for twenty years, having been abandoned by his wife for another, and having made the conscious decision to remain alone for the sake of emotional and mental well-being.

There had been only one, brief, romantic interlude since his wife had left him. The object of his affections had turned out to be a heavy drinker, and apt to use her fists when inebriated. The heartbreak and the bruises had left Archie all the more determined to keep his heart firmly closed. He liked to stay positive, and any upset gave him flashbacks to the day he had found himself a single parent in charge of a small daughter and letting go of their house, to move back in with his mother. The family home, which his hard work had paid for, was sadly no longer a place he wished to inhabit. Suddenly all the family photos on the walls and message boards around the place had seemed like a lie.

He and his wife had married young, as many had done in the nineteen-sixties, in order to have a private place to pursue their courtship, and to get to know one another. It was the only way. He had worked two jobs to furnish the small terraced house near to the factory where he worked. Family planning being what it was in those days, baby Bryony had come along two years into the marriage, just as the cracks were beginning to appear in his relationship with Yvette.

Because the family budget was stretched to its limits, Yvette had found herself an evening job at a local hairdresser's, and it had not been long before she had claimed part of her wages for herself and begun to leave Archie in charge of Bryony while she went out to the local disco on Friday nights. It wasn't surprising: she was so young still, and hardly ready for a diet of housework, clipping coupons and trying to make meals out of leftovers. At the disco, she had met other men who were free and single: men who paid her compliments, on her figure rather than her scrag end of lamb casserole, and who wanted to treat her like a princess. They had cars: Archie could only afford the bus. They smelt of aftershave: Archie smelt of oil and old tyres.

It was nobody's fault that the marriage had fallen apart before it had had a chance to lay the foundations that keep a couple together. Any conversations they had were about money. They never had enough spare cash for a holiday, or even a decent night out. But Archie still smarted from the feelings of rejection, of betrayal, of anger at the unfairness of it all, and he wasn't about to let another woman hurt his pride.

Archie hurriedly pulled a blanket from the bed and put it round his shoulders for the trip along the hall, through the living-room to the kitchen, where he put on the kettle, returning to the living-room to switch on the electric fire. It was on two bars. He reduced it to one. Once he had had his coffee and biscuits and got dressed in the clothes he had laid out on the sofa the night before, he would switch it off.

Best to be on the safe side. It was only the beginning of March, and who knew when the warmer weather would arrive?

The coffee warmed him for now, and as he sat on the sofa under his blanket, he thought of the day ahead. Enid, an armed forces widow in her eighties who lived in the flat next door, had asked him to fetch her medicines from the chemist's, and Robert the retired caretaker who lived on the first floor had just come out of hospital and would appreciate a visit and perhaps his tea cooked. And it would be as well to visit the freezer centre just off the High Street and stock up on microwave dinners, just in case the snow came back. Perhaps they'd have some spicy chicken wings in today. He could always make a dinner of them, with a few oven chips. There was half a tin of baked beans in the fridge.

Archie smiled and rubbed his hands together as he thought of his dinner. Nothing wrong with good, old-fashioned, English grub. He'd grown up on it, and it had never done him any harm. He didn't hold with all this fannying-around type cooking they showed you on TV. In hard times, his mother Florrie had kept him and his eight older siblings going with bread and dripping and hotpot, and they'd all been as tough as old boots. Although the youngest of the brothers and sisters, and therefore invariably referred to as 'the runt', Archie was wiry, strong and compact, with more energy than most men of his age.

Archie sighed and buried his nose in his coffee cup until his glasses steamed up and he couldn't see the rain tipping down outside the window of his eighth-floor council flat. He pressed the remote, and the TV sprang to life. An old black and white movie. Great stuff! One of his absolute favourites: 'Tarzan and the Slave Girl'. One of the most far-fetched plots and sets of outlandish costumes ever to grace the silver screen, and easily the least convincing of all the Tarzan films of all time. Dozens of random slave girls in flimsy costumes, fellows with whips who were dressed like Egyptian priests, and a feisty blonde character called Lola, who managed to give Jane a good run for her money. Tarzan was played by the virtually unknown Lex Barker, Jane by the (in his humble opinion) rather plain Vanessa Power, and Lola (the 'bad girl', but in this case he was prepared to make an exception: she was jolly easy on the eye) by a certain curvaceous and pouting Denise Darcel. Archie chuckled and nipped to the kitchen for a packet of digestive biscuits.

Chapter Five

A GOOD REPUTATION

Archie tried above all to be good. He had his personal standards, and had rarely departed from them, whatever others did. Above all, his good conduct related to females, whom he had been raised to revere. All the more reason, then, why he took it so deeply to heart when a woman erred or strayed. He resisted looking at porn mags in the tobacconist's and ogling young women joggers when he was going along the covered walkway between Eden Tower, where he lived, to its twin, Paradise Tower, fifteen yards away. He never flirted with female neighbours, shop assistants, or staff in the pub along the road, as some of his fellow tenants did, and had never in his whole life made a lewd suggestion to any woman.

Archie also believed in being a good neighbour and member of the community. He said good morning to everyone, whether they answered or not, when walking to the single-storey building between the two high-rise blocks for over-50s which housed the communal facilities: a kitchen, a lounge, a small laundry-room, a disabled loo and an office for the support officer.

The lounge was warm and cosy with an array of comfy chairs. There was a book shelf and a kettle, a drop-down screen for film shows, and a cupboard containing board games. Processing your laundry took at least three hours (the tumble drier being a bit half-hearted), and you could sit with the paper and a cuppa, look at who came in, and maybe exchange opinions on the day's news or how the local football teams were doing this season.

Archie had been raised by Catholic parents who believed in good-neighbourliness, decency, clean living and hard work, as well as treating other people—whoever they were—with consideration and respect. Not all his neighbours were of a similar persuasion. There was the usual percentage of drunkards and spitters-in-the-lift, and people who left their bin bags in the back hallway, the contents spilling across the doorway for anyone to slip on, and for the caretaker to clean up after them. And the few who, in spite of their age, held loud parties until three or four in the morning, and thought it was a fair exchange for their selfish behaviour if they invited those who complained to join in or eff off. Archie was not a man given to complaining, but he was often the first to rap on a door and have a word or two with the offending tenants, explaining to them that the only other option, in case of antisocial behaviour, was a formal complaint to the local authority who ran the estate. It was surprising how many people listened to him, considering his gentle voice and demeanour. He had a quiet authority about him that came from confidence in his belief system, as well as a deep and unwavering thankfulness for the things in life he valued most: love, friendship, music, Nature.

It was his community-spirited approach to life that got him co-opted onto the residents' association committee within the first year of his tenancy at Flat 33 Eden Tower. Before he had been given the flat, he had been sleeping on his sister's sofa for six months, having returned unexpectedly from a ten-year stay on one of the Canary Islands, where he had been working in a restaurant, first as kitchen boy, and eventually as chef and manager. He had adored the lifestyle: the cooking, the conversations with locals, customers and colleagues, the long walks on the beach at night when the restaurant closed, the Sunday picnics and barbecues on the beach. And the warm, sunny weather and sea breezes.

He still often dreamt of the island, of the sand between his toes, of running for a bus in shorts and flip-flops, of the sound of waves crashing on craggy, volcanic rocks. But his return had been sudden and full of regret. A Spanish couple had approached him one day with a proposition: go into business with us, and own your own restaurant. They had shown him the restaurant, up for sale, and it was in a prime position on the road half way between the island's capital and second cities, and not far from a popular beach. The building was in good order, and all the kitchen equipment had been left behind, and was available at a knockdown price. A deal had been struck over a roast leg of lamb and a bottle of wine, and the contracts had been signed. But then, disaster had struck. Archie had turned up to start work the following Monday morning, and the place was deserted. The Spanish couple—and their lawyer—had, it seemed, run off to the mainland, taking Archie's money with them. His savings, earned by the sweat of his brow and put by over a decade: all gone.

Archie had walked along the beach all day and slept there all night, an empty Scotch bottle clutched in his hand. He had wept, when it grew dark and there was no-one else around to see his face, too sad to think of revenge. A conversation with the local police the following day had brought enlightenment. This cruel con had been perpetrated many times before. After the conversation, Archie felt a little better: at least he wasn't the only fool on the island. But there was nothing he could do.

His daughter Bryony, who had gone to the island with him to work in the same trade, having finished her education, had already returned to England, to live with her mother, Archie's ex-wife Yvette, in Coventry. He had been glad of that for, until his sister had been able to send him his air fare home, he had been roaming the streets by day and sleeping on the beach at night, under the watchful eye of the Guardia Civil, many of whom were his friends. He had a good reputation on the island, for he had broken up many a fight with a few quiet words, and escorted many a drunken tourist back to his or her hotel or holiday villa, saving the police a lot of time and nuisance.

Although Archie was now a member of a very different kind of community, he still put in a lot of effort, whilst desperately seeking a job that would get him off Jobseeker's Allowance. He had to keep busy and be useful. Life on the dole made him feel lost. He had worked his entire life, beginning with a two-hour paper round at the age of eleven. He had never been out of work before, and it was not his way. Visits to the Job Centre made him feel tired, old, humiliated and out of the loop. He couldn't understand the time-wasting of job searching online, which yielded adverts that didn't match your experience or skills, and which were hundreds of miles away and at a wage that was the equivalent per week of what he had been earning per day before.

The money he received from the state every week barely covered his expenses and allowed for nothing extra—not even a train ticket to visit his daughter or enough cash to buy a new shirt or Christmas presents for the family. He tried to keep up his spirits, and keep active, and so he was happy to help out, running the weekly Bingo session and a Skittles Club on Saturday evenings, for the neighbours who wanted to mix (most kept to their flats, in spite of his repeated invitations to come and join in the fun).

Every one of the sixty-eight tenants on the housing scheme knew Archie, including the newcomers, and nearly all of them liked him. At last year's residents' association AGM, Big Frank, who lived on the top floor of Paradise Tower with his twin sister June, had referred to him as "the outstanding tenant and member of the community", which was a huge compliment, as Big Frank was often referred to as Mr. Angry by those who remembered a character of that name who had appeared daily on a local radio show, taking those in power to task for various misdemeanours.

Not everyone entertained appropriate thoughts of Archie, though. The person who had come knocking on his door to invite him to join the committee was a woman in her early sixties by the name of Carol, and she had since grown to hate Archie, for the simple reason that she had had designs on him, but that her efforts to seduce him had yielded nothing. Quite the contrary: Archie seemed quite repulsed by her. In the summer time, it was one of their simple pleasures for neighbours to spend an afternoon in the garden of the pub down the road, the Speckled Trout, and Carol and Archie had, by her engineering of seats, often found themselves sitting squashed up together at a bench table.

But no amount of leaning over and displaying a wrinkled, brown cleavage, or stroking his knee under the table, had provoked more of a reaction than a look of shock and an embarrassed, "Well, I'm off to the little boys' room," from Archie.

But Carol had a master plan which she had been hatching for a while, and which she was now about to put to the test. It was do or die: she would 'do', and if she didn't get what she wanted, she would destroy him. A 'woman scorned', and all that jazz . . . It wasn't enough to give up and leave him alone. She would make sure no-one on the housing scheme ever spoke to him again.

The innocent and well-meaning Archie was surprised to find her at his door that first evening, all dressed up and smelling of Old English Lavender. It tickled Archie's nose, and he stifled a sneeze. Carol smiled and asked if she could come in and have a chat, which quite floored him. It was rare for tenants to do more than exchange greetings and spend time in the communal lounge together, even rarer for a tenant to want to get inside another's flat. If he had known what she was after, he would have cowered in the furthest, darkest corner of his bedroom, holding his breath and praying for divine intervention. For Carol was about to meet her match in the estate's newest tenant, Ann-Marie Osborne, and this would only add more fuel to the flames of Carol's wrath.

Chapter Six

WELLINGTON

Marjory, Elspeth and Tim stepped out of Wellington Airport into temperatures twenty degrees above that of home. They had already swapped their winter coats for raincoats. Aunty Christine had issued various instructions over the phone, but mainly to do with clothing: "Four seasons in one day—that's what we say here," she had warned, "Raincoats and sunglasses. Shorts and long-johns. T-shirts and jumpers. If you don't come prepared, don't expect Zooie and me to lend you our stuff. We don't have a *wardrobe* like you people. But I expect you can afford the Wairaranga shops anyway. See ya!"

Aunty Christine's voice was gruff, but at least she was straightforward. Marjory was honestly tired of gatherings where everyone had an agenda—hidden or otherwise. She had been longing to visit her sister for years, but somehow the trip to New Zealand's North Island, and the first face to face meeting with Christine's partner Zooie had been put off and put off until she had all but given up hope. Then Elspeth and Tim had both moved back into the Manor, and their constant moaning, and the strain it caused her husband, had given her the ideal excuse to suggest they left Percy in peace for a while. "And besides," she had said to her husband, as they lay in bed holding hands as they always did before dropping off, "A month or two living such a different way of life might open their eyes. They're so ungrateful, Percy darling. Look at how they reacted to their Christmas presents. I spent hours in Harrods searching for something they'd like, and all Elspeth said was, 'I could have done with a new car,' and Tim said the mobile phone was already six months out of date."

Percy had agreed: the children could do with learning a lesson. Whether it was the fact of being back home again, or whether they still hadn't really grown up, they were both behaving like surly teenagers. "Ring your sister in the morning, darling," he had said, squeezing his wife's hand, "Go as soon as you want. I'll manage. Mrs. Morrish will look after me, and—you know—absence makes the heart grow fonder." "I couldn't possibly be fonder of you than I am, my dearest," whispered Marjory, turning to her husband and putting her hand on his shoulder. "I didn't mean you, darling," answered Percy, patting the hand, "I meant them. Did we spoil them?" Marjory snuggled up. "Oh, no. I don't think we did," she said, patting his shoulder, "At least, I hope not. They've been . . . well . . . *privileged*, I suppose. High expectations. Assuming things would come their way. Assuming they have some kind of divine right to everything. They're still young. They'll learn." Percy smiled. He'd seen photographs of Christine and Zooie in their natural habitat. "Oh yes," he agreed, "They'll learn!"

"So, where's Aunty, then?" asked Elspeth, making a great show of sitting down heavily on one of her four suitcases and scanning the car park. "You know she's not coming to fetch us, darling," said her mother, in a tone of strained patience. Twenty-three hours and fifty-three minutes in the air, plus the journey to Heathrow by car, plus check-in and waiting time . . . And all that moaning and complaining. She was a bundle of jangling, but exhausted, nerves. Tim swore under his breath. "So, mother dear, how are we meant to get from here to whatever little backwater it is she lives in?" he asked, putting three pieces of chewing-gum into his mouth at once and chewing loudly. "Keep your mouth shut, dear," said Marjory, "A fly might get in. There's a bus. The stop's right over there, see? Those orange buses. That's how." "Jeebus! Didn't you arrange transport, Mummy?" asked Elspeth, "I'm exhausted, and I really can't cope with . . . well, *that!*" She waved her arm in the direction of the bus, "All those sweaty people, and we'll be recognized, and then there'll be photos, and I'm really not in a fit state."

Marjory ignored the protests, grabbed the handle of her (only) suitcase, and headed for the bus-stop. The children would have no option but to follow, she reasoned. What she hadn't told them—she didn't dare—was that there were—Christine had warned—disruptions to services, and they would have to take the bus to Molesworth Street, get off by the hideous Beehive and Parliament buildings, walk to Wellington Station, take the Tranz Metro (Wairarapa Line) to Masterton, then catch another bus to Greytown. And there would be a walk at the other end.

Christine had been firm on the phone: "Put it this way, by the time you arrive the kids will be so fed up and tired they'll probably just want to crash, and you can get some peace and quiet. You, me and Zooie can crack open a bottle of wine and catch up." To Marjory, that sounded so good, she felt almost disloyal. Almost. It had been ages since she'd been out of the limelight and had the chance to do something as normal as get a little tiddly with a couple of other women who weren't politician's wives, or parish councillors, or journalists, or stylists.

The bus driver was a little shirty about the number of suitcases they had with them, but when he saw the expression on Marjory's face, and had got the rough edge of Elspeth's tongue, he took pity and helped them stack the cases in the luggage rack, putting Marjory's on top. "Don't worry," he said with a smile, "I'll help you off when we get to town. I'm guessing you're off at Molesworth Street for the Metro, but I wouldn't advise it." He slipped a business card into Marjory's hand. "My brother's a taxi driver. I can give him a quick call if you like. He can take you the rest of that way—that's if you've got cash on you." Marjory laughed. "That's very kind," she answered, "But we'll manage. Got to get used to the way things are done in the real world. Besides, it's an adventure." The bus driver grinned, "Well, the best of British, then!" he said, "You're one brave lady."

"What did he mean?" asked Tim when they had sat down, "Brave? And you talking about adventures?" "Never mind, darling, you'll see," said his mother, turning away to look out of the window, "Just enjoy the trip. It's your first time here. Make the most of it." "First time, last time!" muttered Tim, but he left it at that, and the three of them watched the scenery go by as the bus pulled out of the airport and turned onto the service road. The bus headed west.

Little houses with weatherboarding, painted in blues and reds, industrial buildings, apartment buildings, more than one house with a boat in driveway, patches of greenery—the scene outside the window was a hotchpotch, but fascinating, even to the world-weary Elspeth. She soon forgot to look around to see if anyone had recognized her family. None of the other passengers seemed interested in them at all. When the bus went through a picturesque village, she peered out, fascinated. It was like something from the Wild West, in a way. Wooden buildings with an overhang to the front, making a covered walkway for pedestrians, and the buildings painted in the prettiest of colours: buttermilk, turquoise, leaf green. She longed to get out and sit outside one of the cafés with a long glass of iced tea.

Elspeth was not recovering at all well from the breakdown of her two-year-long marriage to photojournalist Maurie Turnbull. A strikingly handsome Australian with ice-blue eyes, a mop of bright blonde hair, a body to die for and a cast in one eye that made him look like a visionary (which he almost was), he had barged into her life—quite literally—in Covent Garden Market one hot summer's day. She had been standing, talking to a friend on her mobile, when he had backed into her whilst lining up a shot of some street jugglers, apologized sincerely and invited her for lunch. She had often thought about that first meeting, and wondered whether he had realised who she was, but she didn't think he had. She wasn't bad-looking, she'd been nicely dressed—not too Sloaney: elegant in a dress, with a good handbag—and she'd just landed some freelance writing, which meant she was relaxed and in a good mood, knowing she would be able to work from her flat in Bloomsbury.

Maurie's courtship of Elspeth, whom he called Els, with the 's' pronounced as a 'z', had been ardent and rapid. He had managed to get her into bed after the fourth date, which had been a boat trip down the Thames, followed by dinner at a Thai restaurant. He had insisted on walking her home, as he always did, but this time he'd insisted on coming in. "I want to check out your surroundings," he had said, poking his nose into the hallway of her building as she stood holding the door half open. She hadn't been able to think of a reason to refuse. Once inside her flat, he'd pushed her against the wall, circling her waist with one arm while he caressed her neck with the other. She'd melted—she knew that was a cliché, but that was how it had felt— into his embrace, and the rest of the night had passed like a dream.

Mummy and Daddy hadn't been sure at first, until Maurie had dropped a few names, top people he'd photographed and interviewed, and taken them out to a quiet country hotel—a good choice, since they were always trying to avoid the paparazzi—and wined and dined them. They'd been pleased when the couple had told them they intended to get married. Even more pleased when Maurie had whisked Elspeth off to Las Vegas for the ceremony, leaving them only one task: to receive the wedding presents and write the thank you letters.

The marriage had not, however, lived up to Elspeth's expectations. Maurie was out nearly the whole time, chasing stories, or going to meetings. When he came home, all he wanted to do was make love. He was a spectacular lover, but that didn't make up for the fact that he wasn't particularly interested in hearing how Elspeth had spent the time apart. Occasionally, she would ask him to edit her articles (mainly on fashion trends and who was wearing what in London), but although he seemed to want to help, somehow he never got around to it. Then he'd disappeared off back to Australia and hadn't returned. A new job, hunting down stories of tourists disappearing in the Outback. She'd set in motion a divorce on the grounds of abandonment, and he had sent back the papers signed, but nothing else. Not even a note saying he was sorry.

The person who had been the most supportive when Elspeth had turned up at Brandston Manor to give her parents the news was, of course, her mother. Her father had only worried about the papers getting hold of it. Marjory had taken her off to the kitchen, dismissed the staff for the night and made a pot of tea. "You must move back in for a while, so I can look after you," she'd said, looking at the angry, hurt face of her daughter, "I can send Mrs. Morrish round to the flat for your stuff, if you like. Or we can leave it. You can always borrow a pair of my pyjamas . . ."

Images of Maurie flashed across Elspeth's inner vision as she stared through the bus window at the buildings and trees, the people walking along. She pushed them away. She was young. She was abroad. She was going to have a holiday. "Nobody here knows me," she thought, "I can be myself—whoever that is."

"Mummy," she said, in a tone that was less whiney and less strident, "They have nice shops here. Quaint. Take you out to lunch sometime." Marjory risked a small smile at her daughter. Maybe this wasn't going to be so difficult after all. Tim was on his mobile phone, texting. "Send a text to Daddy, could you please, Tim?" she asked, "Just let him know we've arrived safely." "In a bit," replied Tim, tapping away furiously, "Anyway, we haven't arrived safely yet." Marjory turned back to looking out of the window. They'd be in town soon. Perhaps they could all do with a drink before catching the Metro. She'd googled, and found a place called the Sushi Express and Juice Bar which looked quite appealing. It was a bit of a walk from the bus-stop, though. Probably best to head for the Railway Station (which the official New Zealand website described as 'historic') and a venue called Trax Bar. She'd suggest Elspeth change her high heels for something more comfortable and risk getting her head bitten off.

Chapter Seven

GREYTOWN

The bus journey continued in silence, and before long the driver was helping them down with their cases and wishing them a pleasant stay. "Two minutes to the railway station. This way!" called Marjory, and set off. "You're joking!" shouted Tim, "We've got to get a *train* as well?" "Oh, shut up, Tim," hissed Elspeth, shoving two of her cases in her brother's direction, "Put up and shut up. Can't you see Mummy's tired?" Marjory heard her remark, and was both surprised and pleased. Age and experience would bring them closer, as they had been when Elspeth was a girl. And this holiday would lay the foundations of a relationship that, she hoped, resemble a friendship, woman to woman. Tim, she wasn't so sure about. It had been years since he'd first brushed her hand away when she had gone to ruffle his hair. Years since they'd had a proper hug. But she was a woman of faith. It would all work out in the end.

Half an hour later, fortified by a glass of Ata Rangi Craighall Chardonnay and the most delicious pizzas they'd ever tasted, including a Boscaiola that Marjory had ordered, and which the children had half demolished between them, once they'd seen it, they boarded a train bound for Masterton. Trax Bar and Café had been wonderful. They had been able to sit outside in the courtyard, where native birds which, the waiter had informed them, were called tuis, gave virtuoso performances in the trees, and hopped around, pecking up crumbs. The tuis looked black, perched in the overhanging shade trees, except for the curious bibs under their beaks which made the birds look for all the world as if they were carrying around two small pickled onions, but on closer inspection, their feathers were iridescent, in shades of dark blue and green.

Both Tim and Elspeth now seemed more relaxed, and Tim had even cracked a joke or two. He seemed to have taken Elspeth's point about his mother being tired, for he had immediately jumped up to fetch extra napkins when they were needed, and to take close-up photos of the birds on her mobile phone for a souvenir of their first meal in New Zealand.

"Not long now," said Marjory, as she settled down for the train journey to Masterton. The seats on the train were comfortable, and warm from the sun. Tim nodded off, his phone still in his hand, and Marjory and Elspeth sat in companionable silence. At least, Marjory felt it was companionable. She passed her daughter a piece of fudge and got a smile in return that was really quite unusually warm, and then Elspeth, seeing her mother shiver, took off her pashmina and passed it across, saying "Put this round you," which surprised Marjory no end.

At Masterton Station, they had help from two fellow passengers— elderly men in walking gear—to lift down the luggage. They didn't ask whether help was required, they just took hold of the cases and passed them down carefully, one at a time. "Are you OK from here?" asked the older of the two men. Marjory almost jumped, and moved swiftly to grab her case. "I mean, do you need a bus-stop or a taxi number?" the man added, smiling. Marjory blushed. "I think we're OK," she replied, "Thank you." She tutted at herself when the two men turned away with a friendly wave: she was *so* distrustful. She fished around in her coat pocket for the piece of paper with the bus details on it. The bus stop was in Church Street, and it took twenty-five minutes to Greytown—to the Community Supermarket on Main Street. It was the only large shop in town, her sister had explained: Elspeth would *love* that!

Christine had told her to ring when they got off at Greytown and she would cycle down and walk them to her place. "It's just off Main Street," she explained, "And the walk will do you good after sitting so long." "We'll have a few suitcases," Marjory had interjected, "Fine. I'll hitch up the trailer," answered her sister, "One of the kids can take charge of it." Marjory was about to explain that the 'kids' might refuse, but she decided that her sister could deal with that issue. She'd probably tell them that it was a case of 'drag it or leave it behind'.

The sun came out—a late afternoon blaze of glory—when they got off the bus outside Greytown's supermarket. They took off their raincoats and stood on the pavement, trying to keep out of the way of shoppers, while Marjory got hold of Christine on the phone. It was Zooie who answered: "Oh, hi there tourist!" she said brightly, "Hold on a mo . . ." Marjory heard her talking to Christine in the background. After a few seconds she came back on: "Chris says to wait in the park across the road. Find a bench. She'll come find you. See ya soon!" Zooie hung up without waiting for an answer. "Come on, you two," said Marjorie, "We're to wait in the park." Both Tim and Elspeth groaned. "No, it's OK," said their mother, "It's just across the road. Come on! Last one to a bench is a rotten cabbage!" She felt strangely light and carefree as she trundled her suitcase—and one of Elspeth's— across the street and walked through the iron gates and under the trees. Tim and Elspeth followed, trying to race each other, actually laughing at last, though they were out of breath.

"Here you are, Mummy," said Tim, a rare smile on his face, "Best bench in the park. In that it's the nearest, as you see. And it's Peth who's the rotten cabbage: I got here first." Marjory smiled back and sat down. She looked up at the cathedral roof of trees above her, wondering what species they were. Christine would know. She probably had a book of New Zealand trees. Tim and Elspeth looked up too. "Jeez, is that a *parrot*?" said Tim loudly, shading his eyes, "Where?" asked Elspeth, following his gaze to a branch halfway up the tree directly in front of them on the other side of the path. "I can see it too," said Marjory, looking up at a bird with a bright red head and chest that looked like a snood, and a bright yellow tum that she had at first taken for a plastic shopping-bag the wind had blown there.

"It's a rosella," came a gruff voice from a few yards away, accompanied by the squeak of a bicycle, as Aunty Christine came into view, red in the face but grinning, "*Platycercus eximius.* Try whistling at him." Elspeth got up slowly from the bench and approached the tree. She gave a low whistle. The rosella repeated it exactly. Christine joined Elspeth and made a noise a bit like a fire alarm going off in the distance. The parrot copied. They both laughed. The parrot copied that too. "Come here, you," said Christine to her niece, and she enveloped her in a sweaty hug. Elspeth hugged her back with almost equal enthusiasm. Marjory looked on, delighted. Tim got up and strolled nonchalantly over to his aunt, who grabbed his arm and pulled him into the hug. "Tim and Elspeth in a group hug? Well, I never!" remarked Marjory, and before anyone could say anything, she joined them. God, it felt good to get some unconditional love!

Christine pulled away first, leaving Marjory and the children still holding onto one another. It was a good three seconds before they broke it up, slowly. "Well, come on then you lot!" shouted Christine, "Zooie's got dinner on. You must be famished as well as tired out. Follow me!" She grabbed her sister's arm and, walking far more slowly than her accustomed march, she turned towards the park gates, leaving Elspeth and Tim to gather up the suitcases, load them into the large trailer attached to the back of the bicycle—which looked ancient, and almost as heavy as the wire mesh trailer with its four solid wheels—and catch up as best they could. "Come on, Peth," said Tim, "You can sit on the bike. I'll pull."

Chapter Eight

CAROL PAYS A VISIT

"Hello Archie," said Carol, brandishing her customary bottle of Lambrusco and a sheaf of papers, "Do you mind if I come in? I'd like us to have a chat." "Of course," said Archie, not quite managing to hide his embarrassment, for he had already taken out his false teeth for the night, "Go through, Carol." Archie was glad he hadn't yet put on his pyjamas and dressing-gown, but he was wearing the slippers his grand-children had given him for Christmas, with their images of Animal from Sesame Street on the uppers, and he noticed Carol smirk at the sight of them.

Carol pushed her way in, brushing Archie's upper arm with her bosom. At six foot, she was almost a good five inches taller than he was. Archie felt goosebumps rise on his arms, and gave an involuntary shiver. Carol walked purposefully along the hallway, swinging her hips in what Archie thought was a quite unnecessary way (though he tried not to stare), and into Archie's living-room, where the TV was showing a favourite old western. He put it on pause, which was his way of hinting that he intended to finish watching it shortly, and moved some clean laundry and his blanket off the sofa so that Carol could sit down. "Would you like a cup of coffee?" he asked his guest. "Oh, well—I've brought this with me to share . . ." she said, waving the bottle of Lambrusco at Archie, "But OK then, yes please—that would be very nice," simpered Carol, arranging her pink linen skirt across her stockinged knees and leaning back against the cushions.

Archie went into the kitchen, put the kettle on and spooned instant coffee into his two best cups. He stood at the window while the kettle boiled, trying to remember when was the last time he'd entertained a woman without the sound of breaking glass or a door slamming. His marriage had broken down when his daughter was seven, and he'd only had that one brief fling on the island. Cherry had come in alone and flirted with him while she ate a meal, paying him extravagant compliments with lashings of sexual innuendo: "Your leg is gorgeous, but I prefer a nice, big sausage . . ."—that kind of thing. Vulgar, but somehow impossible to ignore. What had made him fall prey to her charms was the one thought that kept running through his head: "Have I lost the knack?" Cherry had subsequently turned out to be married. It had taken him a year to discover this fact. She had also claimed she was on a business trip. She was the director of a holiday company, she said, over in the Canaries checking out the best hotels, and had hinted that it might be nice if he joined her when she went to other destinations in future. She had seemed so sincere.

It was Archie's sister, his senior by a year and possessed of instincts that were almost supernatural, who had smelt a rat and looked up the girlfriend online. She was, in fact, the wife of a local businessman who had recently won the national lottery. Evidently they had enough money for her to be able to take several holidays a year. When Archie toured the local bars and did a little digging himself, he had discovered that she had quite a history of holiday romances, her preference being for men who worked long hours, as they were less likely to see her out and about with rivals for her affections. When Archie had discovered this, he'd been very angry. If he had known she was married, he'd have run a mile. He'd taken a vow there and then to remain a bachelor and keep out of trouble and, apart from a few half-hearted looks at dating websites for the over-50s during visits to the local library, he had kept it.

So now, as Archie stood looking out at the falling rain, he realised he was finding it really quite awkward to have a woman come into his personal—and very private—space. Especially one towards whom he felt such a strong aversion. What if Carol pounced? Could he handle it like a gentleman? Or would he crumble and make a fool of himself?

Or worse: not be able to get rid of her and end up pinned against a wall? "Come on, Archie," he said to himself, bracing up like a soldier on parade, "There must be fifty ways to let a woman know you don't fancy her."

Archie carried the cups into the living-room and placed them on the coffee table. Carol gave him a huge, toothy grin, as if he'd served up champagne and caviar. He ignored the grin, returning to the kitchen to fetch the packet of chocolate biscuits he'd been saving up for Friday, when Pete the support officer dropped in for his weekly visit.

Pete was one of Archie's favourite people. Kind, hard-working and respectful towards older people, he had a way of dealing with problems (lost keys, stuck lifts, issues with benefits) that made you feel safer and less anxious. He was there from nine to six every week day, and if you had a difficult phone call to make—for example, an electricity bill that seemed too high and needed challenging—he was happy for you to use the office phone, and to take over when things got tricky, and speak up on your behalf. Tenants panicked when Pete went on holiday, for the replacement support officers were less popular. They were kind, and they meant well, but they came and went every few hours, and they didn't have Pete's inside knowledge of how things were for the tenants: the worries that consumed them, the things that upset them—and more importantly, what you could do to cheer each one up.

Pete was the only other person—apart from Archie's daughter and a few council workmen—who had set foot inside his flat since he'd moved in. Now there was Carol, sitting on his sofa as if she was in for the long haul, sipping her tea and crunching her way through her third chocolate biscuit. For the first half an hour, she talked about the weather, the cost of living, and who on the estate was suffering from which ailment. Archie listened, nodding and adding a word or two when it seemed appropriate. Then Carol tried to talk about soap operas, of which she was an avid fan. She watched them all: 'Eastenders', 'Coronation Street', 'Neighbours', 'Home and Away' and 'Emmerdale', though she drew the line at 'Hollyoaks' because she said there was too much sex in it. When she said the word 'sex', she smiled at Archie, and her eyes ran up and down his body, which made him shudder. "I think I'd better shut the window," he said, "There's a terrible draught in here . . ."

Carol asked Archie which was his favourite soap opera, and he replied—being a truthful man—that he thought they were all a load of rubbish. Carol seemed shocked, but took a gulp of coffee and said, "So, what *do* you watch then?" Archie mumbled something about westerns and nature programmes, and asked her whether she'd like another cup of coffee. Carol smiled and refused, saying she'd come about a different matter. "I want you on my committee," she said, with what she probably thought was a winsome smile, "I've noticed you do a lot of shopping for people, and helping them out. The committee's a bit thin on the ground at the moment, what with Basil passing away, and Tom O'Brien moving out, and I was hoping you'd come and help us."

Archie said he'd just pop out to the kitchen to top up his coffee, and she could tell him all about it. Carol beamed and started shuffling through the papers she'd brought with her, as if it was already a *fait accompli*. And perhaps it was. With Archie's background and character, it was always going to be hard—even impossible—for him to say no, when presented with an opportunity to be helpful. But as he stood again at his kitchen window, waiting for the kettle to boil, he breathed a deep sigh: he knew that if he took on the residents' association, it wouldn't be a five-minutes-a-week job. Little did he realise where it would lead him. Many times over the next two decades, he would look back to that moment of decision and wish he had said no, and think how much more peaceful his life would have been if he had.

Archie appeared in the doorway of the living-room, a resigned look on his face. "OK, then. What is it you want me to do?" Carol bared her long teeth in a truly shark-like grin. "Just you come and sit down, and I'll show you," she said, and patted the seat next to her.

The Gnomes took great risks by choosing to settle in urban areas, or by staying when a village became a town, a town became a city . . . They had been instructed to prepare, and which of them knew where the good men would arise?

Some Gnome bands chose wooded areas and parks within cities, to be close but not too close, but their burrows were crushed by the developers' diggers, and those who tried to escape became separated from each other and were never seen again.

The Great Leader of the Gnomes sent out a message by carrier dove warning his brothers to be more careful. Some quit the towns and cities for the hills and mountains, covering hundreds of miles on foot, travelling by night.

For millions of Gnomes, it was too late. Their souls wandered in Ether, cold and alone . . .

One journeying group was spotted in Germany, crossing a mountain path, by a man by the name of Phillip Griebel, who made animal figurines to decorate people's gardens, and who was on a walking tour. Herr Griebel quickly sat down and made sketches of the Little Men from memory. When he arrived in his home town of Gräfenroda, he went straight to his workshop and began to make several designs for "Gartenzwerge" or garden dwarves. Having no idea that Gnomes existed, he had mistaken the band he had seeing scurrying into the undergrowth for dwarves . . .

These were supernatural creatures, Griebel was sure, and their effigies would bring good luck. At least, that is what he told his customers . . .

Chapter Nine

THE TROUBLE WITH CAROL

Carol moved to Eden Tower when the council estate where she had lived for twenty years and raised her two children began to sink, and her daughter and son had graduated from the local university, found work and bought their own homes. Her daughter Suzy was a GP in a local practice, and her son Ben ran the housewares department of one of the city's largest department stores. The house, on which she had lavished so many years of tender loving care, no longer felt like home. Because the estate was on the edges of the northern side of the city, and therefore far away from the sight of tourists and business people working in the centre, or visiting it, the council had filled the houses which became vacant with families who had fallen foul of themselves and the police, for reasons of crime and antisocial behaviour. The once neatly-tended gardens were, for the most part, full of rubbish, and drug dealers and their clients hung around the streets and bus-stops. The post office and local store had been robbed on numerous occasions, once—recently—at gunpoint.

When her husband, a tutor at the local college, left her for a younger colleague, she kept her end up for a while. She got a group of tenants and homeowners together with the support of the local neighbourhood forum, and they started to do litter-picks twice a week. They formed a residents' association and began to lobby the council for better 'street furniture' and for the small circle of grass in the middle of the estate to be improved by means of raised flower beds.

When the four flower beds were put in place, and planted up by the council, they lasted two days before someone came along in the night and tore up the plants, dumped them in the road and trampled them. Carol and her ninety-year-old neighbour Alice bought more plants and patiently replaced every one, but each time the vandals returned. Lamp-posts were replaced by the council, and two benches were installed on the grass, but people drove stolen cars into the lamp-posts, and broke the wooden seats of the benches.

One day, when Suzy came home for tea, she found her mother crying in the kitchen over a cup of tea that had gone cold. "Mum," she said, putting a gentle hand on her mother's shoulder, "You're not going to win this one, though you deserve a medal for trying. And you're tired out. Maybe it's time to think of moving? And maybe to somewhere that's a bit calmer?" Suzy had done her homework. She'd been aware of the her mother's difficulties and disappointments for a while—in fact, her own car had had its tyres slashed on more than one occasion whilst parked on the street in front of the house, in spite of the 'GP on call' sticker on the dashboard—and had been asking around. She thought she might have found a place where her mother could live more peacefully, among her own kind, and still play a role in the community. A patient had been singing the praises of life on over-50s housing schemes, and had got her thinking.

A month later, Carol packed up her belongings to move to No.22 Eden Tower, on the other side of the city. The housing team had been sympathetic. Carol was a model tenant, and they liked to place good people where they could be what they called 'proactive'. Carol and her ex-husband had not bought the family home: her husband had nurtured the hope of promotion at work, and the possibility of buying a private property somewhere leafier. She was glad now, because it meant she was eligible to apply for a one-bedroomed flat. It would free up their four-bedroomed home in the north of the city for a family with young children, and there was a dearth of such properties. The whole process of transferring her tenancy took so little time, she barely had a minute to feel sentimental or nostalgic about closing the chapter on a life that had taken so much of her time and energy. She left the neat garden as it was: where she was going, there was no garden, just a balcony, which she intended to use for storage.

And so it was that at the age of fifty-seven, Carol Manley found herself with a new 'mission field': the seventy neighbours who lived in the two towers she would call home until she was eventually carried out, feet first, or moved to a care home.

Like Archie Prescott, she immediately got stuck in. She wooed the committee, which consisted of four strong-minded women and two men who were on the way out, and began to collect new friends around her. But there was a convenience store next to her building that sold cheap booze, and it was not long before the committee meetings, which had once been serious and sober, and full of intent, began to resemble a girls' night out at the pub. The vodka, Lambrini and cider flowed. Basil, who was a long-standing committee member and its Treasurer, had stopped coming and told Pete the support officer he wanted nothing more to do with it. He had gone into hospital for a routine operation not long after, and had passed away before ever returning to the estate. Tom O'Brien, who had been the work horse of the committee, the one who moved furniture and climbed up ladders to hang party decorations, had moved home to Ireland. In the absence of the men (it must be said), it wasn't long before the bitching and backbiting began, and Carol, who had been restrained in her behaviour as long as her children were paying frequent visits, found she had a weakness both for the booze, and for the bitching.

She saw Archie as a kind of insurance policy against the uncertain future. He was reasonably attractive, and had loads of energy. He seemed quiet and compliant. He never seemed to say no to anyone, even when you knocked on his door in the middle of the night asking if he would use his phone to call the engineers because the lift had broken down (again), or because someone had fallen over drunk and was blocking the front door. It wasn't that Carol was in love with Archie, or even fancied him. She felt in need of a man to do things for her, and she was afraid of being alone. Getting him onto the committee was only the first step in her plan to marry him. She was sure he would not resist. "I'm a good catch," she told her reflection in the bathroom mirror as she applied mascara and lipstick, and plenty of hairspray, "Good figure, good boobs, good pair of legs—what more could he want? It's not as if they're queuing up at his door . . ."

"So," said Carol, fixing Archie with steely grey eyes, "We'd like you on the committee. Any objections?" Put like that, Archie found it impossible to anything other than nod agreement to her proposal. "And we've decided to give you the job of Treasurer. Here are the books. They're a bit of a mess, I'm afraid. You'll manage, won't you?" Archie's heart sank into his worn-out slippers. He scratched his head and mumbled, "I'll do my best," before finally standing up to indicate to Carol that he considered her visit at an end. Carol stood and patted Archie on the arm. "Well, I'll leave you to it then, Archie. Committee meeting tomorrow night, six o'clock in the lounge. See if you can manage a short report by then, hmm? Income, expenditure since the last meeting—that sort of thing."

Archie followed Carol down the hall. She was swinging her hips again, which he didn't think did much for her as she had what could only be described as a low centre of gravity. At the door, she turned and went to kiss him on the cheek. He was so surprised, he dodged left and the kiss landed on his ear. "Well, good night, Carol," he said, "See you tomorrow." Carol turned as she reached the lift door and gave him what he thought was a rather silly wave. "See you tomorrow, Archie," she said with a playful grin that was so alarmingly full of teeth, "Have fun!"

Chapter Ten

CONSTITUTIONAL

Well stuffed, and buffered against the chill by buttered kippers, wholemeal toast with damson jam and several cups of tea, the Secretary of State went downstairs to the Great Hall, where Roger the Labrador was lying on a blanket in front of the open fire. "Come, dog!" called Percy, and Roger sprang to his feet and trotted to his master's side, burying his wet nose in his outstretched hand. Roger had only been with the family for a year. His predecessor, another black Lab called Minty, had been with them for six years. They always got their dogs from a local breeder, but Roger was the first that Percy and Marjory had been to choose by themselves, the children both having lost interest in family pets.

Roger was affectionate and a little bandy in the legs. He had a long muzzle, and one ear that stuck up higher than the other, giving him an air of being constantly on the alert, which he wasn't particularly. He just knew the routine and was ready for what came next. Sleep, food, and walks in the late morning and late evening: the first with a family member (usually Marjory), the second with one of the gardeners, unless Percy particularly wanted to get out of the house—for example, to make a call on his mobile phone he didn't want anyone else to hear.

Percy wasn't particularly attached to Roger, but then, he didn't keep a dog for any other reason than that it was a family tradition. Most of the family portraits pictured a dog as well as its owner. Several lords of Brandston had been painted in hunting gear with a retriever, greyhound or terrier at their side—one with an Irish wolfhound. Ladies of the Manor were painted seated with a lapdog. Percy hadn't had his portrait painted yet. This was partly to do with his being always so busy and travelling to London and back, and partly to do with self-consciousness. Whereas the lords of old rather liked to be painted, warts and all, their grey hair (or wigs) sticking up at odd angles, their knobbly knees or paunches in full view, those of the twentieth century had opted for a portrayal of themselves that was more impressionistic.

Percy's father and grandfather had had their portraits done in Fauvist style, and from the waist up only. And whilst they had opted to be painted in dark jackets, with shirts and ties in neutral colours, their faces shouted from the breakfast room walls, full of Brandston smugness and self-confidence, in brutal shades of red, green and orange. Percy knew that neither style was for him, but could not think of a style that might be. Marjory had suggested watercolour. His children had suggested a photograph done in a studio. As far as Percy was concerned, they could see to it when he was dead.

Percy would have been nonplussed to know what to wear, how to pose. His face was round, flat, pink and shiny. His neck was the same width as his face, and too short. His body was short and square and round. He had no paunch to speak of, but his love-handles hung over his trousers at the hips. His arms and legs were short, but his hands and feet were disproportionately large and clumsy. His fingers were like long, fat sausages. Photojournalists had long ago despaired of taking a flattering picture of him, and had been glad when he became unpopular. Now the most unattractive photos were the ones they dragged out time after time: the sliding, foot-dragging walk, the smirk, the head on one side with the dim-but-trying-to-concentrate expression. How would an artist depict him? The only time he truly felt at ease was walking under the trees, in the shadows, in a suit of green Harris tweed and brogues, his face and body dappled, broken up—a Cézanne, all in sage greens, greys and creams, perhaps. With Roger leading the way. He had occasionally found himself wishing he were a dog. They led such a simple life.

Percy put on Roger's lead and brought him to heel. They walked together across the marble floor and out through the front doors of Brandston Manor, as so many lords and their dogs had done before them. Upstairs, the servants were already clearing the breakfast things, airing the bed, dusting and polishing ready for their master's return.

Man and dog went down the stone steps and round the side of the main building, where a gravel path led through the topiary and kitchen gardens and away from the back of the house towards the meadow, the stream, the perimeter wall, the farmland, the open countryside. Patches of snow crunched under Percy's leather soles. The air smelt like steel. Small birds huddled in the trees and shrubs, their shoulders hunched against the cold. Percy let Roger off the lead and sat down in the first of the three gazebos in a row, facing away from the house, that his mother had had built and planted with winter-flowering jasmine and roses.

Once Roger had sniffed around and done his business, they would be ready for a hearty walk. Percy took a deep breath and wriggled his shoulders to let out the tension. At last he could be himself. He allowed the sense of freedom and space to invade him. Today, for a few hours, he wouldn't think about any of the subjects that plagued his mind. He would pretend he was Roger, and try to blank out.

The chill spring wind ruffled the patches of soft, thin, fluffy, blonde hair that still remained on the back and sides of Percy's round, pink head. He looked up at the sky, where storm crows flapped audibly. They reminded him of his teachers, and the way their academic gowns used to flap as they tore down the corridors of his old school, on their way to the staff-room at break time. He wondered if it was anything to do with getting older that everything reminded you of something else. You could never just look at something—just look at it, with no connotations, no implications, and no memories crowding into your mind. He supposed that was why so many people went to the most far-flung, unexplored places they could get to on holiday. If you could find a place where nothing reminded you of anything else in the past, how relaxing that would be!

He found himself thinking of Marjory and the children, to whom he would be speaking after his walk. When he thought of them, he saw them in his mind's eye, waving as they went through airport security: his wife with her large, round sunglasses and her coral-pink headscarf tied under her chin and round her neck, like a 1960s film star, his children failing to follow their mother's example of turning and waving goodbye to him at the last moment. They were not happy with the choice of New Zealand as a retreat, at the prospect of a fortnight or more with Aunty Christine and her partner Zooie, their 'green' lifestyle.

Marjory's cousin Christine was an eccentric, and a recluse. Zooie, a native New Zealander and retired airline pilot, had been her companion for over thirty years. They were happy, sun-tanned, grey-haired recluses who did everything together. "There'll be nothing to do!" the children had moaned at dinner, even though they had been the first to complain of the presence of F5, whom they referred to 'riff-raff', and to suggest getting away from Brandston Manor. "Whatever happened to those nice chaps from the local force who used to look after us?" his daughter had asked, whilst picking alternatively at her food and her nail varnish. "They've been cut," his son had remarked, "Along with half the army. Daddy's fault." "Now that's not very fair . . ." Marjory had started to say, but Percy had shaken his head at her, as a signal to change the subject.

"Anyway," Marjory had said, brightly, always supportive of her husband, "We can hire a car and go and visit the Lord of the Rings thing. You know, the place where they filmed the . . . films. Hobbiton, Edoras—all that. I know *I'd* like to see it. They have people in costume . . ." Her voice had trailed off as first Tim, then Elspeth, tutted and pulled their napkins from their laps and dumped them on the dinner table: the family's signal that things were becoming a little emotional. "Well, I think it's a splendid idea, darling," said Percy, beaming at his wife, who beamed back, "You know how busy Daddy is with everything. Nothing much happening here to interest you. And Aunty Christine will be thrilled to see you." He was about to say "see how much you've grown" but bit back the words at the last moment: his children would not have taken the joke well.

Already the children felt aggrieved that they were back, living at home, having stuffed up (as he saw it) in the outside world. Elspeth's failed marriage was the talk of the town, and Tim's business going to the wall was even more of a disgrace. This did not make for a peaceful atmosphere. In addition, the rules of the house: no parties except by agreement, guest list to be supplied for security clearance purposes, noise levels to be kept reasonable, overnight guests to sleep in their own rooms, etc. were a topic leading to arguments that had ruined many a weekend family breakfast.

The air inside the Manor had remained as frosty as the wintry air outside, up to the day of Marjory, Elspeth and Tim's departure. Not between Marjory and Percy, of course—they were always united and on warm terms with each other—but between parents and offspring. It had all rather put a damper on Percy's birthday party. "Not to worry," said Percy out loud to himself, as he blew on his gloved hands and shifted his numb behind on the bench, preparing to begin his walk proper, "Not to worry. No point in worrying. No point at all. Keep it together, old chap."

Percy Brandston got up a little painfully from his seat and called, "Come, boy! Come, Roger!" The Labrador bounded up and stuck his nose into Percy's outstretched hand. Percy clipped his lead back on and headed towards the topiary garden, where the holly, myrtle and bay laurel spirals and diamonds (inspired by the family crest), perfectly sculpted, stood in their ranks, either side of the gravel walk, their tops iced by the frost. The sight of them reminded Percy that his head was feeling cold. He fished around in his pocket, drew out his tweed cap and put it on. "Right, old boy," he said to Roger, reaching down to pat the dog's soft, smooth head, "Let's be off!"

Man and dog trotted off side by side, falling into step with each other. Up in the sky, the crows cawed loudly and circled, watching.

Chapter Eleven

CO-OPTED

And so it came to pass that Archie Prescott found himself press-ganged onto the Residents' Association Committee, to take his place side by side with Carol Manley and five other tenants. For Eden Tower there was Carol, Archie, Big John Bloor (who spent most of his days riding around the area on a majestic and ancient motorcycle) and Ronald Greeley, a fifty-five-year-old postman.

Ronald was still working at the local mail sorting office. His son Bobby lived with him. Bobby, a rather shy young man, was unwaged, and spent most of his time doing volunteering with a local conservation group. He had once lost a week's benefits because he'd slipped into a stream, gone home to change, and been an hour late to the Job Centre to sign on. He had been ejected by the security man for swearing at two members of staff.

For Paradise Tower, there were three ladies, all friends of Carol's: Mandy, Evie and Veronica. Archie referred to them as the three witches, but only in conversation with Pete the support officer, who was discreet. All three were known for their constant complaining, and for their aggression when crossed. Woe betide the person who left their washing in the machine ten minutes too long if one of *them* was waiting! Evie was the worst. She had been known to go for weeks without speaking to a particular tenant, for no apparent reason. She had a permanent frown on her face, and kept her arms tightly folded against her flat bosom most of the time, even when walking, as if she mistrusted the world. She took instant dislikes to new arrivals on the estate for reasons such as "I don't like the way he smiles" and "Her voice sounds like a neighing horse".

Veronica, who looked like a piece of old string, all thin and sinewy, had known Carol for years. They had been work colleagues before retirement, and often went shopping together. She and Carol could often be heard to arrive before they were seen, by their identical braying laughs, and their imminent arrival was invariably announced, as it were, by the clouds of cigarette smoke that billowed before them.

Mandy was the extra one, invited to go shopping whenever either Carol or Veronica was unavailable. She didn't seem to have much of a character to Archie. She did her hair like Carol's—in a yellow blonde bubble perm—wore the same kinds of clothes (jeans with tights and court shoes, shapeless floral print blouses and dun-coloured cardigans) and always seemed to echo what Carol said. Archie thought she could have picked a better person to emulate.

Carol, Mandy, Evie and Veronica thought it was fine to have a party every couple of weeks and get everyone blind drunk. This worried Archie, who knew how many of the tenants had problems with alcohol, and how many were either on the verge (because of worries of various kinds) or were trying hard to quit, or had quit and needed to stay off the booze. With his experience of restaurant work on a holiday island, he was quick to read the signs of alcoholism, and the facial expressions people got when they were offered a drink and were desperate to refuse. He also knew that, once a culture of drunkenness and fighting took hold, the estate would be hell to live on.

It wasn't just the tenants, but their visitors. Drunks attracted other drunks: he'd seen it before. When he'd first moved in, there had been three old men in the building who were inveterate boozers, and there had been shouting, swearing and fights several times a week, going on late into the night, urine and worse in the lift, doors kicked in, litter everywhere. The three men had ended by falling out. One had died, one had been carted off by relatives, and the other had gone into a home. Nobody wanted to see a repeat of that.

Carol was the most vociferous in complaining about bad behaviour on the estate. And she never hesitated to confront suspects and give them a ticking off. She had several times humiliated elderly men who got into the lift smelling of alcohol, or urine, or body odour, or all three at once.

But Carol and her cronies seemed unaware that they were on the same slippery slope themselves. Archie saw it as some kind of sexism: they simply thought they were still 'ladies' however they behaved, that they were being trendy by having a 'girls' night out' (or in), that they were somehow better than the men who did the same kind of thing. Raised by a mother who had never had so much as a drop of sherry at Christmas, though she had been happy enough for her husband to have a glass of stout by the fire on a Friday night, he—who by no means considered himself a fuddy-duddy or a killjoy—was genuinely shocked by the way these women, his age or older, behaved when they'd been at the vodka.

It was into this unhealthy culture that Archie, at a time of life when he would have preferred a smooth sail, was dropped, like a piece of meat into a piranha-infested river. The first committee meeting at which he was to be present took place on a Monday afternoon in September at two in the afternoon. Archie walked into the community room to find the ladies already there, and himself the only gentleman present.

It soon became clear, from what he overheard as he entered the room, that the other two men had resigned, and it was only in conversation with each of them over the next few days—whispered conversation in the laundry room—why they had chosen to do so. "I just can't stand the noise," said Ronald Greeley, shaking his head. "They just, well, cackle. Especially when they've had a few drinks. Goes straight through me, like a knife. I get a headache. Anyway, I've done my time. Three years is enough. But if ever you need to talk, or have a moan, knock on my door. The kettle's always on." Big John Bloor had been reticent at first: "No reason really," he said, looking down at his shoes, "Sorry about that. I wish you luck and all that."

"Ah, come on John, there's got to be more to it than that," Archie gently probed, "Man to man, what's put you off?" "It's the drinking," said John with a sigh, "Every meeting. And I've been on the wagon since last new year. Doctor's orders." "Sorry," said Archie, "Just wanted to know what I'm up against . . . Take care now." "See you," said Big John. He did sound tired and depressed.

Archie didn't like sitting there surrounded by women. Not that he was in any way anti-women, but it reminded him of too many evenings on the island, waiting for the female customers who'd come on holiday without their partners or husbands, or in groups, to get a move on. Especially the hen parties. Practically falling off his stool with exhaustion while he waited for them to finish up their cocktails, knowing that when they did they'd want walking back to their hotels or apartments. He was always the last, left to lock up, and the streets were dark and dangerous. It was one of his self-appointed civic duties to accompany the women—off their heads with booze, sun and excitement—safely home. There were pickpockets, muggers and worse who lurked in the shadows, and more than once he'd had to get into fisticuffs to defend the possessions—and dubious honour—of holidaymakers. Not only that, but on many occasions the women had tried to seduce him at the end of a walk, which was something he had not appreciated at all. Nothing less of a turn-on than a sangria-sodden, sweaty stranger, burnt red from too much sun, pressed up against him, grabbing his crotch and slurring into his ear.

Not that he expected any of the women on the committee to pounce on him, but the two bottles of vodka and one of Lambrini already open on the table worried him. "Anyone for a coffee?" he asked his colleagues, keeping a straight face as he headed for the kitchen. Carol giggled. The other three were silent, watching. "We've put a glass out for you, Archibald," called out Carol, "Come on, lighten up a bit!" Archie ignored her and made himself a cup of coffee. He went and sat down. They had pushed two of the square tables together. He sat as far away from Carol as possible. This meant he was next to Evie, who sniffed at him audibly as he sat down. "Is she smelling me?" Archie thought, "I had a bath last night and I put aftershave on. Maybe she doesn't like it." He tried to catch Evie's eye to give her a smile, but she was facing front with her nose was in the air. Clearly he was guilty of something, but he honestly couldn't be bothered to ask what. It might be the shape of his chin or the size of his shoes she'd taken exception to, for all he knew.

"Can we get on, please Carol?" asked Archie, getting out his biro, ready to take notes, "Only I've got something to do afterwards." Carol glared. Archie decided to press the point: "Is there an agenda? Only, I didn't get a copy . . ." The ladies laughed, and Evie said, "Hark at him! What's an agenda when it's at home, then?" Archie was feeling brave. "There should be an agenda," he insisted, "And minutes taken. Otherwise how can you do things properly?" Carol and Evie snorted. "D'you really think the people who live here care about things done properly?" said Carol, "They just want to get together for a drink and a bit of entertainment now and then. A singer, or something."

Archie decided that it was 'in for a penny, in for a pound' and, raising his voice above the derisive laughter coming from the women around the table, he said, "We have a lot of people here who have problems with the booze, and a few who've given it up. I think we ought to be thinking about our health more. What about skittles, or a bit of gardening? Or a nice lunch with soup and a ploughman's?"

Carol and her friends fell silent. "Are you having a go?" asked Carol, going red in the face. "Well, if the cap fits . . ." said Archie, going equally red. "Excuse me," said Veronica, her first contribution to the conversation, "Are you making this personal?" But Archie was not in the mood to back down. All he knew about the dangers of too much drinking came flooding back, including all the times he'd seen men and women making arses of themselves on the island. "I think the committee should be setting an example, yes," he ventured, "Haven't you been voted on to take some kind of a lead?" Evie turned to him with a look of pure hatred on her face, "Well, nobody voted for *you*!" she spat, "You're just here to . . . Well, to . . . Carol? What's he here for?" she asked, turning to her friend, who was sitting tight-lipped in her chair, her wineglass halfway to her mouth. "Do you know, Evie, I can't for the life of me remember!" said Carol, "But I tell you what: if he thinks he can do a better job, let him try it. Come on, you lot, I'm off to the pub. Meeting's over. I resign!"

Carol stood up, pushing her chair backwards with such force, it tipped over. And of course, first Veronica, then Evie, then Mandy, followed suit. Picking up their half-full bottles, they swept out of the common room, banging the door behind them. Archie was left all alone with nothing but his cup of coffee, their empty wineglasses, four chairs to put to rights, and a redundant biro. He shook his head in disbelief. After a few minutes, he got the accounts book out of his bag and opened it. Then he got out the receipts and the petty cash book. He might as well use the time to do something worthwhile.

Having driven the Gnomes underground, so to speak, the Humans now became enamoured of their effigies. Soon everyone in Europe who could afford a garden gnome was proudly displaying their own: beside a pond, on top of a rockery, in the doorway of a decorative windmill, as the centrepiece of a rose bed.

New designs appeared, including the infamous 'Mooning Gnome'—an almost blasphemous misrepresentation of the real thing—depicted with his trousers down and his buttocks in full view. This character was particularly favoured by those with nosey neighbours . . .

Meanwhile, the souls of departed Gnomes were forever seeking a home: a new body in which to live again. The advent of the garden gnome gave them the opportunity they had waited for. All it took was for a garden gnome to be loved and treated with respect for the miracle to happen . . .

Chapter Twelve

ARCHIE UNSETTLED

Archie Prescott couldn't sleep. He lay with his eyes closed, flat on his back, and tried to relax, beginning with his toes, the way the teacher had shown the class at a yoga 'taster session' he had recently attended at a nearby church hall. His toes were too tight under the sheet and blanket tucked in at the foot of the bed, so he kicked both legs to make more room. He tensed his feet and ankles, then let go of the tension. He felt the tingling sensation. He repeated the exercise with his legs, his hips and bottom, his back, his chest, shoulders, arms, and finally his neck and head. Now his body felt heavy and warm, and he gave a great sigh as he waited for sleep to take him.

It didn't. It wasn't anything to do with the committee meeting three months before. Sleep eluded him—as it had for the past three nights, in fact—for the simple reason that there was no way he could stop thinking about Ann-Marie Osborne, his new neighbour, in a flat directly under his, three floors below on the fifth. His head kept filling up with images of her: her rounded calves and slim ankles, her warm smile, her eyes, the colour of which, he suddenly realised, was the same as the paper towels the council provided for the communal kitchen and loo. A very unusual shade of green: eau de nil, or light sage, possibly? Her firm, ample bosom, her long, slim fingers, and her expression whenever she was looking at him, and listening to him speak. Nobody focused on what he said the way she did. He liked that about her. So many only struck up a conversation with him so they could talk about themselves: their ailments, their grand-children, their dodgy boilers.

He hadn't imagined it. In a group—say, over waiting for the laundry—when he spoke up, there was a sudden alertness in her shoulders, in her face, like an infusion of energy, or of concentration. As if what he was saying really meant something. Not just the ramblings of an older person. He had never thought of himself as very intelligent, or very interesting, but Ann-Marie seemed to find him riveting. Archie smiled a little smile in the dark.

She was four years his junior at fifty-five. Why was he even thinking about the age gap, as if he were thinking that far ahead? "Silly old me!" said Archie out loud, chuckled and gave a little cough, "What am I thinking? She's just a nice lady. And the new kid on the block: that's all." He remembered how, whenever a new pupil arrived at St. Gabriel's, his old school, half the pupils (depending on whether the latest arrival was male or female) would be mooning around for weeks. "It's just novelty, that's what it is," he said, "Anyway, why would she be interested in an old codger like me? She's just nice and friendly. Or maybe my voice is a bit too quiet. It's been a while since I really bothered about making myself heard."

Archie tried turning onto his left side, which was his normal sleeping position, but then his pyjamas got somehow twisted around and his feet started to itch. "Itchy feet? Hehehe . . ." Archie laughed so loudly that his upstairs neighbour knocked on his bedroom floor. "Sorry!" he called out, reaching over to switch on his bedside lamp. He lay looking at the light filtering through the red and blue Spiderman shade. The lamp was a gift his grand-children had given him last birthday. "We were going to get you Superman, Grandad," his grandson Miles had said. "But Katie and me, we thought . . . Well, he's got a lot of muscles. So . . ." Katie, Miles' little sister had chipped in, ever the diplomat, "So, because Spiderman is really braver anyway, we went for him instead." That had made Archie laugh. Spiderman: yes! Skinny arms and legs like a spider, bit of a tummy in the middle, spot on.

That got him thinking how nice it would be to be able to spin a line and swing from one building to another, all the way to the supermarket and back. It would save a fortune on bus fares. Or, swinging all the way to the airport, then using his sticky spider feet to glue himself to the underside of an aeroplane bound for somewhere warm and sunny . . .

He imagined himself lying on a golden beach under a lapis lazuli sky without clouds, propped up on his side, cocktail in hand, sand between his bare toes, and Ann-Marie in a swimsuit with a plunging neckline, lying on a pink towel with a pattern of roses. He had seen her with a towel like that on top of her laundry bag. She certainly likes roses, he thought. Ann-Marie looking up into his face over the top of a pair of sunglasses, licking an ice-cream cone. A little blob of ice-cream on the tip of her nose. Himself leaning down to lick it off, then moving downwards to kiss her plump lips . . .

Archie sat up in bed with a jolt. Cursing under his breath, he swung his legs out and jammed his feet into his slippers. He angrily grabbed his dressing-gown and flung it round his shoulders. Then he marched to the kitchen and switched on the kettle. While the water was coming up to the boil, he took up his accustomed station at the window, looking down into the garden, trying to breathe more slowly and calm himself down.

The moon was almost full—all but a sliver hung in the clear sky—and its silvery light picked out every detail of the scene below. The leaves and branches looked as though they had been dipped in some kind of dark metal. No breath of wind stirred them. There in the middle of the garden sat the bench. Trevor's bench, named after the neighbour who most often sat on it. Trevor, whose growing fragility and unhealthy colour betrayed the terminal cancer he was still trying to overcome. Archie and Trevor were good mates, both supporters of the same local football team, both fond of a coffee and a Kit-Kat over the newspapers. Both confirmed bachelors.

The bench was empty tonight. It was rare for any of the tenants to go out after dark, even though that part of the garden had been fenced off by the council, to give them all somewhere safe to sit, free from litter and the drug paraphernalia that had once made the area so unattractive to relax in. "I know what I'll do," thought Archie, going to the cupboard where the mugs were kept, "I'll get dressed and take my coffee down there. A bit of fresh air is bound to help me drop off."

During his years on the island, he had often been up late, going for long walks, or just sitting on the rocks by the sea after a long shift in a steamy, roasting-hot kitchen. He knew better than to try and force sleep when it would not come. Better to go with the flow, enjoy the comfortableness of one's own company, and the night with its flavour and its scenery. The night, to Archie, was an exotic country, a place where being alive felt right, no matter what yesterday had brought, no matter what was in store tomorrow.

He dressed warmly, made up a strong coffee in a thermal mug with a lid, slipped the end of a packet of chocolate digestives into his jacket pocket, grabbed a sofa cushion and let himself quietly out of his flat. Two minutes later he emerged from the lift, took the back door out of the block and headed for the bench. The grass was damp, but he liked the feel of the coolness seeping up through the cloth of his old, brown, corduroy slippers.

Archie placed the sofa cushion at one end of the bench and his mug on the arm, and sat down, wriggling his back into the slats at the back of the bench. The wood felt good, like a firm massage. He stretched out his legs, cracking the left knee, which had a little arthritis, and took a deep breath. All was still, all was well. He was alone with his coffee and the moonlight. The occasional vehicle slid by at the end of the road with a soft hiss, on the wet road.

The air smelt of old wet leaves, and of the old-fashioned lavender he and Ann-Marie had planted beside the bench the week before. Seconds later, very faintly, but growing, as his nose became accustomed to its new environment, the indescribably heavenly scent of roses wafted to him. Three bushes planted in a triangle in the bed three feet in front of the bench: a white, a pink and a yellow. The white rose was called Ice Cream, the pink was a Rosemoor, and the yellow with hints of peach, which was nearest to him, was of course a Whiskey Mac, chosen by Archie himself in memory of his mother, whose favourite variety it had been. He loved the way it was possible to separate the three scents from one other by their hints of apple, of spice, and of cucumber. It was his mother who had taught him to take time and smell the roses. He had been delighted when, the first time Ann-Marie had noticed they were flowering, she had knelt down on the grass, regardless of her white trousers, and plunged her nose into an Ice Cream bloom, exclaiming: "Now isn't this the loveliest thing in the world?"

It had crossed Archie's mind at the time that the loveliest thing he'd seen for a long time was Ann-Marie with her head in a rosebush, but he had shaken it off, muttering something about filling up the bird bath, and made a quick escape. He had returned a few minutes later to pick up the conversation, regretting his lack of self-composure.

"The Three Graces", Ann-Marie had christened their three rosebushes, blushing as she had explained the reference when she noticed his blank expression. "I'm sorry, Archie," she had said, looking down at her feet, "I forget sometimes that not everyone's been raised on ancient myths." Archie smiled and asked, "So who were they then, the Three Graces?" "Oh," said Ann-Marie, "Promise you won't take me to task for lecturing you, if I tell you?" "Never!" said Archie, "I could probably tell you the name of every holy saint and martyr from my school days! And it's good to learn new stuff. Keeps the old brain fresh . . ." Ann-Marie and Archie were sitting on the bench in the sun, having one of their long conversations. This was happening with increasing frequency. They just got on.

Ann-Marie lifted her face to the sun and closed her eyes. "Well, now," she said, in her sweet, quiet voice, "They were three gorgeous women, called Euphrosyne, Aglaea and Thalia . . ." "That's a bit of a mouthful!" interjected Archie, smiling. "Well, yes, I suppose . . ." said Ann-Marie, "Anyway, they were goddesses. The three daughters of Zeus. They were a bit like you, in a way . . ." Archie laughed, "How's that then?" he asked, intrigued. "Well, they presided over the banquets of the gods and made sure everyone was having a good time. Just like you do, when we have a get-together in the common room." Archie was flattered—and fascinated by listening to his friend. "They were said to represent beauty, charm and joy." Archie turned to Ann-Marie and looked at her. "That last bit is you, I think," he said, surprised at his own daring, "You've cheered me up a lot since you came along." "Yes, but I don't think Carol and Veronica like me very much," whispered Ann-Marie. She looked away into the far distance, a wistful expression on her face.

Ann-Marie was very educated and had several times been the butt of sniggers and comments from Carol and Co. when she had let slip a long word or a literary or classical reference. Archie had been guilty of a snort himself on the first occasion, when she had laughingly referred to spring-cleaning her flat as "cleansing the Augean stables". Then he had heard Carol's laugh of derision, and her "What's she on about then?", and seen how Ann-Marie's face had gone red, and her smile had been wiped off. He had felt ashamed, as he realised with a start that he was in danger of being infected by Carol and her friends' spitefulness. "After all," he told himself, "Education's a good thing, so why put someone down if they have it?"

His respect for Ann-Marie had increased considerably when she had turned to Carol and answered, "You've heard of Hercules, haven't you? Well, cleaning out the stables was one of his nine labours that he had to complete. Shovelling horse muck. Only, he was clever. He diverted a river through the building and let the water wash it all away. I wish it were that simple when I get into the shit!" Veronica had actually nodded in sympathy, which had occasioned another of Carol's glares, but Carol herself had had nothing more to say. Archie knew her tactics: she would go the underhand route and spread it around that Ann-Marie was a snob. And it would take a long while for her to win people back over as a result. Carol was still a force to be reckoned with on the estate.

From then on, Archie had made a point of being himself with Ann-Marie, and allowing her to be herself with him. When the big words came out, and the quotations from Shakespeare, he asked her about them. In return, he was teaching her about gardening, of which she knew so little. It was developing into a fruitful friendship in more ways than one.

Archie drank in the night air and its mingling fragrances, and realised that his interest in Ann-Marie had already grown into something that involved a certain fascination, a desire to know her better, to make space for her in his life—and a sense of responsibility for her well-being. He drank his hot coffee and ate his biscuits, and shook his head over himself. He was a humble man, and did not think it necessarily followed that if he took an interest in pursuing friendship with another person, they would feel the same. He had at times missed out on opportunities to make friends because of his reticence, which others sometimes mistook for self-sufficiency, or a lack of warmth in him. "No fool like an old fool," he muttered to himself, "Just make sure no-one else notices, especially her. Better to keep things the way they are, nice and simple."

Archie put down his empty coffee cup, and the packet of biscuits. There were three left, and he intended to save them for his early morning cuppa. After a while, his eyes began to droop, and his head to nod, and he fell into a deep, calm sleep. He had not meant to fall asleep, but because he did, the whole future of the nation changed that June night. For it was an hour later, in the darkest hours before dawn, when lavender and roses scented the air and the moonlight dipped the garden in magic, that Archie Prescott first made the acquaintance of four elderly gentlemen who had travelled far, seen much, and had much to say. It was on that night that Archie met Norman, Nigel, Nick and Ned Blackthorn.

Chapter Thirteen

AFFINITY

Archie, already considerably stiffened from his doze on the bench, stiffened even more when he realised he wasn't alone. A small, warm body was snuggled against his side. He could feel the slight changes in pressure as the creature—whatever it was—breathed deeply and slowly. "What the . . . ?" he asked himself, "Is it a cat? A small fox? What do I do?" He began by matching his breathing to that of the creature, in case the slight movements he was making woke it up. Then he slowly moved his head, so that he could look down and to his right. He could not at first believe what he was seeing.

At this pivotal moment in the story of Archie—and Percy—it is vital that it be made clear that Archie felt a peculiar affinity to all small creatures, perhaps because of his own smallness, relative to most people. Growing up with the nickname 'Runt' does something to you. All his life, he had espoused the cause of those whose size or height made them vulnerable, or put them on the fringes. Whereas his brothers and sisters had preferred robust dogs or cats as pets, and romping in the park, he had always been the one to bring home an injured fledgling and nurse it for days in his room, to spring the mousetraps at night when the family were asleep, to spend his time on family visits to the zoo sitting in front of an exhibit called Mouse City: an octagonal glass case containing a huge structure resembling a doll's house with ladders to the windows, which contained several dozen of the small rodents. While his siblings clamoured for ice-creams and a ride on the elephant, Archie could be found lying on his tummy in the grass, observing butterflies and beetles, and shooing away anyone who came close enough to risk frightening them off.

That's not to say that Archie loved everything just because it was small. He had drawn the line, for example, at the cockroaches (whistling and non-whistling) which had infested his apartment on the island, hiding in the toilet bowl and dropping on his face in the night. Neither did he love sand flies, mosquitoes or midges. But if something was small, beautiful, useful and kindly-disposed, he was its champion.

Archie had a face straight out of Snow White and the Seven Dwarves. A craggy face, a long, hooked nose, a wedge-shaped chin, put together with his height and compact body, made him a perfect Santa's Helper for Christmas parties. He had first played the role at the Christmas party his mother had organised at the nearest old people's home when he was only eight years old. Archie had loved the costume so much he had worn it for the whole fortnight of the school holidays, to the amusement of his brothers and sisters, who had given him all kinds of extra chores to do, using their knowledge that he was familiar with—and fond of—the story of 'The Elves and the Shoemaker'. They hid his proper clothes, and informed him that he would have to work to get them back, and then he would be free. Innocent Archie had been found by his mother, dozily sweeping out the grate in the parlour, at two in the morning, in full uniform. His eldest brother Bernard— always the ring-leader—had had his ears boxed.

The creature was clearly visible in the moonlight, even though the moon was doing down, and it was dark. Silver light picked out a dark mass that looked like a jacket with silver buttons and a belt with a large buckle, fat legs in dark green trousers, tucked into sturdy brown leather boots (one ankle crossed over the other), a woollen scarf (crimson), a chin and a nose of equal length and of similar shape to Archie's, smooth brownish skin, and a tall, crimson, pointed hat. Archie was not completely surprised—for reasons which will shortly become clear—but he was worried about reacting appropriately. And—wonder of wonders!—on closer inspection, he found that, leaning against the gnome—for of course that is what the creature undoubtedly was—on the far side was another gnome. And leaning against him was a third, while a fourth lay curled into a ball, his bottom pressed against the third gnome's side, like a book-end. They were all four fast asleep.

"I don't know what to do," thought Archie, and because it was his philosophy in life that if you don't know what to do yet, do nothing, he stayed still and enjoyed the moment. He also rehearsed in his head things he might say if they woke up. They might panic, in which case he must immediately reassure them of his good intentions. They might become aggressive (though he doubted it, whatever J.K. Rowling's portrayal of their character might be). They might want something. Archie was a hospitable and generous man, so the first action he took was to sneak the remaining chocolate biscuits out of his left pocket, slide out two biscuits, break them in two and lean over very slowly and carefully to place half a biscuit on the lap (if 'lap' is the appropriate word) of each gnome. How keen was their sense of smell? He guessed that it must be acute. If they woke up to the delicious smell of chocolate digestive, that would be a pleasant experience. And they would know that he was on their side. He sincerely hoped they didn't prefer custard creams or fig rolls. If, indeed, they had ever tasted human-made biscuits. Did they scavenge? Or did they have burrows, and cook for themselves somehow?

Each little fellow would have been approximately a foot tall standing up, he reckoned. They must have good upper body strength to pull themselves up onto the bench. He did wonder why they had chosen to sleep there, and whether they had done so in awareness of his presence. Perhaps they wanted to talk? They must have voices, for the two in the middle were now snoring quite loudly. Archie's thoughts ran off in all different directions, but they were mostly pleasant, for he had—he was now sure—already established a good relationship with the little men.

Not long after Archie had become the sole member of the Residents' Association Committee: its Chair, Secretary, Treasurer and Social Secretary all rolled into one (though Carol and Co. had never passed over the bank accounting, so he was left to manage as best he could without funds), he had had a chat to a number of other men on the housing scheme, and in particular to Ronald Greeley, and Big John Bloor, and together they had come up with a scheme to make something of the garden. It wasn't really a garden at all in those days: just grass and a few straggly shrubs in one corner. Archie's mother had taught him a lot about cultivation, and the pleasures of gardening, and it was time to put that knowledge to good use.

They had begun one cold but bright March morning, having borrowed some tools from a tenant who had once had an allotment but could no longer work it, and a couple of litter picks obtained from the caretaker, a friendly chap by the name of Dave. They pruned the shrubs, bagged up five sacks of litter, pulled up ivy and weeds, and dug four beds: one for flowers in front of the one bench, and three for vegetables.

The following day, a Sunday, they had turned out again, this time in the sleet, to dig a fourth bed. Archie had insisted on a gnome garden. "What's an English garden without gnomes?" he'd asked the guys, over a cup of tea after work, the five of them ensconced in the common-room's high-backed armchairs, muddy boots off, their toes in woolly socks gradually getting their feeling back. "I grew up with gnomes," said Ronald, his eyes drifting left as he remembered his youth, "My dad put them all over the back garden. If you put them in the front, they got stolen. There was a pond with three gnomes in a row with fishing-rods. Even one on top of the bird-house." Big John confessed to having stolen a gnome from a front garden on the way home from school one day and giving it to his mother for Mother's Day. "She loved that gnome," he said, laughing, "So much so my Dad put it in her coffin with her when she passed away. He'd painted him up in the Aston Villa colours, which I don't think she'd have approved of, as she was a Blues fan. Used to call him Doug, because he had a spade in his hand. Doug—Dug—d'you get it?" They shared companionable laughter. It was a good moment.

Every day from then on, at various times, as if by the action of some psychic connection, the men would gather in the common-room, ready for another few hours of effort. And within the space of a few months, the garden was showing signs of the transformation. Wherever they planted a perennial, it would thrive. Fruit trees, planted only a foot tall, would thrust their branches towards the sky. Even the grass became lusher and greener. It was as though the garden knew it was loved. And other tenants would come down to spend a few minutes on the bench, to congratulate Archie and his friends on their determination, to hand them a chocolate bar or a can of pop. Two or three of the older ladies, who went out weekly with relatives, came back from garden centres bearing gifts: a herb plant, a packet of marigold seeds, a tray of pansies, a bare-root rosebush.

When Ethel, who had lived on the second floor of Paradise Tower, passed away, three of the ladies took up a collection, and handed over the money to Archie. "Get something nice for the flower-bed, please," said Joan, the eldest at ninety-two, "In memory of Ethel. She loved her roses. They've got some nice ones at that place on York Road. You know, the one with the café? Just an idea. And maybe a couple of buddleias, for the butterflies and bees?" Archie had taken their suggestions on-board, which is how the Three Graces came to be there in June of that year, spreading their colour and fragrance, and cheering everyone up—at least, those who were open to being cheered up.

Carol had been sceptical: "You won't be able to keep it up," she'd said to Ronald and Big John, when Archie wasn't there, "People always start things, but they always give up. It's a commitment. Plus, all these beds you're digging—you'll have to put the grass back if you don't keep them going, otherwise the place'll look a right mess." Ronald and Big John had looked subdued when Archie arrived on the scene a few minutes after Carol had left. He'd seen her leave. "What's up, lads?" he had asked them, "Been listening to a motivational talk, have you?" First John and then Ronald cracked their jaws and smiled. "Come on, then," said Archie, "Fish and chips on me afterwards!"

Archie was the kind of man who flourished in the face of opposition—another effect of having had to fight his corner growing up—and he found it easy to motivate others as a result. "Let it go over the top of your head" he was fond of saying, and "You can't win some of the people any of the time". And he had a way of carrying others along with him until they caught his enthusiasm. He was more influential on those around him than he realised, being a modest man, and not given to thinking of himself as a leader.

So it was that the Eden and Paradise Gnome Garden began to emerge from the mud that spring and summer.

Chapter Fourteen

NEW ARRIVALS

Archie was consistently encouraged and supported in his vision by Ronald, Big John, Viktor Novak—a Pole who lived on the fourth floor of Eden Tower and who had first come to England in his teens to serve as an airman—and a new arrival to Paradise who went by the name of Banton. Was that his first name, or his surname? Nobody knew. Nobody knew much about him at all, except that he had a glamorous and willowy girl-friend called Alicia who made him delicious African-Caribbean food, the mingled savoury smells of which drove everyone on his floor crazy when it wafted out onto the landing three or four times a week.

Occasionally, Big Frank came out to make sure they had a cup of tea or coffee, but he couldn't leave his sister June for long: she'd had what he described as a 'collapse' over Christmas, and not yet recovered her energy. "June says hello," he said as he delivered a tray of hot drinks to the bench one afternoon, when the wind was blowing so strongly it took their breath away, "She can't come down, but she's sent you this." He rummaged in his coat pocket and took out something wrapped in newspaper. "Your first one, I believe," said Frank, handing it over to Archie, who was blowing his nose for the umpteenth time. The wind always got into his sinuses.

Archie took careful hold of the small parcel, and removed the first layer of paper, then a second and a third. Whatever the gift was, it was valuable to June, and therefore he gave it the care it deserved. When he saw what was inside, he laughed out loud, a carefree, delighted laugh: "Well, well!" was all he could think of to say, as he held it out so the others could see. In his hand was a classic garden gnome of the 1960s. You could tell, because he was smoking a pipe, whilst leaning on his spade. Modern gnomes are not usually depicted smoking. The expression on his face was rather inscrutable. He wasn't smiling, and his eyebrows were raised. If one were to take a guess at what he was thinking, it might be something along the lines of: "I'll get back to my digging when I'm good and ready, OK?"

There was a minute's respectful silence, while the men inspected the figurine. Viktor was the next to speak: "Does this gentleman have a name?" he asked Big Frank. "Yes, he does," Frank replied, clearly impressed that this mattered to Viktor, "June got him as a joke wedding present when she married her late husband in 1968, when her favourite band was Pink Floyd. That was the year Syd Barrett left them, because of his mental health. So she called this little fellow Syd. Syd with a 'y'. Not that we've ever had to write it down, or anything . . ." He blushed.

"Welcome to the Gnome Garden, Syd," said Archie gravely. Together the men went over to the designated area, where they had built up a rockery with bricks and stones dug out from other parts of the garden, and Ronald solemnly placed Syd on the side facing the shrubbery, halfway up. "He'll be able to look at the birds from there," said Banton, laughing. They fetched their hot drinks, and stood looking at Syd, leaning on his spade and smoking. "He looks a bit lonely, don't you think?" asked Big John. The others nodded. "Well, I've got to be off in a bit," said Archie, "Need a few bits and pieces up the High Street." "I can give you a lift," said Big John, "Got a spare helmet, if you're interested." Archie guffawed, "My God!" he exclaimed, "Haven't been on a bike for . . . ooh . . . got to be thirty-five years!" "All the more reason!" said Banton, "Mi old but mi nuh cold, as my granny used to say!" "Meaning, there's life in the old dog yet?" laughed Archie. "More or less, dog," said Banton, smiling.

Big John and Archie went off for their bike ride, and the other men cleaned the tools and put them away for another day. Syd—who was a gnome of the Willow clan, those who wield tools and are known for their physical endurance—kept his lonely vigil in the garden until tea-time, getting used to his new surroundings, glad to be out in the open after twenty years of living on a windowsill—until Big John and Archie reappeared, their pockets full of little friends to keep him company. They had found four more gnomes—not in the garden centre, but in a shop called Moneystretcher, which had a surprisingly well-stocked garden section. They were from the same company, and had the same faces and beards, but different stances. They had been the only ones on the shelf, and John and Archie hadn't had the heart to separate them.

These four, which Archie and Big John laughingly agreed must be cousins, if not brothers, were immediately given the names Norman, Nigel, Nick and Ned. People passing by in the shop were curious to see two grey-haired men having a serious conversation about garden gnomes, and highly amused when they stopped to listen, and heard them giving them names. By the time they had gone through the checkout, the men had decided on the character of each gnome. Norman would be the eldest, steady, peaceable, forgiving and wise. Nigel would be the bossy one, always wishing he'd been the firstborn, always jockeying for position. Nick would be the adventurer, itchy-footed, the gnome for whom a garden was not enough. And Ned, the youngest, would be rather shy and anxious, always ready to point out the risks inherent in any project.

John and Archie were spot on, in fact: the four were indeed brothers, and noble Blackthorns, upholders of tradition, warrior bards, centuries old. And their characters were pretty much the way the men had outlined them. They had once had five other brothers, but they had been lost in battle, their souls left to drift until they could anchor themselves once more. And that would not be until there were more statues on the rockery. For that is how a gnome's immortality works. When humans provide a safe haven for gnomes, and place their effigies there, the ghostly souls of gnomes are drawn to them, and they can live again.

These four had already come to life, thanks to an employee of Moneystretcher called Aziza, who had unpacked them from their box in the stock-room, taken a shine to them, and kept them on a table in the staffroom for a few weeks, with tinsel around their necks, to show her colleagues she wished them well at Christmas. They had been there for a month, greeted each day by most of the staff members, until the manager had said it was time they were sold. The day they had been placed on the shelf in the shop was the day Archie and Big John had bought them, so there had been no unpleasant hiatus for the brothers, whose souls had taken root within their terracotta shells as a result of the respect Aziza had shown them.

When John and Archie took the gnomes out of their pockets and carefully placed them on the rockery, each (at John's suggestion) facing one of the four points of the compass, they knew they had found a good home.

Archie did not see their little eyes following him as he took one final stroll round the garden before going in for his dinner. He felt eyes on him, but looked up at the windows of his neighbours' flats to see who was watching. Nobody was out on their balconies. No curtains were twitching. "Need a sit-down," he said to himself, and went in.

As the sun dipped down below the horizon, the five gnomes began to whisper to one another. And when the moon rose, they stepped down from the rockery and began to explore their new territory, exclaiming over the work the human men had done, gathering up the snails and slugs they found and making a delicious supper of them, which they shared under a holly bush, safe from marauding cats. Later on, the local fox came for a visit with her cubs and, while Syd played with the young foxes in the shrubbery, she gave the Blackthorns as much information as she could about the locality, its benefits and its hazards. Meanwhile, Archie made himself a supper of Cornish pasty and chips, and settled down with 'Match of the Day'. When he phoned his daughter later on, the first thing he told her was: "I've got gnomes in my garden." Little did he know!

Chapter Fifteen

TOPIARYPHOBIA

Percy didn't like the topiary garden, although he wasn't sure why it would make a grown man cower. It made him feel insecure and anxious. Perhaps it was the towering sculptures of greenery, which resembled statues, but were not human figures, or even animals. Perhaps if they had had deer or lions on the family crest, instead of spirals and diamonds, the topiary garden would have felt more welcoming.

He was supposed to entertain nothing but positive feelings here. His father had told him, on the rare occasions when they had walked there together, that the geometric shapes should inspire a "profound sense of family pride". And of course a sense of personal responsibility: "You must never allow this place to go to the dogs, no matter what happens, Boy," his father had admonished him, "Everything you do must be to raise this family higher, to increase its influence, and to secure its future."

Why the spirals and diamonds? One might well wonder. There was a leather-bound book of drawings in the Manor library, made by the ancestor—another Sir Hugo—who had had the privilege of designing Brandston's coat-of-arms, and submitting his designs for approval to the College of Arms and the Court of Chivalry. In it were various ideas, sketched out in black ink on parchment: lions, leopards, even a hare (there was an ancient colony of hares on the estate) represented the animal kingdom. Then there were the supernatural creatures: gryphons, mermaids (no apparent reason for their appearance), and an irate-looking satyr. Percy had often wondered about the satyr and laughed over him, guessing that old Sir Hugo had been feeling randy—and frustrated—the day he had drawn him.

From turning the pages, it could be surmised that Sir Hugo had grown tired of creatures—or perhaps been told they were out of bounds, or already taken by another family—so had changed tack. Trees came next: oaks, of course, apple-trees (the estate had once had its own apple orchard) and a blasted oak. The latter, he guessed, had probably been drawn on a bad day. Perhaps a tree on the estate had been struck by lightning. Why trees had not been chosen for the shield, Percy could not guess, and there were no notes in the sketch-book to tell him.

Next, strawberries had appeared on three successive pages, drawn with and without leaves. By googling, Percy had learnt that the strawberry represented both purity and sensuality, as well as abundance and fertility, modesty and humility. Perhaps, though, they had merely been Sir Hugo's favourite dessert. Clearly, the strawberries had yielded no fruit, for their idea had been abandoned. After all these pages of attempts, there was one on which naked women had been doodled, lying in various inviting positions. Percy always laughed out loud when he came to this page. Sir Hugo must have needed some light relief from his onerous task, which would decide so much concerning the future of the family, or at any rate how its members perceived themselves, not to mention outsiders.

Sir Hugo's final few pages had been drawn with a new quill. You could tell. The lines were sharp and clean, and there were no blots. And he had decided to play it safer and go for geometric shapes. First, he had attempted hearts, and then crossed them out. Percy guessed why: hearts were out of the question; they were just asking for trouble. People would think you were a 'softy'. Lightning forks came next—a good choice, and attractive, but clearly not attractive enough to Sir Hugo. Perhaps he had thought they might attract bad luck, or divine judgement: a lightning strike on the Manor House which would of course have had no lightning rod in those days.

At last, the diamonds had appeared on the parchment, and among them the spirals, turning both clockwise and anticlockwise. Percy had done his research and discovered that, while the choice of diamonds was easy and obvious (they symbolized wealth and perfection as well as strength, in that only diamond can cut diamond), the choice between left spiral and right spiral held deep significance. A right spiral (that is to say, going clockwise) often symbolized ascendancy, spring going into summer, the sun's influence growing. A left spiral could mean the opposite: a decline in every sense. While the Brandston spiral had four complete turns, which symbolized endurance, Percy failed to understand how Sir Hugo could have made the mistake of choosing a left-turning spiral. Perhaps it had meant something else at the time: going in a different direction from his peers, for example. Adherence to the Catholic faith, at a time when Protestantism was more popular—or safer. Or independence of thought. It was a fascinating subject.

The quartered coat-of-arms, finished and complete with its motto, was drawn in full on the final page of the sketch-book. "The family calls on you to be strong and diamond-hard," it spoke to Percy, "To make money, and to go your own way, even if it seems to lead in a downward direction." As Percy remembered all these things, he felt fear jab its icy-cold finger into his stomach.

Percy had got into a habit of feeling afraid in the topiary garden in the presence of his father, the twentieth-century Sir Hugo, and the habit had never been broken. He was trembling now, and feeling rather faint. He took his hip flask from his coat pocket and took a swig of brandy. Roger was racing up and down the gravel paths that formed a square within the area. "I wish I could change places with you, Rog old chap. So much is expected of one . . ." said Percy under his breath. Roger must have had very acute hearing, for he immediately slithered to a halt, did an about-face and came bounding back to his master. Roger stood leaning against his master's leg. It seemed to Percy that dogs might be sensitive to their owners' feelings.

In the centre of Brandston Manor's topiary garden stood the three-hundred-year-old marble fountain, with its three toga-clad women pouring water from ornate jugs, and its family coat-of-arms and the motto: *familia fortis vocat*. Percy's father, Sir Hugo, had translated this as 'the family calls for strength'. Percy had never felt strong in his entire life, though he had had to tough it out, or "man up" as his father put it, on many occasions: at school, at university, in his career. However, he had taken his father's dictat seriously, even after he had gone into politics, which had been on a whim, after a girl he admired had been seduced into bed and suggested it to him. On waking in the morning, she had looked at him and uttered these fateful words: "If you can get me into bed, Percy, when so many have tried and failed, you should be in government. You could talk any*one* into any*thing*, just about. You utter cad!" She had given his cheek a good, hard pinch before getting out of bed and leaving. He had made the mistake of feeling flattered, and had got in touch with the local Tory party office the following day, whilst still hung over on champagne and sex.

His illustrious family history, as well as his military background (he had served for a short time in the Navy) had guaranteed him promotion through the ranks, and he had become, first a Member of Parliament, having been heavily backed by the local party, then Leader of the Party—a singularly unsuccessful one, rapidly replaced when his lack of charisma had caused them to fail dismally in a general election—and eventually a cabinet minister at the age of fifty-three. He had been introduced to Marjory Bland at a cocktail party at the local party HQ when his state of bachelorhood had raised eyebrows during his campaign to become an MP. There were many in his party who suspected any single man over the age of twenty-five of being a homosexual. Paranoia abounded where conformity to what party members called "family values" was paramount.

He had been fortunate in Marjory, for she had liked him from the outset, though he had often asked himself why. Perhaps it was his quiet voice—the only one in the whole room—or his baby face, or his low stature. Marjory was just a little over five feet tall, and other men dismissed her, nicknaming her "the moustached dwarf". It was true, she did have a slight shadow on her upper lip, but Percy, charmed by her attentiveness to his every word (probably explained by the fact that she had to concentrate to hear him against all the haw-hawing), had thought it unimportant. She was a girl, she had a big chest, and she liked him. And moreover, when he had summoned up the courage to ring her parents' house phone the following day to ask her to accompany him to Ascot, she had accepted with enthusiasm. After a short courtship, which both sets of parents had been closely involved in promoting, they had been married.

There had been little physical contact before the wedding, for Marjory was a responsible young woman who knew the value of her maidenhood in the circles in which she moved. This had made the wedding night, in a hotel in Venice, with gondolas gliding up and down the canal under their balcony, very exciting indeed. Percy, who had made love several times before, had been glad of his self-imposed six months of celibacy when Marjory had appeared beside the four-poster bed, clad in a white lace night-dress, her upper lip waxed to nakedness, and had shyly requested, "Percy, make me a real woman."

Marjory's purity, coupled with her devotion to her husband, had kept him enraptured—and faithful—all their married life. He had loved her through and through, and she had loved him in return. He found he was missing her dreadfully.

"*Familia fortis vocat*," said Percy to Roger as he looked down at the panting dog, "Sod this, let's go and frighten the crows off the cabbages!" Roger woofed his agreement. And Percy Brandston, Lord of the Manor, fortified by brandy, set off, Roger trotting by his side, in the direction of the yew archway that connected the topiary garden to the kitchen garden.

Chapter Sixteen

HURUHURU

The walk to Christine and Zooie's cottage wasn't as unpleasant as Marjory had anticipated. Firstly, her hands were free of luggage; secondly, the children were following and taking responsibility without moaning; and thirdly, Christine was in high spirits and shortened the walk by drawing her attention to various points of interest along the way—an ancient oak tree, struck by lightning so many times people thought it must be magical, the home of a neighbour who made her own stained glass, its windows full of rainbow patterns and colours, and a pond where neighbours had built a hide to watch wild birds. "We have Sunday bird-watching every week," said Christine proudly, "And we've started a photography club. Get our photos in the papers sometimes. Well, and here we are," she said at last, stopping at the end of a driveway, "Welcome to Feathers!"

Marjory stopped and looked along the driveway, to the house they would be calling home for the foreseeable future, and was immediately charmed. It was a single-storey Victorian cottage, freshly painted in white and mint green, standing in the middle of the property, surrounded by gardens. There was a wooden fence to the front, behind which was planted a hedge of escallonia that gave off an exquisite scent. Antique lace café curtains hung at the windows. The corner of a verandah could be seen on the right-hand side of the house. Tall trees of many different varieties grew at the back of the property, sheltering the house from the frequent high winds and hailstorms to which the area was prone. Beside the gateway, a wooden sign hung from a wrought iron bracket attached to a wooden post painted in mint green. On it was painted what Marjory now recognized as a rosella bird, and the words 'Feathers' and 'Huruhuru', its Maori equivalent.

Tim and Elspeth, laughing and panting, hurried up behind their mother and followed her gaze. "Oh!" exclaimed Elspeth, "It's really pretty!" She looked at her Aunt and put her hand to her mouth. "I mean, it's even prettier than I thought it would be . . ." she explained. "Yeah, right!" said her Aunt, "I bet you thought you were coming to a shack!" "It's beautiful, Aunty," said Tim, coming to his sister's rescue, "But where on earth are you going to put us all?" "You'll see, Timmo," said Christine, clapping Elspeth on the back at the same time, "We've got it all sorted, never you worry. Come on! Zooie'll think I've run off!"

Christine strode off along the driveway, and her visitors followed slowly, taking time to drink in the prettiness of the place. The air was fragrant with the scents of green growing things and the salty tang of sea air. Elspeth felt as though she was really breathing for the first time in her life, and that her heart had stopped pounding for the first time in a year. Tim took note that the fence could do with a lick of paint, and thought he might ask his Aunt to show him how. At twenty-six, he knew he was a complete duffer when it came to anything practical. There was something about this place, he felt, that made you want to get going and achieve something you could see and touch.

Christine led the way around the right-hand corner of the house, along the verandah, with its hanging baskets and terracotta planters, through a wooden door and into the kitchen, which was flooded with afternoon sunlight. There was a table in the centre with a green and white gingham cloth and six bent-wood chairs, a sink with worktops either side, under a café-curtained window, a tall dresser with green and white crockery, an Aga, and a sunburnt woman, medium height and build, with blonde hair that was turning grey, and a huge, welcoming smile on her face, wiping her hands on an apron. "Meet Zooie, the love of my life," said Christine, going to the woman and kissing her on the cheek, "Zooie, meet my sister Marjory and her kids: Elspeth and Tim." "I'm very pleased to meet you all," said Zooie in a voice every bit as raucous as Christine's, "Would you like a cuppa first, or get your stuff into your rooms?" Tim was the first to respond: "Hello Zooie, it's nice to meet you at last," he said, moving forward and taking her hand. Zooie laughed. "Some *kid!*" she exclaimed, "Why, you're a grown man!" Tim laughed at this: "When people say *kid*, I always think of goats! A cuppa would be great, but could I please use the bathroom first? I wouldn't want to sit in your kitchen smelling like one!" At this, everyone laughed.

In the flurry of activity that followed, all the visitors got a wash in Feathers' green and white bathroom, and everyone got a hug from Zooie. Christine disappeared outside to bring in the luggage and dump it in the guestrooms, and then they all sat down to tea. Elspeth preferred coffee, but tea from a white teapot with a pattern of green leaves, poured into an antique Majolica cup and saucer that had been made to look like cabbage leaves, was somehow appropriate. And the tea was delicious. "Do you know?" said Elspeth, when there was a gap in the conversation, "I get the feeling everything tastes better here . . ." Zooie, who sat opposite her, smiled: "Something to do with the air, maybe?" she said, "I've travelled a fair bit in my time, and I think you're right, everything does seem to taste better here."

"The air at home is awful," said Tim, "Except after snow or heavy rain. We're quite a way from the city, but even so . . . We're dying by slow poisoning." "Oh, Tim!" said his sister, "Don't be so dramatic!" "No, Peth, I mean it," said Tim, "I've been thinking for a while that I might try to get away from England all together, even though I suppose I love the place. It doesn't smell good, or taste good, or . . . well . . . *feel* good to me anymore. Not like when I was a boy. And people look so *jaded*. Look at Mummy for example. I'm sitting here now, looking at her across the table. Closest I've been to her to take a good look for, well, too long. And I can see how tired she is. And how much she needed to get away . . . Isn't that right, Mummy?"

There was no answer, and the children looked at each other, concerned. It was true: she did look tired, and not just from the journey. "Mummy?" said Elspeth, but Christine put a finger to her lips: "Give her a minute, love," she advised, "Anyone for more cake?" Three plates appeared under her nose, and she tutted in mock seriousness: "Greedy lot!" she said, and cut three more generous slices.

Marjory sipped her tea and nibbled on a slice of Zooie's moist carrot cake, letting the sound of conversation fade into the background. She was beginning to feel more relaxed, but with a small knotty core of anxiety somewhere that was still telling her she ought to be doing something. "Could I have a wander in the garden?" she asked, turning to her sister. Christine took a good, long look at Marjory, evidently working out whether that meant a lone wander, or accompanied. After a minute, she said, "Come on then. You can have a wander while I check on the birds." Marjory smiled gratefully. Funny how, after all these years, her sister could still read her. They got up from the table. Elspeth and Tim made to follow, but Zooie laid a hand on their arm and whispered, "Sister talk, I think. Let's have another slice of cake, shall we?"

Christine led Marjory to the far end of the garden, where the tall trees created dappled shade and there was a rustic bench, a somewhat weather-beaten garden gnome in a red jacket and blue trousers, fishing with a rod and line in a stone bird bath. "Just you rest there, Sis," she said in an uncommonly gentle tone, "Bingo Birch, our gnome here, will keep an eye on you. I'll go and feed the birds, but I'll be back in ten, and we can either sit here quiet together, or you can talk. No pressure, no worries." She pressed Marjory's hand gently, and went off in the direction of what looked like large shed, with an aviary tacked onto the side of it, though no birds were in evidence. She guessed her sister kept the bird-seed there. Marjory sank down onto the bench, stretched out her legs and arms, and smiled at the garden gnome, who appeared to be looking straight at her. After a few seconds, she began to feel strangely self-conscious under his gaze and, turning her face upwards, seeking the sunlight, closed her eyes.

And that is how her sister found her ten minutes later, dozing, the shadows of leaves and branches playing across her face, as if they were dancing. Christine was about to sit down when her sister awoke and smiled. "Thanks Chris," she said, her voice already sounding younger, "I think I needed that. I love your garden gnome, by the way. I'm sure he was keeping an eye on me while I was napping!" Christine went over to the bird bath and patted the gnome on the head. "He's an antique," she said, "And an important member of the family. Name's Manfred Willow. I'd give him a little bow or a wave before leaving, if I were you." Marjory got up from the bench, took her sister's arm and said: "Shall we go in? Tomorrow's early enough for talking, don't you think?"

The two women returned to the kitchen, where what was left of the carrot cake sat on its Majolica plate in the centre of the table, and Zooie was flipping coins with the children to see who would get the last slice. "My God, you people know how to scoff cake!" exclaimed Christine, grinning, "If you're still hungry after all that, I'll get the lolly cake out of the fridge and see if you can make yourselves sick!" "Lolly cake?" said Elspeth and Tim in chorus. "You wait and see," answered Zooie, looking and sounding mysterious.

Chapter Seventeen

AN EXPERIMENTAL GARDENER

Three full-time gardeners, a father and two sons, kept Brandston House—and a local children's home—fully stocked with vegetables. When there was a glut of parsnips, lettuce or asparagus, Marjory gave them to the gardeners to sell from a stand in front of the tied cottage on the edge of the estate where they lived with Mrs. Billett the Elder, who had never had her hands on a trowel in her life, preferring to shop or go to the hairdresser's.

William 'Bill' Billett and his elder son Frank were traditionalists who always planted, tended and harvested by the book. Their marrows and cauliflowers were the envy of the neighbourhood, and they always came away with a handful of prizes including 'Best of the Best' from local competitions. Andrew, the younger son, on the other hand, liked to experiment, and was often to be found in the glasshouses poring over seed catalogues when on his break. His father and Frank found this amusing as well as unnecessary, but believed he would grow out of it if left to his own devices. So he was allowed the Old Glasshouse on the east side of the kitchen garden, and the overspill vegetable bed beside it for his experiments.

The Old Glasshouse was a Victorian build, with fanciful wrought ironwork, pretty stained glass windows here and there, hand-painted with designs of herbs in flower, and a door that tended to stick in damp weather. Andrew Billett had installed a small wood-burning stove in the middle, and a broken-down old armchair, thrown out during a spring-cleaning of the nursery when Tim had followed Elspeth to boarding-school at the age of eleven. Andrew was seven years Tim's senior at thirty-three, and people in the surrounding villages had long ago decided he was an eccentric. Why else ride around on a tricycle when everyone else had a car?

Andrew had crossed paths with his employer on several occasions, but tended to keep out of Percy's way, both men being rather reticent. Percy was no conversationalist, and Andrew rather empathized with that. A nod and "Good day!" was about as far as they got. Percy showed no interest in vegetables until they were on a dinner plate, or in the people who grew them, so it was always Roger who preceded him when Andrew found them walking in the vicinity of the Old Glasshouse: Roger, galloping so fast on his bandy legs that he tended to skid to a halt and bump his nose on whichever object got in his way—usually the water butt or Andrew himself.

Young Mr. Billett always kept a dog biscuit or two for Roger. He wished that, once in a while, the family would let Roger loose on his own. He guessed the dog would come straight to him, and he would have loved a bit of company over his midday herbal tea and home-made veg pasty. The Billetts had two dogs of their own: golden retrievers that they bred to generate extra income, but Andrew preferred old Roger, who was always wagging his tail and sniffing around as if, in a previous life, he had been a gardener himself. The retrievers were, by contrast, lacking in enthusiasm and a sense of fun. Too much time spent chasing after dead ducks, most likely.

On that fateful Sunday in April, Andrew had come into work, even though it was not in his contract. He often did so when he had a new variety to pot up, so that he couldn't be accused by his father and Frank of wasting time Monday to Saturday. He'd taken delivery the previous day of a box of seeds he'd bought online, and couldn't wait to get cracking. He knew that the types of salad leaves he was going to try out would be a first for the Brandston estate. They had exotic names: mizuna, kailaan, komatsuna and tsoi sim. If his father had known he was planting anything Japanese, he would have had a blue fit. If asked, he would say they were types of lettuce. His dad had only just about got used to rocket and lamb's lettuce, because their mum had served them up with the reassurance that they had come from Marks & Spencer.

Andrew was washing pots and trays under the outside tap when Roger came racing round the corner of the glasshouse, slid on a patch of mud and landed at his feet with a yelp. "Roger!" said Andrew, quickly kneeling down to examine the dog, who was shaking his ears and looking more than usually confused, "You daft dog! One of these days you'll break a leg or knock yourself out!" Roger began to lick Andrew's face, as he firmly but gently felt the animal's limbs. Andrew laughed: "All right, all right! No harm done. Calm down now," he rubbed Roger's hairy tummy and gave his silky head a pat.

"Where's your master?" Andrew asked Roger, "Where is he?" Roger looked up at him quizzically then, slithering and having trouble getting his balance, he got to his feet and looked around. Andrew laughed again: it seemed Roger had a short memory, and had forgotten he was meant to be going for a walk with a human. "Go find!" called out Andrew, pointing in the direction of the garden. Roger paused, his head cocked, for a few seconds, then came trotting up to Andrew, looking at the jacket pocket where the young gardener always kept the dog biscuits. "You're less daft than you look, eh Roger?" said Andrew, a grin on his face almost as wide as the dog's. He still wanted to make sure Roger was all right, so he took a biscuit from his pocket and launched it in the direction of the hedge. At least if Roger overshot his mark, he would have something softer to bump into.

Roger watched the flying biscuit, his hind quarters bunched and ready, until it was in mid-flight, then took off in the direction of the hedge. He was fine, it seemed. But just as he was about to poke his nose in among the greenery, he stopped, froze, lifted his ears and sniffed. He looked back at Andrew. "What is it, old chap?" asked Andrew, "Do you smell a rabbit?" Roger shook his head, not looking back. "Well, well!" exclaimed Andrew, surprised. "A fox?" Roger shook his head again. "Bird? Stoat? Badger? Rhinoceros?" asked Andrew, beginning to laugh with amazement, as Roger kept on shaking his head.

Intrigued, Andrew walked slowly towards the hedge, trying to see what had caught the dog's attention. But it was a yew hedge, two feet thick, dense and dark. He didn't want to risk putting his hand in, in case it was a badger, or a vagabond mongrel, so he took a bamboo cane and poked it in. At this, Roger turned to look at him, and growled, baring his teeth. "What the . . . ?" exclaimed the gardener: what was the Labrador upset about? He tried calling Roger away, but the dog remained stock still in front of the hedge, so he backed off, fetched a folding canvas stool from the glasshouse, and sat himself down a few yards away with his pots and trays and his bag of compost, and got on with his work.

Five minutes later, Percy caught up with them. He'd guessed his dog was visiting the young gardener, having seen Andrew's tricycle parked beside one of the larger glasshouses, where they grew the oranges and lemons, and had taken the opportunity to sit in the glasshouse and puff away on a pipe. Marjory didn't like him smoking in the house, and even in her absence he was respectful of her wishes. Tucking his empty pipe into his side pocket, he sauntered towards young Billett, smiling but looking down at his shoes, which shone in the sunlight that was now beaming down on the scene and making things look a bit more spring-like.

Andrew was bent over his bag of compost, so Percy coughed quietly and wished him a good morning. Andrew jumped up from his stool and returned his greeting, touching his cap. "Good morning, Sir," he said, then appeared to be about to say something else. "What is it, young Billett?" asked Percy, taking a step closer. Whatever Andrew had been about to say, he seemed to think better of it, for he replied, "Er, looks like more snow on the way, Mr. Brandston. Or maybe sleet. By mid-afternoon, Sir. Or later . . ." Then he rubbed his composty hands together, and stood looking down at his muddy wellington boots.

"Yes, indeed, Billett. Indeed. Quite possibly," replied the Lord of the Manor, "I hope Roger hasn't been giving any trouble," he added, stretching out the conversation, thus making it the longest they had ever had. "Oh! No, Sir! Not . . . really," answered Andrew, "He's a bit excited about something he's found in the hedge . . ." Andrew pointed towards the hedge, where Roger was still frozen in his vigil, his nose six inches from the foliage. "Oh, is he now?" remarked Percy, "Rabbit?" "No, Sir," replied Andrew, "He says not." The young man blushed furiously, "I mean, I don't think so, Sir . . ." "Ah well," said Percy, "Mustn't keep you from your work. Daft dog, that one, eh?" Andrew took a few seconds to nod his agreement.

Percy Brandston called his dog to him, and Roger eventually came, his obedience training stronger than his inquisitiveness. Percy clipped on his lead, smiled at Andrew and turned away to continue his constitutional. Once they were out of sight, the gardener went poking about in the hedge for a good while, walking round it and looking for animal tracks. But there was nothing to be seen but a small piece of green cloth caught on a twig, which he pocketed.

Chapter Eighteen

ARCHIE AND FRIENDS

As the chill of night and the damp of approaching dawn crept into Archie's bones, still he made no movement. He was longing to cough, but he took little dry swallows to suppress the reflex. He sat for twenty minutes with his bottom going numb, waiting for the gnomes to wake.

It was the gnome at the far end, the one curled on his side whom Archie recognized as Ned, who stirred first. Archie heard a small yawn, slid his eyes right, and saw him stretch out his legs, point his toes (which must have been difficult in boots with hard, round toecaps) and wriggle over onto his back. This woke the gnome next to him, who also yawned and stretched both arms and legs. The third gnome did the same, elbowing the one leaning against Archie, who made a sound rather like the hoot of a small owl, and opened his eyes.

The first thing he saw was Archie looking down at him. Archie smiled, keeping his lips closed—something he remembered about smiling at primates and not showing one's teeth—and said, "It's all right, little chap—it's only me: Archie," which seemed appropriate. The gnomes must, after all, have been observing the human activities taking place in the garden ever since their arrival. And some of those activities might actually have impressed them, he was sure. For whereas most tenants did little more than glance at the work in progress in the garden, Archie and his friends had been tireless in their efforts to make it both attractive and productive.

It had taken Archie and the other men a week to construct the gnome garden. First, they had dug out the turf and, using bamboo canes and a piece of string, they had marked out a perfect circle. Next, they had made a narrow trench around the perimeter, and placed rocks along it, leaving no gaps, so that it formed a barrier against encroaching grass. Then they had piled in small logs, twigs, earth, compost and finally bark chippings. As they had created height, so they had also created a spiral with more rocks, until the design was complete.

The design was something Viktor knew from his childhood in Poland. His grandparents had grown fruit and vegetables by stacking up logs and covering them with earth all their lives, and had shaken their heads over his parents' views on factory farming being more efficient: "People will come back to the old ways before my grandson grows a beard, you mark my words!" his grandfather had proclaimed, wagging a finger. And he had been right, as he always was. 'Now everyone is talking about hugelkultur," Viktor had told Archie and the others, "As if they invented it! How did our ancestors survive? They grew their food this way!" Archie had been fascinated to learn how it worked, and it made perfect sense. The wood rotted away inside the mound, releasing nutrients which fed your crops, and it also soaked up rainwater so you didn't have to get out the watering can so often.

Bobby, Ronald's shy son, had been mightily impressed by the project, and had come down with his father to help dig up the bricks that were to be found everywhere in the garden, only inches below the surface of the ground. The estate had once been part of a brickworks. He had stayed for a cup of tea afterwards, and offered them with a list of bee-friendly plants for the new flower beds they were planning. "What you're doing is *really* important," Bobby had said, with real passion, "Bees are dying out everywhere and nothing works in Nature without them. It's a tragedy!"

"He takes things so seriously," Ronald had said after his son had departed to hear a talk on creating a wildflower garden at a local eco-centre, "A lot of dads would tell him to go out and get a job—any old job—but there are things he refuses to do. Yesterday a job came up, working in a supermarket, pushing credit cards at people. He said he'd rather die than be responsible for more people getting into debt.

The more I listen to him, the more uncomfortable I feel. But we all need a shake-up sometimes, don't we?"

Neighbours who had passed by when the men were building their spiral 'Hugelkultur' garden had had a lot to say, and none of it complimentary: "What you gone and dug up that grass for? And what's all them twigs? Bleedin' mess!" one old chap had said angrily, "You youngsters don't know what the hell you're doing!" They had had to laugh after he'd gone: at anything between fifty and sixty-five they hardly qualified as 'youngsters'! It had given them quite an energy boost, as well as a feeling of rebelliousness that they had enjoyed. As Ronald had put it: "We're breaking new ground here, guys! No wonder we're getting into a heap of trouble!" Ronald had cheered up a lot these past few weeks.

It seemed Archie was right, for the gnome blinked a few times and grinned back—a full smile with two rows of perfectly even, sharp, white teeth. "Ned Blackthorn, me," he said in a sleepy voice, "Pleased to meet you. I say, properly at last." The gnome wriggled his bottom on the hard seat, then raised and rubbed each small buttock in turn, and gave a sigh, "Hard bench, sore back quarters. Give a good rub. Go on!" he said to Archie, pointing to what he could see of Archie's 'back quarters'. Archie did as he was told, amused and touched at the gnome's interest in his comfort.

Ned Blackthorn, who Archie could see—now that all four were sitting up straight—was the shortest of the four, and also the slenderest (if 'slender' were at all a word that could be applied to a gnome, for they were all of them solidly built, with bulging muscles, thick legs and round bellies). Ned looked up at Archie and saw him surveying the line-up: "Furthest from you, Norman. Eldest brother. Next, Nigel. Next, Nick. I say, your small friends in the garden, for removal of slugs and snails by proper method, and other conveniences."

Archie was impressed by how well the gnome spoke English, for it seemed it might not be his first language. "Thank you," he said, nodding his head, at which all four gnomes, who were now fully alert, nodded back: "It is always our duty, but in this case a pleasure," said the one called Norman, his voice an octave deeper than his brother's, and pleasantly calm and rumbly, "Blackthorns are diplomats. Necessary in times of breach in relationship between our two kinds." Norman nodded his head twice, and Archie, who could be a diplomat himself when dealing with people he respected, nodded twice back.

Archie was completely fascinated. Blackthorn: did they take their surnames from trees, then? It seemed somehow likely. He wondered how many other families of gnomes there might be, and found himself making a list in his head of all the types of trees he knew. He was about to ask the question out loud, when he was pre-empted. Nigel, the second eldest Blackthorn, spoke next: "People will be awake soon, maybe already. It is time for gnomes to go to earth. Say farewell and depart." He hopped down from the bench, did a full stretch on tiptoe and touched his toes. The others followed suit. Each in turn bowed to Archie, and he bowed back. "I hope to see you soon," he said quietly, "I was hoping so much . . ." Nigel turned back, already three feet away: "We will be in touch soon, *breganti ash*—by the Power of the Sacred Nine," he said, his face grave, "Gnome ways, you will see! *Flabaaray!*" All four gnomes disappeared into the gloom of the shrubbery. There was a rustle of dry leaves under their little feet, and Archie was left alone.

Chapter Nineteen

A MOMENT

It turned out that Aunty Christine's lolly cake, of which Marjory, Elspeth and Tim caught a tantalizing glimpse, stayed in the fridge until the following day. Tim suddenly gave a deep yawn, and Zooie got up from the kitchen table and said, "Let's get you unpacked. You must be cream-crackered! Follow me!" She led the way through one of the kitchen's two internal doors into a hallway which turned a right-angle and took them to an annexe, built onto the back of the house, where there were two guest rooms. "My ex built this on before disappearing off into the sunset," she explained, without sentimentality, "Ladies, to your left. Gentleman to your right."

Zooie opened a duck-egg blue painted door on either side of the hallway, and early evening sunlight flooded the space, making them all blink. "OMG! This is gorgeous!" exclaimed Elspeth, walking into the room she was to share with her mother. Marjory was surprised. She had not told her daughter they would be sharing, fearing a refusal. She flushed with delight. The room *was* gorgeous, and moreover the sleeping arrangements would work, for her sister had placed an old Japanese lacquer screen between the two single beds, which were in any case at right angles to each other, rather than side by side.

The room itself was as neat as the proverbial pin, with its varnished pine floor, round rag rugs in a dozen different shades of blue, duck-egg blue quilts and pillows, and white lace curtains, which fell to the floor and were tied back with duck-egg blue velvet bows. In front of the window there was a small table with two bent-wood chairs with white velvet cushions, and on it were items for letter-writing and a Japanese lacquer tray with a carafe of water and two antique glasses, engraved with bluebirds. How it had been possible to find room for a wardrobe was beyond Marjory, but wardrobe there was in stripped pine. She turned to Zooie in amazement: "The house looks so much smaller from the street!" she exclaimed, "But it's so spacious!" Zooie laughed delightedly, "Cottages here are often like that," she explained, "The plots are narrow but go back a long way, so you can get a lot on them. We're lucky though: this is one of the biggest on the road. There's a stream at the back, behind the trees, and it takes a bit of a meander away from the house just behind here. We've got a good lot of land. I'll show you tomorrow, if you like."

Zooie left Marjory and Elspeth to unpack and wash in the bathroom at the end of the hallway, and went to get Tim settled in. Both doors remained ajar, so they could hear his enthusiastic comments and Zooie's responses, and their laughter. "Woohoo!" they finally heard Tim yell, as they heard a creak of bedsprings as he flung himself down, "This is the real deal!" "Glad you approve, Timmo," said Zooie, "Supper's at eight. Tell your mum and your sister, all right?" "No problem, Aunty Zooie!" exclaimed Tim joyfully.

Marjory and Elspeth, who were hanging clothes in their wardrobe, turned to each other, their eyes huge with surprise. "Mummy," said Elspeth, putting her hand to her cheek, "Tim sounds *happy*!" "He does, doesn't he, darling," answered Marjory, "I really do think we might all be happy here, don't you? Your aunts are so . . . well, cheerful and . . ." "I think the word you're looking for is 'laid-back', Mummy dear!" said Elspeth, but without sarcasm for once.

She paused and, reaching down, took her mother's hand, taking from it the coral pink silk blouse Marjory had been about to hang up and placing it carefully on the hanger herself. She gave the hand, which was warm and rather damp, a gentle squeeze. "There's something I need to say . . ." said Elspeth hesitantly, looking down at their joined hands, "Look, I know I've been an awful grouch . . . and, quite frankly, a bit of a bitch to you of late . . ." Marjory was about to protest, but her daughter stopped her by rushing on with her speech:

"I have! And none of it was your fault. All you did was support me in my choice of husband, which meant a lot to me at the time. Some of my friends said some terribly spiteful things—before and after—but you never did. I suppose I was horrible to you because I had some stupid idea you should have known he would . . . leave me . . . and told me not to marry him . . . or something . . . but I was really wrong. I suppose what I'm trying to say, in my usual emotionally inept way, is that I'm sorry, Mummy. Can we be friends again . . . please?"

At this last sentence, Marjory crumpled completely. All her self-control abandoned her, and she burst into tears and, grabbing her daughter by the elbows, pulled her into a strong embrace. Elspeth began to sob too, and they wept loudly, letting out all the pent-up tension of years.

It wasn't long before Zooie and Tim appeared in the doorway, closely followed by Christine, all three of them looking on in something between amazement and terror. "Everything all right in here?" asked Christine, her voice hinting at anxiety, "Don't tell me you don't like your room, because Zooie and I aren't about to do a swap. Ours is full of noisy parrots who only shut up when *we* tell them to!" Everyone laughed, and Marjory and Elspeth both reached for the packet of tissues sitting on top of Marjory's handbag, bumped heads and rubbed them ruefully, smiling at each other. "Couple of blockheads! Like mum, like daughter!" laughed Christine, relieved.

Nobody asked why the women had been crying, for they guessed from the body language of both that it had been some kind of reconciliation scene. Both of them had lost their usual stiff-backed, tight-lipped look, and their smiles were radiant. Tim felt his eyes fill with tears, but didn't his emotions show. There would be time for him to heal the breach with his mother and sister. All in good time. This was not his moment, he realised with a jolt. The old Tim would have waded in and insisted on being a part of every scene. This was a brand new Tim, and he felt that he had at last grown up.

"Did you say 'parrots'?" he asked his Aunts, turning to follow them, "Nobody has parrots in their bedroom apart from Long

John Silver . . ." "Oh," said Zooie, looking back at Tim over her shoulder, "Chris and I do. But the parrots are for later. Go and have a shower, Timmo—you smell of long-haul, and Chris and I have high standards!" She laughed at his worried face as she watched him sniff his armpits, "I bet you scrub up pretty nice all the same. So, off you go and don't use up all the smellies. See you at eight! You guys are already showing signs of being high maintenance. We're going to need time to ourselves till dinner-time!"

Tim left his Aunts to their tasks and went to have a long shower. As he passed his mother's bedroom door, which was now shut, he could hear soft voices and a flow of conversation that made him feel as though everything would be all right, now they had arrived at Feathers. His last thought, as he let a good, hard jet of warm water begin to wash away, not only the journey but England and all its troubles, was whether his father was OK. "You should have come with us, Pa," he said out loud, "But I suppose the damned country can't manage without you . . ."

Chapter Twenty

COFFEE AND BISCUITS

It came as no surprise to Archie when he woke the following morning, went to make his usual wake-me-up cup of coffee and found all eleven gnomes (he and Big John had been adding to their collection whenever the opportunity arose) sitting on his settee, as real and alive as anyone could be. In the morning sunlight, he could see their faces properly for the first time—their 'alive faces', that is.

They had not all come from the same manufacturer, and some had been too smooth, bland and Disneyesque to be very convincing. Two in particular, whom he had named—on a whim—Cholmondeley and Hugo, had ridiculous orange trousers and ladybirds on their bright yellow hats, as well as inane expressions. In real life, their clothes were natural shades of a burnt orange that reminded Archie of lilies, and a yellow that was reminiscent of forsythia. The ladybirds on their conical hats were crawling up and down, perching every now and then on the very top and spreading their wings as if to catch the sun.

"Good morning, gentlemen," said Archie gravely, bowing deeply. The gnomes responded in the same way. Cholmondeley and Hugo wobbled and fell over, ending up in a heap. It seemed they were the clowns of the group, for the others laughed uproariously, winking at Archie, so that he felt comfortable joining in. "Well, it's a long time since anyone made me laugh this early in the morning!" exclaimed Archie, looking from one gnome to the next, and tying his dressing-gown in a knot. It was chilly in the living-room.

"We have come to visit, as promised," said Norman, bowing again. Archie bowed back, thinking "If I have to keep bowing like this, I'll soon start to feel dizzy!" Ned, the youngest of the Blackthorn brothers, who—perhaps because he had spent a couple of hours leaning up against Archie on the garden bench—evidently felt *at* home with him, spoke up next, a big grin on his sunburnt, rosy-cheeked, bright-eyed face with its long whiskers that stuck out like a guinea-pig's: "We have come to make you acquainted, friend Archie," he said, "To teach you our ways and to make you safe." "Oh, that's . . . fantastic!" Archie answered, "I'm honoured! And I'm full of questions! You can't believe how many questions I've got buzzing around in my head!" Nigel tilted his head on one side, quizzically, poking Hugo—who was two gnomes away on the sofa—in the eye with the tip of his hat. Hugo made to protest, but Cholmondeley poked himself in the eye with his finger, screamed and rolled off the sofa onto the carpet, where he lay kicking his legs like a footballer trying to get a penalty decision. Hugo rubbed his eyes, gave a lopsided, soppy grin and rolled off on top of his friend—"Brother, maybe?" thought Archie—knocking the wind out of him. Clearly the gnomes were accustomed to making their own entertainment. Archie was a little worried about the ladybirds, but they somehow managed to remain firmly fixed to their respective hats until the comedy show was over.

"Rude interruption excused," said Nigel, waving a finger at the clowns, who were now both trying to climb back onto the sofa, and pulling each other back down by their braces. "Gnomes wear braces?" Archie had time to think, before he turned his full attention to Nigel, who was doing a mock glower that made him look quite fierce. "*Mun-tili manni*, sit down before you wear out your floor covering, pay heed and learn!"

It was clear that what Big John and Archie had said about the four Blackthorns and their respective characters was pretty near the mark, at least from what Archie had seen so far: "Nigel *is* the bossy one!" he thought to himself, as he sat down, and then got up again, about to ask permission to get his morning cup of coffee. All the digestive biscuits were gone, he remembered: it would have to be custard creams. Never mind. "*Mun-tili manni* has no sour tea!" said Norman, leaning over to Nigel to explain, "Let him get his cup, or he will not learn or remember our teachings." Nigel nodded, and Archie, already the good pupil, bowed low and went off to the kitchen to fortify himself. He had not been in training of any kind since he'd learnt Spanish cookery on the island. He hoped he would be up to the mark. He didn't see Nigel being the most patient of teachers. But perhaps it would be one of the others who took him in hand. He hoped it would be Ned, who seemed the nearest to himself in personality.

As Archie poured boiling water onto his 'sour tea', he wondered what that strange, foreign phrase the gnomes had used to describe him could mean. "Stupid old git, maybe?" he said to himself, chuckling, "Or 'old man of the garden'?" He stirred in the milk and sugar and hunted in the cupboard for the custard creams. He emptied the entire packetful onto a plate, and carried them to his guests. Within minutes, the biscuits had gone, and Hugo and Cholmondeley were having a burping competition, which made his friends clap their hands and shout encouragement. Archie sat back in his armchair, sipped his coffee and waited for lessons to begin.

Chapter Twenty-One

AN AVID STUDENT

"To begin with," said Norman, "We shall each tell names. Then you may tell." "Tell what? Just my name?" thought Archie, finishing his last mouthful of coffee and sitting to attention, "This is a whole lot better than a committee meeting all by myself, anyway." Norman introduced himself first as "Norman of the Blackthorn Clan", followed by the other ten gnomes in turn: Nigel Blackthorn next, then Nick and Ned, Cholmondeley and Hugo Birch, Terry Alder the Mushroom-gathering Gnome (only three inches tall and the guardian of a flourishing lemon verbena plant halfway up the gnome garden), Syd Willow of course—still looking proud to have been the first—and two gnomes who held cup-shaped orange toadstools, twins who went by the names of Sigmund and Sigfrid Rowan, and lastly a grim-faced gnome dressed from head to boots in dark green, who growled out in a bass voice that his name was Alevin Yew. At least, Archie assumed that was the spelling, given that gnomes had the surnames of trees.

There was silence in the sun-filled living-room, until Norman nodded his head at Archie and said, "Now you may tell." Archie gave his name as "Archie of the Prescotts", and the gnomes nodded to each other. "He has no tree," remarked Syd, shaking his head in sorrow. "He will," Norman reassured him, "And it will be a blackthorn, for diplomacy." "You have a woman?" asked little Terry. Nigel, who was sitting next to Terry, nudged him with his elbow and tutted: "Not yet!" he said. Terry hung his head until Ned, sitting the other side of him, patted him reassuringly on the knee. "Archie will have a woman soon," he said. Archie flushed bright red, thinking of Ann-Marie, but put her out of his mind in his effort to concentrate.

Surprisingly, it was Alevin Yew who spoke next, pulling on his beard: "Know, *mun-tili manni*, that there are many of us, many. All over this world, in many places. But not so many as we were. Ah, no! Not so many. So many burrows destroyed. So many clans scattered. And we fear, yes, we fear. You!" he suddenly pointed his finger at Archie, who nearly jumped out of his seat, "Friend of Gnomes! Hearken and learn. Teach others. There is still time!" There was a silence, then Alevin gestured to Archie. He took it as a signal to speak, and asked: "Time for what? And this *mun-tili* that you call me: what does it mean?"

The gnomes nodded to each other, as if they approved of his questions. "You ask well," said Alevin, "And so I will answer. First, I say—and we all—that there is still time to be saving this world. You know what I mean. Floods, fighting, one set against another, all in fear. There is much that can still be done, and gnomes will help. We taught your leaders in ancient times. Your druids, your poets, foresters, farmers: they learnt from gnomes the great respect. There is still time, I say. Second: you will be taught Gnomish also. You will be a messenger between gnomes and human people. We see you; we see your work in the garden. We have trust in our hearts towards you, Archie Prescott . . ." Here, Alevin paused for breath, and Hugo, who had begun to wriggle in his seat and look as though he was bursting to speak, clapped his hands and shouted out: "*Mun-tili manni*! The man who is learning to give proper account of himself. The man who will be safe for gnomes. The man who is learning to be safe! That is what it means, Archie Prescott! And I am glad!"

Archie felt he had just been paid the compliment of his life, and bowed to the gnomes three times. Just one corner of Alevin's mouth began to lift into a smile, but then he sighed. Cholmondeley clapped a hand over Hugo's mouth before he could catch his breath and continue, and laughed: "Hugo speaks much but his heart overflows. That is why. He feels it inside, the hope. This hope is strong in him, in me. It is the hope of the Birch clan. That is why we make jokes, play the fool as you would say. With hope, a person needs much fun. It makes a balance."

Archie nodded, completely in agreement. He remembered the phrase 'a healthy sense of the absurd' from somewhere, and found he was saying it out loud. Syd leaned towards him, putting his pipe, which had been in the corner of his mouth but was unlit, into his pocket, and searched Archie's face intently. Archie wondered where Syd had left his spade, but didn't ask. "I know your meaning, Archie Prescott," he said, nodding his head up and down vigorously, "It is good to laugh, for life can be grim—for us, for you. A person also needs to drink when his throat is dry . . ." This time, Archie really did jump up from his chair. "What was I thinking?!" he exclaimed, "I'm so sorry! What would you like? I mean, what do you like to drink?" Nigel Blackthorn stood up on the sofa, facing Syd, and shook his little fist at him: "Ibni!" he shouted, and stamped his foot, which made him fall over onto the floor. Archie dived to pick him up, but Nigel put out his hand in a fending-off gesture, and got to his feet and straightened his hat, which had gone crooked. Cholmondeley and Hugo were giggling, but Alevin shushed them.

"Nigel Blackthorn is angry," pronounced Alevin in a tone that Archie was sure held a grain or two of laughter in it, "Syd Willow has asked for drink. He has shamed our good host by asking. He will sit in silence!" Archie looked sympathetically in the direction of poor Syd, who was the latest to hang his head in shame, the tip of his tall red hat reaching past his toes. "Nigel Blackthorn says 'Ibni'—Brother Gnome—before he falls from his seat," Alevin concluded.

Everyone, including Archie, who was getting the hang of it, nodded sagely. Nigel, who had managed to climb back onto the settee unaided, though both Hugo and Cholmondeley had offered him a helping hand, looked at Syd and said, "Nigel sees Syd's sorrow and is satisfied." Syd breathed a great sigh and looked up. Archie was sure he saw a tiny tear on the gnome's cheek. It seemed the gnomes took their

respect for each other, and for etiquette, very seriously. He wished he
could say the same of the humans he knew.

Ned Blackthorn, who had not yet spoken, held up a sack, which
he had been using to lean against. His eyes were red, and Archie had
noticed he seemed in danger of dropping off to sleep every moment.
"Ibni!" he said, "Ned Blackthorn has been busy while the world slept.
He has made for you a drink." He opened the sack and drew out a
leather flask with a flourish. Every gnome got to his feet and Archie
followed suit. "Birch wine!" shouted Norman with unusual excitement
in his voice. "We will drink to hope!" "We will drink to the clans!"
exclaimed Nick. "To men becoming safe!" yelled Archie, quite carried
away by the moment. "This beats the pub any day!" he thought to
himself. The flask was passed round, ending up with Archie. It was
tiny, but when he lifted it to his lips, the most delicious drink filled his
mouth. He swirled it around, and swallowed.

"What thinks the Friend of Gnomes of our friendship drink?"
asked several of the gnomes in chorus. There was a complete hush
as Archie searched for the right words to describe the garden scents:
herbs, summer flowers, soft fruits, that were playing a tune on his taste
buds. At last he spoke: "Well," he said, "Well . . . well . . ." A blissful
smile came over the face of Archie Prescott, at the same time as his face
took on a look of longing. "Well?" echoed Ned, his voice sounding
remarkably like Archie's, "What more is there?" Archie's voice came
from deeper in his chest this time, "A woman!" he said, "Definitely a
woman!" At this, the whole room erupted in gales of laughter which
continued for so long that Archie and his friends almost forgot they
had serious business to discuss.

It was dark before the gnomes left, and Archie was in such a state
of excitement that he forgot to put on the television, and almost forgot
to eat, until his tummy rumbled audibly. He hunted around for the
spiral notebook he used for the residents' association and turned to
the back page. He sat at the kitchen table with a cheese and onion
sandwich and a cup of coffee, and made notes of as much of what he

had learnt that day as his tired brain could remember. It was midnight before he finally tumbled into bed, and he was asleep within seconds. He dreamt of Ann-Marie, and this time they were standing in the centre of a grove of autumn trees, hand in hand . . .

Chapter Twenty-Two

WHERE IS ROGER?

Detective Sergeant Jim 'Brillo' Jackson kissed his wife and children goodbye and got into his car with more energy than usual. It was six o'clock in the morning. There was a chill in the air, but the wind had dropped in the night, and birds were singing with voices that sounded joyful. He wound down the car window and stopped to listen as he checked his mobile phone for messages before turning the ignition key.

Jim was a keen birdwatcher whenever he got the time, and he could recognize every call: thrush, blackbird and greenfinch. He had shown his daughters how to build bird tables and nesting boxes, and his wife Danuta kept their garden well stocked with nuts and seeds. The girls—Julia and Bethany, nine and seven respectively—already knew how to make the nuts and seeds into 'fat cakes', and how to make sure the smallest birds got their share, in spite of the squirrels.

Jackson had never wanted to leave the town where he had lived all his life. He had met Danuta at the local Royal Society for the Protection of Birds group, and she felt the same way. What more could there be to life than a loving home, tending your garden, going for long walks at weekends and doing your bit for Nature? They could neither of them understand why so many people went haring off all over the place and moaned if they hadn't had a holiday abroad for a while. "I don't know why we say 'haring off'," said Danuta, "When hares have a lot more sense about where to go!"

Danuta had been delighted for Jim when he had told her, in whispers so as not to wake the girls, what his assignment for the following day was going to be. "Take your wellies, love," she said, snuggling into his warm, solid back, "I'll make you a flask and sandwiches. What fillings would you like?" Jim turned over carefully, so as not to accidentally pull his wife's long hair, and put his arms around her. "Any filling you like," he whispered caressingly, breathing into her ear, "What filling do you like best?" Danuta stifled a giggle in her husband's chest and slid a hand down the bed. "I think you know the answer to that question," she said.

What with the spring chorus of birds in his ears, and the afterglow that had stayed with him as he had slept the previous night, Brillo Jackson was feeling on top of the world. He started up the car, and set off for the police station, where he was to compare notes with his partner for the day, Detective Constable Farisi Kayatta. His younger daughter Bethany had insisted on lending him her Tatty Teddy rucksack for his flask and sandwiches, but he knew that Farisi would not laugh at him: she regularly turned up to work with paintings her own children had given her that practically covered the wall above her desk, and three or four friendship bracelets escaping from her sleeves.

Brillo and Farisi checked in with the boss, and set off for the charming village of Brandston. On DI Masters' advice, they took a marked police car, and one from the top of the range: the only Lotus in the garage, it was usually used for high-speed chases. "You're driving to impress," he said, an ironic smile on his face, "You should take the best of the bunch: it'll get you past the Men in Black." On the way to pick up the vehicle, the two detectives argued companionably about who would be in the driver's seat: "I'll drive," said Jim, "Then you can make sure I don't get lost." "No, I'll drive," answered Farisi, "You lot are always saying men navigate better than women." In the end, they agreed to stop off halfway and change over. They worked out the mileage to Brandston and split it in two, which put the changeover point at a Happy Chef roadside restaurant. This pleased Jim, who loved his second breakfast. "There won't be time for that!" said Farisi, "Dogs can travel fast, you know!"

It took an hour to get to the village, and they stopped to consult a map showing the boundaries of the Brandston estate. "We should head east, I reckon," said Farisi, "That will put us near the church at the end of this boundary wall here, and there's a car park next to it." Jim agreed.

The village was stunning in the morning sunlight, and Jim craned his neck to see whether the horse chestnuts on the triangular green in front of the Saxon church were showing any signs of budding. Not yet, but then, there was still the risk of another freeze. Farisi parked the car and they got out, stretching and yawning. Jim got their wellingtons from the boot of the car. "Right," said the detective constable, "Let's get going. There's a footpath or bridleway along most of the boundary. This should be a lovely walk, and I'm in danger of forgetting why we're here." "Me too," agreed Jim, putting on his gloves, "It's gorgeous out here. No wonder Roger didn't want to come home."

The pair strode off in the direction of the finger-post in the far corner of the car park that marked the beginning of the footpath. They took note of the time, and got ready to look for clues, which left things pretty wide open. How do you find a dog in the middle of the countryside? Other officers had already done a door-to-door, which had yielded nothing. Roger the Labrador was well-known in the village, and if anyone had taken him in, they would presumably have reported it straight away. "Missing Dog" posters had already gone up too, with a reward. Their best hope was that he would be spotted by a rambler or a rider with a mobile phone.

"Why is it so important to find Mr. Brandston's dog, Sarge?" asked Farisi, as they negotiated a muddy part of the narrow path that had nettles and brambles either side. "Well, it's a question of the bite marks," he answered, "They want to eliminate him as a suspect." "That's crazy," said his partner, lowering her voice, "They have photos: they could measure the bite of a dog the same size and age, surely?" "I was told they've done that," said Jim, "Maybe there's more to it than that." "Maybe," agreed Farisi, as they stopped to look around a spot where the boundary wall was lower than its normal eight feet. At some point, this part of the wall had collapsed, and it had been mended with dry stone. The rest of the wall was made of limestone and, apart from the occasional gap at its base, made intentionally so that water would not collect, and here and there an iron-reinforced wooden gate, it ran in a solid line around the estate.

"Wonder what happened here?" remarked Jim, bending down to examine a heap of small branches and twigs at the base of the new part of the wall, "Subsidence? An attack by the peasantry?" He paused, and hunkered down, then snorted with puzzlement, "Hang on, what's this?" He began to take photographs and put down yellow markers around the pile.

Farisi Kayatta already had her hand in her pocket when her partner asked, "Could you pass me an evidence bag and a pair of tweezers? I think I've found something." Carefully, he poked the tweezers handed to him in among the twigs and drew out a small object. He put it into the evidence bag. "I'm going to need a few more bags," he said. Farisi handed them over. "What have you found, Sarge? Don't tell me we've struck lucky already!" she breathed, moving closer, looking for footprints around where Jackson was squatting, putting more small objects into the bags. "A load of something or nothing," he replied, shaking his head in disbelief, "Give me a minute."

Eventually he stood up, rubbing the backs of his legs, ten bags in his hand, each containing the items he had retrieved. "Look here," he said, holding out the bags to the detective constable, and she took them, expecting to see clumps of dog hair with blood on them, or drug paraphernalia, or perhaps a torn up document. "We need more light," she said, squinting at the contents of the bags and moving away to where the sunlight cast a patch of brightness onto the path, "Got your torch on you?"

The detectives sat down side by side on a convenient log, and Farisi took one of the bags and shone a torch on the contents. She made a little *tsk* of surprise. "Pass me another one, Sarge," she said. "They're all the same, Detective Constable," said Brillo, but did as she asked. "What the heck are they, though?" she said, using the tweezers to take one from its bag. "Well . . ." answered Jackson, taking his time finding the right words, "I think what we are looking at is a collection of very small balaclava face masks, hand knitted in black wool, and of the three hole variety. In case you aren't familiar with this type of head-gear, that means one for the mouth . . ." "And one for each eye," Farisi interrupted, "My husband rides a motorbike." She continued to examine the small object she was holding four inches from her face. "Except that this has five holes," she said, "It appears to have ear holes too."

The balaclavas were muddy, as if they had been trampled on. "So, what do you think?" Farisi asked her partner, "Something or nothing?" "Well," said Jackson thoughtfully, "We can't rule them out as evidence just because they're nothing we can relate to a dog's disappearance that we can work out, just now. But I think it's unlikely Roger the Labrador's run into a band of tiny bank robbers and eaten them." Detective Constable Kayatta laughed. "Or that he's been kidnapped by an army of Barbie dolls in urban guerrilla outfits," she quipped, "Let's get on, shall we? It's getting a bit chilly and my seat's getting damp."

Jackson and Kayatta put the evidence bags into a larger bag, marked up the label, tied caution tape around the area, leaving room for people to walk along the path unimpeded, took a few more photographs of the scene from different angles and continued their patrol. It was noon before they found the next clue, which was to puzzle them even more.

Chapter Twenty-Three

VEGETABLES

Percy Brandston had intended to give the kitchen garden of his estate no more than a cursory glance, but it was not to be. For as soon as he and Roger went under the woven willow archway that marked the boundary between the topiary garden and the kitchen garden, Roger barked loudly and reared up on his hind legs, straining at his lead. Percy's immediate reaction to this was fear: his constant companion. He had embraced the paranoia, spread by the tabloid press—and other bodies that had something to gain by keeping the general public in a heightened state of anxiety—that there were terrorists lurking everywhere, ready to jump out and blow you up.

He cowered back against the yew hedge, let Roger off the lead and surveyed the area, his eyes flickering from side to side and up and down as if he were suffering from a bad case of nystagmus. Nothing appeared to be out of the ordinary. The tool shed was padlocked, and its window shutter was bolted. Rows of winter cabbages, sprouts and cauliflowers stood serenely under the now milk-white sky. It occurred to Percy that more snow might be on the way. Nothing stirred, except for Roger, who was galloping along between two rows of polytunnels in the direction of the shed, and the crows which, as ever, circled overhead, cawing loudly.

Percy pulled his mobile phone from his pocket, hit first the number one button and then the call button, and put it to his ear. A male voice answered: "Sir," it said. "Possible intruder in the kitchen garden," said Percy in a loud whisper, "Come immediately." "Sir," said the voice again. F5's finest were on their way. Within seconds, Percy heard the sound of several pairs of feet running fast in heavy boots on gravel. He immediately felt reassured. All he had to do now was to collect himself, stand out of the way, and watch.

Five security guards, Glock Seventeens out, came charging across the topiary garden towards him. The one at the back was out of breath. Percy made a mental note to have him fired. The one at the front looked as though he had worn a Marines uniform at one time, and he had. Percy knew his history, shared over an off-duty glass of port in the library when he had first arrived. It was the one in charge: Marcus Pripson. Pripson had one of those rugged, steely-eyed faces that made Percy Brandston feel safe. He would rather have had him on his side than any Marvel superhero. Pripson had an impressive scar that ran all the way down from the middle of one eyebrow to the middle of his chin. Percy was intrigued, and had longed to ask him how he'd got it, but he was afraid he might be too squeamish to be able to listen to the story. Percy almost wished he had a scar to show for his life in politics, but he carried any scars he had on the inside: scars from people who had let him down, scars from people he had let down himself. But he was fortunate: his lifestyle offered plenty of distractions, and then, there was Marjory . . .

Pripson came to a halt beside his employer and waited for his men to catch up. He carried a machine-gun as well as his pistol. They arranged themselves in a semi-circle around him, a few feet away, in 'ready for action' poses that reminded Percy of a title sequence from a James Bond film. Pripson spoke into a miniature walkie-talkie on his wrist. All in code: Percy couldn't understand a word. Then, without a word to one another, the F5 men—actually, to Percy's surprise, one was a woman—spread out across the kitchen garden. "They've been *deployed*," said Percy to himself, relaxing. "I recommend you return to the house, Sir," said Pripson in an undertone as he glided past, a sleek shadow in the weak sunlight. Percy wasn't about to retreat to the house, though. He wanted to watch.

He was a little disappointed when, half an hour later, Pripson returned to him and reported that there was no danger. "We've carried out a full sweep of the grounds, sir, and found nothing. We will, however, step up our patrols for the next twenty-four hours and then review the situation," said Percy's head of security, "I will attend on Monday morning at 0800 hours for the usual briefing. I wish you a pleasant day, sir." Pripson touched the peak of his cap and was gone, marching fast towards the out-building where his office was situated. The four who had been with him, along with six other officers, came strolling past a few minutes later, chatting about this and that and ignoring their employer, who had sat himself down on a bench and was waiting for Roger to tire of what he was doing.

The dog, still on alert, was walking round and round a wheelbarrow parked beside a potato bed. Every now and then, he would try to get his front paws on the side of the barrow and see into it. As far as Percy knew, F5 had not checked the barrow. Why would they? What could possibly lurk in a wheelbarrow that could pose a threat to a Secretary of State? Finally, tired of calling Roger, usually so obedient, away to him, Percy got up, followed him over to the barrow and looked in. He was puzzled by what he saw, and stood scratching his head. Roger looked up at him, his head on one side, waiting.

There was half an inch of water in the bottom of the wheelbarrow: melt water most likely. There were also two other objects in it. They looked like toys. Perhaps Billett the Elder had a grand-child, and had let it play in the garden. That would, of course, be a sackable offence. Percy, forgetting to be afraid, took off a glove and picked up the object nearest to him. It was a Meerschaum smoking-pipe, beautifully crafted with a pattern of oak leaves, and evidently an antique. But it was only an inch and a half from top to bottom. It couldn't be a child's pipe, surely? Percy couldn't imagine Billett approving of a child smoking, let alone allowing it to smoke a pipe. And to allow a child to smoke a pipe in his employer's garden: it simply didn't seem likely. He shook out the water that had collected inside it.

Percy did what he always did with random objects he found: he pocketed it. He had quite a collection in his desk drawer in the Manor library, and often went through it, remembering the occasions when he had slipped a photograph, a piece of cutlery, a bar of soap or something a little more valuable into a pocket, only realizing what he had done on his return home. The second object was, it turned out, a pair of hand-knitted green mittens, connected by a narrow woollen plait. This he could not understand at all. A child might take off its mittens, but would leave them dangling by their thread from either sleeve. And anyway, the mittens were way too small to fit a child of an age to walk.

The mittens followed the pipe into Percy's pocket. Roger was now becoming quite badly behaved, running back and forth, back and forth, between the wheelbarrow and the shed, barking himself hoarse. He had scattered gravel onto the vegetable beds and now Percy saw that he had done his business right next to his master's feet. "Heel, Roger! Heel! Bad dog!" shouted Percy. Roger would not come to heel. He went over to the shed and sat down, his ears up.

"Enough, Roger!" yelled Percy, following him over to the shed. As he drew closer, he could have sworn he saw someone peeping through the yew hedge: a little old man, about a foot tall. "Impossible!" said Percy to himself. He put Roger back on the lead and dragged him away, smacking the dog on the nose. Roger whined and resisted, but eventually came to heel, and they proceeded on their walk. Somehow the mood had been broken, but Percy soon recovered his aplomb. He was looking forward to the next part of the excursion, which would take them into the meadow and down to the stream.

Chapter Twenty-Four

HOUSE OF PARROTS

Showered and rested, Marjory Brandston and her daughter tidied their room and went to knock on Tim's door to say it was nearly dinner-time. They guessed he would fall asleep, and the sleepy voice that answered their knock proved they had been correct. "Come!" he called, and was in mid-yawn when they entered his room. "Oh, this is amazing!" exclaimed Elspeth, surveying a space that was as different in style from the room she was sharing with her mother as possible.

Whereas the women's bedroom was all pastel shades and lace, the room in which Tim lay stretched out on a patchwork quilt all the colours of the rainbow rubbing his eyes was a riot of colour. The room was painted in rich shades of red and orange. The ceiling, which was about eight feet high, had been completely covered in a mosaic made of small pieces of glass and pottery, which had been placed so as to form a sun design, complete with rays. There was no ceiling light. Standard lamps stood in all four corners of the room, the white wood stems carved to look like totem poles, except that they were clearly modern and the design was of lizards, red and orange, twining round each other and climbing upwards.

The window was hung with bamboo blinds, which were down, showing their hand-painted pattern of parrots in flight. "My goodness, Tim!" said his mother, "It's all a bit overpowering, isn't it?" Tim smiled a tired smile, "Well, actually Mother, I always wanted a room like this when I was a boy. It's . . . Well, it's an adventurer's room. It makes me want to get out and explore. Save endangered animals or something." Marjory did remember her son wanting such a thing, but she hadn't taken him seriously. Decorating a room like this wouldn't have been at all the thing at Brandston Manor. Everything had to be kept more or less as it always had. Heritage, and all that. She wondered how sleeping in a room with antique furniture, oil paintings of pale children and pheasants, and wallpaper with floral patterns might have affected her children.

She remembered how cowed she herself had felt when her future in-laws had shown her round the house and she had entered the master bedroom for the first time. Her future mother-in-law, Lady Sylvia, had told her that she and Percy's father had already moved to the east wing, to a room overlooking the stables. Marjory was used to antiques, of course, but this was overwhelming: the four-poster bed with its carvings of slaves carrying water jars, and the portraits of Brandston matriarchs in particular. Everything was somehow too weighty and reeking of history. And the faces of the women in their pale grey or blue silk peignoirs looked down as if they were waiting to see if she would do her duty by her husband and produce at least one male heir. She had never got used to that bed, or those eyes. In the end Percy had had the offending bed moved, once his parents were both dead, to one of the guest-rooms, and replaced it with a modern bed, in which they had both revelled. And he had exchanged the portraits—not without a gentle protest—for paintings of floral displays and cornucopia.

"I adore this room!" declared Tim. "I could sleep in it forever!" "Well, you've got to get up now," said his sister, smiling down at him, "It's half-past seven, and I feel like a wander round the garden before dinner. Are you up for it, *Timmo*?" Tim returned her smile: "Lead on, *Elso*!" he replied. Elspeth grimaced. Marjory led the way to the kitchen, with Tim and Elspeth following, *Timmo*-ing and *Elso*-ing each other under the breath, like a couple of kids. She couldn't help but be pleased that they had at last got back their sense of humour.

Marjory coughed politely before pushing open the kitchen door, having seen how affectionate her sister and Zooie were with each other. She found them leaning up against the counter, their arms around each other, looking at the local newspaper, their faces close together. She was happy for her sister. Christine had had a tough time at school, and at university. New Zealand had been a brave new start for her, and it had eventually paid off. She had been with Zooie through thick and thin, after a few false starts in romance. They had met while volunteering at the site of an oil spillage, which had brought many injured birds to a local beach.

"Well, well!" said her sister, staying exactly where she was, "If it isn't some nice, clean people come for supper! What have you done with my sister?!" Marjory laughed. She had thought she looked a bit of a fright, having washing the mousse and spray out of her unco-operative hair and left it to dry naturally. And she hadn't bothered with full makeup: just a dab of mascara. "Have you slept?" asked Zooie, turning to switch on the kettle. "We haven't, but *Timmo* has!" said Elspeth. "Ah yes," laughed Zooie, "The Great Timmo! Do you like your room, young man?" Tim repeated that he adored it and could sleep in it forever, and both women looked pleased. "That's sort of a retreat room we made," said Christine, looking at Zooie, who nodded, "For when one of us gets a bit grouchy. However it might look, we're not joined at the hip, are we, my darling?" "Not likely," agreed Zooie, "That room has saved us from a fight or two, I can tell you. We call it the boudoir. That means a room for pouting in, you know." Elspeth gave her brother's arm a playful punch, and said, "Well, you've put the right person in there, then!"

Marjory sat down at the kitchen table, while Elspeth and Tim went outside, where they strolled round the garden, and came back to sit on the back verandah. "The kids look OK," remarked Christine. "Oh, they'll be all right now, I think," said Marjory, "It was all getting a bit on top of us back home. All a bit irritable. We could do with a boudoir of our own. You're so sensible, Chris. I could have thought of it myself, but I . . . well, I didn't." "Come on, Sis, no brooding now," said her sister, patting her on the arm as she passed by to take bread from a wooden bin, "You're on your hols! Live it up!"

At eight o'clock precisely, they all sat down to dinner together. It was raining cats and dogs outside, but Christine and Zooie assured them that fine weather was forecast for the following day. The meal was delicious: grouper fish baked with garlic, peppers and white wine, with a potato gratin, followed by apple-filled crepes. This was all served with bottles of a light, fresh New Zealand lager, which stood waiting under the open window in the biggest ice bucket the guests had ever seen.

"Beer with dinner," said Timmo, reaching across for another bottle, "Whatever would Daddy say?" Marjory, fearing he would follow this up with a critical remark, jumped in: "I think he'd say, have a jolly good time, darlings, don't you?" "Of course he would," agreed Elspeth, holding out her plate for a second helping of crepes, "That's just what he'd say." Tim took the top off his beer and poured it into his glass. He raised the glass for a toast: "To Daddy, then!" Zooie and Christine followed suit. "To good old Percy, who makes my sister happy, and helped produce these two fine offspring!" said Christine. Elspeth touched her glass gently to her mother's, and slowly they, too, raised their glasses. "So what do we say, then?" asked Zooie, smiling, "I can hardly call him Daddy, can I?" Tim looked thoughtful. "Well, I'm sure we all send him our good wishes . . . I know, let's drink to boudoirs everywhere!" Everyone smiled and five glasses touched over the remains of the dinner. "To boudoirs everywhere!" they all said, grinning at each other.

"Aren't we a crazy lot?" said Christine, "Now, who's going to help with the washing-up?" She could have added that there are no servants here, thought Marjory, grateful that Christine was not the type to say such things. It seemed she and Zooie had found real happiness together, and that was wonderful, and rare, and made Marjory so glad, she felt she could burst. "Tell you what," she said, going up to her sister and giving her a quick hug, "Why don't you leave it to me? Elspeth's been longing to see the famous parrots . . ." "Well, if you're happy with that, Sis," replied Christine, "Thanks. Come on, kids, come and meet Captain Birdseye and his feathered crew!"

Elspeth and Tim got up from the table and followed their aunts. The corridor that led to their rooms had another door just beyond the kitchen that they hadn't noticed before. Through it was a short hall with two doors opposite one another. The left-hand door was open, and led to a living-room at the front of the house. Brother and sister got an impression of pine, sheepskin rugs and lots of books, CDs and house-plants. Two comfortable old horsehair sofas, one opposite the other and a extraordinarily beautiful, wicker, peacock chair, freshly stained in peacock blue. The right-hand door was closed, and it was this door that led to the room occupied (most of the time) by Christine and Zooie. Zooie opened it.

Immediately, there was a chorus of screeching and whooping, and a flapping of wings. "Go in!" said Zooie, giving Elspeth and Tim a little push, "They're not going to bite!" The visitors entered, and were astonished to see that the whole of the wall opposite was an unbroken expanse of window, and that in front of it stood a large cage containing five parrots, all of them fluttering wildly and making a fuss. A double bed and a small wardrobe were squashed into the remaining space. Everyone sat down on the end of the bed and waited for the birds to calm down.

"There's a pair of long curtains we can draw between the birds and the window," explained Christine, "But they like them open so they can see the garden and the sky. We get a lot of advice from the Parrot Society, so we know what we're doing, and don't stress them out. Eh, fellas?" she said, turning towards the birds, which had settled on their perches and were eyeing up the humans in the room. A blue parrot with yellow goggles called out, "Pieces of eight!" and Elspeth and Tim collapsed in merriment. "That's Captain Birdseye," laughed Zooie, opening the cage and coaxing him onto her outstretched arm, "He's the boss. We got him first, from the rescue centre. The green one with the red cap's called Matey . . ." "After the bubble bath," chipped in Christine, " . . . the white sulphur-crested cockatoo is Solomon, the red is Barbarella, and that moulting bundle on the far side whose feathers look like school marble flooring is poor old Marilyn. She came from a bad background, and she makes the most of it to get attention. Don't be taken in! She's on a strict diet, 'cos she'd eat till she burst if we let her."

"Are they all rescued birds?" asked Elspeth, watching Matey bouncing his head up and down as he watched her. "Yes," replied Zooie, "We help the local Parrot Society out. Captain Birdseye's a permanent fixture, but the others will probably find good homes in a week or two, when we've given them a bit of TLC and the vet's checked them out." "So, how many have you had?" asked Tim. "Ooh . . ." said Christine, "That's a tough one. Off-hand, maybe a couple of hundred over the years. We're emergency foster parents. There are other folks who have big aviaries and give them a proper home. Some go to zoos and wildlife gardens and sanctuaries. We've been meaning to turn the shed into an aviary for a while, but somehow we never get round to it."

"Well, I think it's splendid," said Tim, "But I think I'm about to sneeze . . ." "No problem, Timmo," said his Aunt Chris, "I was going to suggest a cuppa in the living-room, and here's your Mum just in time." Marjory appeared at the door. "I've already made a pot of tea, Chris," she said, smiling and looking relaxed, "And I've carried it to the living-room." "You're a star!" said Zooie, "I'll get out the albums and the kids can see what we've been up to, and maybe pick out a beauty spot or two they'd like to visit while you're all here."

By eleven o'clock everyone was yawning, so they said good night and retired to their rooms. Tomorrow they'd be going on their first excursion together, and everyone was looking forward to it. Marjory and Elspeth went straight to sleep. Tim lay for a while with one of the corner lamps on, looking at the sun mosaic on the ceiling of his room and thinking that perhaps it was time to take stock, make plans for his future. He decided that, so far, it seemed New Zealand might be a very pleasant place to make a fresh start.

Chapter Twenty-Five

A Significant Kiss

When Archie Prescott woke up the following morning, he almost couldn't believe that he was alone. He put on his dressing-gown and checked the flat for gnomes, but no-one was there but himself. He felt more alone than he had ever felt in his entire life. As he sat at the kitchen table while the kettle boiled, it dawned on him that he wouldn't be able to see his little friends unless they decided it was the time and the place for a meeting, and it made him a little melancholy.

But Archie had never been one to brood or feel sorry for himself. He drank his usual two cups of coffee, listened to Smooth Radio for a bit, singing along to the songs he knew, then went for a bath and a shave. It was eleven o'clock when he found himself, scrubbed up, smooth-chinned and dressed in his best jumper and trousers, standing in his front hall, ready to face the world. "I'm going to go and see Ann-Marie," he said, surprising himself. He hadn't gone to all that trouble with the thought that today would be the day when he made his move, but something told him his decision had been brewing ever since he'd drunk Ned Blackthorn's birch wine.

Archie went back for the garden plants catalogue the postman had delivered the previous day, to give himself an excuse, and let himself out of his flat. He took the stairs rather than wait for the lift, which he could hear was stuck on the floor below, where two of his neighbours were having a conversation, one in the lift, and one out. It was a bright, fresh morning, and the stairwell smelt of disinfectant. The caretaker had already been on his rounds.

Outside Ann-Marie's front door, Archie paused and smoothed down his hair. Then, his hand shaking ever so slightly, he rang the bell. A few seconds later, he heard Ann-Marie's light footsteps in the hallway. "Ann-Marie? It's only me, Archie," he called out, to reassure her. One never knew who might come knocking. There was a woman in the block who was forever trying to borrow money. Ann-Marie opened the door and stood there smiling, dressed in a pink dressing-gown with a pattern of roses, her hair a little messy, an attractive flush on her face. "Oh, Archie! What a nice surprise!" said his neighbour, checking the landing for other people, "Sorry about the night attire—I've been doing a bit of housework before getting dressed. Would you like to come in? *I* won't be embarrassed if *you* won't!" Archie was pleased she felt so comfortable with him that she would receive him in this manner. "Thanks, Ann-Marie," he replied, stepping across the threshold, "I've come because that garden catalogue's arrived and I thought maybe you'd like to help me choose a few plants . . ." "Sure thing," she said, turning away, "Just turn the key in the door, would you? I'll put the kettle on. Make yourself at home."

Archie felt very manful, being asked to make sure the door was secure. In fact, he always felt particularly manful around Ann-Marie. He followed her to the kitchen, where she pulled out a chair from the table and invited him to sit and relax while she made coffee. "Your flat's a lot tidier than mine," he said, and then kicked himself: what would she think of him now? That he was messy? "I mean, it's so well-organised," he said, admiring her bulletin board, row of canisters and pyramid of round cake tins, all in shades of pale green. He was relieved to find that she hadn't done out her entire flat in pink. The impression he'd got, walking from the front door to the kitchen, was of cool pastels, but nothing overwhelming and—mercifully—no mauve, a shade he loathed.

"Well," said Ann-Marie, leaning up against the counter, where the kettle was beginning to seethe, "I haven't had much to do since I moved here except get organised—at least, until I met you . . ." She blushed. "I mean, I was wondering what to do with my time until I saw what you were trying to achieve here, and thought 'he could do with a bit of support'. You know, I still can't quite believe that there's only you getting properly involved. The neighbours seem OK—well, most of them—but I get the impression they live for the TV, food and drink and a bit of a moan when they get the chance . . ."

Archie nodded, "There's a few who have family who take them out, and they tend not to get involved much. And a fair few who keep themselves to themselves for various reasons. Bad experiences with people in the past, that kind of thing. I've heard a few sad stories . . . But you're right, and it's frustrating. Anyway, things are looking up: there's you, and there's me, and that's twice as many as when I started, so things must be getting better. Actually, a couple of other people are looking like they might help get a new committee together . . ." Ann-Marie gave Archie a charming smile, and pulled the catalogue towards her, turning it sideways so they could both see the pictures. "But for now it's just you and me, Archie," she said, in a happy voice. And so they spent an hour choosing between various types of prickly shrubs for the boundary hedge, varieties of vegetables, and herbs to add to the collection they were building up gradually in planters outside the common-room door. Ann-Marie noted down the names of the plants, while Archie drew a plan of the garden on the back of a wallpaper off-cut, marking where everything would go.

The pair were enjoying themselves so much that it took them by surprise when suddenly both their tummies rumbled at exactly the same moment. They both laughed. "Did you have breakfast?" asked Ann-Marie. Archie shook his head: "I don't do breakfast," he explained, "Just coffee and biscuits. I'm not great at remembering to eat, to be honest . . ." "Nor me," admitted his neighbour, "Sometimes I wake up in the middle of the night starving and realise I forgot supper. It's lunch-time now, isn't it? Would you like a bacon and egg sandwich?" Archie was pleased: "Now that would be a real treat!" he said, "Are you sure you don't mind? I'll return the favour one day," he promised. "I hope you will!" said Ann-Marie, holding Archie's gaze for a few seconds longer than normal. This time it was Archie's turn to blush.

"Actually," said Archie, "I was wondering whether you'd like to go to the garden centre with me when I go to fetch all this stuff. They've got a café at the one that's nearest. I could run to a cuppa and a cake. Get us away from here for an hour or two. That's if you don't mind . . ." "That would be lovely," replied Ann-Marie, her smile getting wider, "Shall we go tomorrow? I mean, if you've nothing else planned . . ." "Why not?" said Archie, smiling back, "I've got enough in petty cash from before, and there was enough earmarked for the garden to cover the list we've made."

And so it came to pass that Archie Prescott proudly walked with his new friend Ann-Marie Osborne to the bus-stop the following morning, in golden sunshine. They managed to find everything on their list, taking their time at the garden centre to admire the statuary, fountains and the colourful plants and trees, and over a pot of tea and a slice of fruit cake. Curtains twitched when they arrived back home and lingered in the garden with the cups of coffee Archie brought down, sitting on the bench with their purchases around them. The gnomes watched from their rockery, the smiles on their faces threatening to crack their plastic and terracotta: this was all just as it should be.

The following day, the third in succession that Ann-Marie and Archie had spent together, they met early in the garden to plant the pyracanthas, sage, lemon verbena and buddleias they had chosen together, taking their time to choose the right spots, and to earth up the roots. "Well," said Archie when they had finished, "That's brought a splash of colour in, hasn't it? It's amazing what a few plants can do for a place." Ann-Marie agreed. "Have you had enough for today?" she asked, "Only, I made a nice casserole last night and I wondered, well . . . I was going to watch a film and have a relaxing evening. Would you like to join me? I'll understand if you've had enough of my company . . ." Archie turned to his friend and held her gaze: "I don't think I could have too much of your company. That would be nice."

The pair soon settled down on Ann-Marie's comfortable sofa with their bowls of lamb casserole, which she said was one of her specialities. It was also one of Archie's favourites. Archie was pleased that neither of them spoke much during the film: he hated it when people had a problem with companionable silence, and was relieved to find that Ann-Marie seemed to share his views on the subject. They began the evening at opposite ends of the three-seater sofa, but when the film ended, Ann-Marie went to fetch a cup of coffee, and when she returned, she sat herself down in the middle. Archie felt a stab of panic, but she seemed to have done it quite naturally. And so, when at half-past ten he rose to go and she accompanied him to the front door, it seemed to him the most natural thing in the world to lean in and kiss her gently on the lips.

"See you tomorrow, maybe," said Archie, taking his time to stand up straight, Ann-Marie's face looked so lovely close up. Ann-Marie gave Archie a kiss back, lingering a little longer than he had. "I hope so, Archie. I certainly hope so . . ." she said.

After his friend had closed her door, Archie stood outside on the landing for a minute or two, listening to her retreating footsteps and the sounds of washing-up in her kitchen, before running up the stairs to his own flat, feeling like a much younger man. He slept like a log, the delicious flavours of Ann-Marie's casserole—and her kiss—still on his lips. Somehow, brushing his teeth would have seemed like sacrilege.

Chapter Twenty-Six

ANN-MARIE TAKES STOCK

Archie's kiss, which was remarkably soft and sweet, took Ann-Marie completely by surprise. And that she found herself kissing him back surprised her even more. She had not been aware of doing anything more than respect and admire him up to the point when their lips met. But as she dreamily washed up the dinner dishes and thought of him, she realised that it honestly wasn't as simple as all that.

Memories came to her in sudden flashes: noticing his bare forearms stretched across the table when he had taken a cup of coffee from her while they waited for their laundry, his hands with their long, spatulate fingers curled round the cup, the set of his shoulders when he was picking up wooden ninepins on a Saturday evening, and a certain affectionate quality in his voice when he spoke to her . . . She could not avoid admitting to herself that he had taken root in her heart so gently and so gradually that he was already inside without her noticing it.

Ann-Marie's emotions as she realised this fact were mixed: first, a sort of quiet joy, because he was worth it; second, absolute terror that she was in danger of falling in love; third, excitement, that her heart could still feel such a thrill; fourth, a determination that nothing should go wrong. The friendship was too precious—Archie was too precious—to risk wrecking it. "We probably shouldn't . . ." she said to herself, then: "Oh, oh, oh! I feel like a teenager all over again!"

This was a woman who had risked her heart before and been hurt, and hurt others too: a woman who had forced herself to become a realist. It was not sensible to expect anything good to last forever—at least, when it involved people. She was too honest with herself to think she could love someone without ever hurting them. And Archie, to Ann-Marie, was special: a gift from God to those who lived around him—to the sad, the lonely, the bored, and the disappointed. Archie could brighten up the day for all but the most hardened of cynics, with his chirpiness and boyish smile.

Ann-Marie touched her lips, where Archie's kiss still lingered, and tried not to think that, if that kiss was anything to go by, he would make a tender and patient lover. That thought, though, led to the release into her mind of other fears: what if he didn't *take to her*, when it came to the crunch? What if the sight of her undressed was unattractive to him? It had been years since a man had seen her in anything revealing, let alone in her underwear, or even without that to cover her. She laughed at herself—out loud—as she found herself mentally rummaging through her lingerie drawer for anything remotely alluring. She'd been wearing what fashion magazines were calling 'utilitarian underwear' for years, and not minding if the colours ran, so that most of her items were a kind of greyish-pink . . .

"Silly me!" Ann-Marie rebuked herself, drying the dishes and putting them in the cupboards, "It was probably just a friendly kiss. I'm reading too much into it. And I probably shouldn't have kissed him back. He went so red in the face! He was probably more embarrassed than, well, excited. Come on Fanny-Ann, pull yourself together!" She finished up in the kitchen and poured herself a glass of water to take to bed. As she hopped in under the quilt, she picked up her book—a novel by Sarah Waters she had been looking forward to reading since she had ordered it from the library a fortnight before—looked at the cover, and said: "Right! Come on, book! Take my mind off my silly notions, please!"

She opened the book, turned to Chapter 1, and took a sip of water. She read the first page four times before she could make sense of it, and the second page three times, but eventually the narrative of 'Affinity' pulled her in and she let her thoughts of Archie drift away. Time would tell, and the worst thing she could do was to become obsessed, or force the pace of things. If it was love, it would take its own course.

Books had been Ann-Marie's friends since her unhappy childhood, and she had got through many a heartbreak and trauma by hiding between their pages. She enjoyed nothing more than to curl up in bed with a good book: something that took her far away from her life. Somehow, in the morning, she felt readier, having travelled a distance in her imagination to a world inhabited by others and back again, to face the demands of her daily life.

She had been married once, many years ago. Her husband had died in a pile-up on the motorway, hurrying home at twenty miles over the speed limit, but he had been careful with money, and had left her with enough to live modestly on, without worry. She volunteered in a charity shop at weekends, when most of the volunteers wanted time off, and made extra pocket money doing occasional sewing: taking in and letting out seams, turning up hems, mending zips. At the moment she had more sewing than she really wanted, because the recession was making her customers more frugal: rather than throw away an item, they were coming to her to have them altered.

Ann-Marie had dated men occasionally over the past two years, but had been disappointed. The ones who came on to her were mostly drunk, or on the rebound, or looking for someone to complain to about their ex-wives or ex-girlfriends, just wanting to bend an ear. Because she was quiet and soft-looking, with her pillow-like figure, they sought her out for comfort. Nothing wrong with that, but when she wanted something in return, they had nothing to give her. They were somehow too full of anger or sadness—or both—to have room for empathy. Not that she blamed them: she had listened to their stories, and could understand why they had ended up so full of self-pity. Many had had families who no longer wanted them around, or had lost their jobs to younger men, or were still holding on to the dreams of their youth, refusing to let them die. They had been Men with a capital 'M': tough, hard-working, resilient, and it had brought them nothing.

There were two she had felt quite hopeful about when she had first met them, because they seemed charming and genuinely interested. But the first had wanted to get into bed with her on the first date, and become angry when she refused, citing the fact that he had—on his own insistence—paid for their lunch out at a local pub and driven her home because it was pouring with rain. She had told him she was not for sale. The second had sat for two hours complaining about his ex-wife, his children, his job and his lack of a social life. When she had ventured a comment, he had stared around the restaurant until she was finished, continuing his monologue without making reference to anything she had said. And he had laughed mockingly when she had talked about the charity shop and her tailoring.

As she drifted off to sleep at around two in the morning—Sarah Waters' novel being almost impossible to put down—Ann-Marie stretched out under the covers and said a little prayer for Archie and for herself: "Help us to know how to go about this and not make mistakes, please," she asked, not sure who might be listening, but in faith that Somebody Up There was, "And please be with Archie and give him a good night's sleep. And help us to be friends, whatever else happens."

Had she but known it, Archie was lying in his own bed, three floors above where she lay, saying his own prayer, which was a little different in style: "Oh God!" prayed Archie Prescott, "Please help me understand the gnomes properly, and Ann-Marie as well. I don't deserve her but if it's your will for us to be together, that would be very nice indeed. Amen."

Neither Archie nor Ann-Marie was religious, but like so many of their generation they had been brought up on Sunday School, 'Songs of Praise' on TV on a Sunday tea-time, and Christmas carols. Their faith, such as it was—more of a bowing to the deep mysteries of life than any kind of belief system or set of answers—ran deep. "I wonder if Ann-Marie's saying her prayers," said Archie to himself, "I wonder how she'll take to Norman and Co . . . ."

Archie and Ann-Marie closed their eyes within minutes of each other and, for once, both of them slept deeply and peacefully through the night, not even waking when the postman rattled their letterboxes at six a.m., or when Big John shouted loud morning greetings from his balcony in Eden Tower across to Big Frank, who was putting nuts into the bird feeder on his balcony in Paradise Tower. "Oy! Frank!" yelled Big John. "Yeah, John, what's up, mate?" his neighbour yelled back. "What going on with Archie and that Ann-Marie then?" bellowed Big John. "Your guess is as good as mine!" Big Frank bellowed back. "I would if I were him!" bawled Big John, making his hands into a loudspeaker. "So would I, mate—so would I!" trumpeted Big Frank. At that point, Big Frank's sister June called him back inside. "Gotta go, mate!" he yelled to his neighbour. "See ya!" yelled Big John, and went inside for his breakfast.

Chapter Twenty-Seven

A Fresh Start

It was the advent of Ann-Marie that helped Archie Prescott get things on-track as far as the residents' association was concerned. Once they had sat down for an informal chat over the washing one Sunday afternoon, and Ann-Marie had asked why Archie was doing the account books, and the Saturday night skittles, and the Bingo Club, and moving the furniture, and reporting repairs—and everything else that went with being a committee member, and discovered he really was on his own, she was on the case.

The first move was to obtain a copy of the standard constitution, which she did, by phoning someone at the local authority. According to the document, any three concerned tenants could call a special general meeting and co-opt a committee of three people: a chair, a secretary and a treasurer. So all she and Archie had to do was find at least one neighbour who was willing to step up to the mark, preferably three or four.

With so many people living so close, and with a vested interest in the housing scheme being a decent place to live, finding willing helpers ought to be easy. Ann-Marie said words to this effect to Archie, as they emptied the tumble-dryer. "Not on your life!" said Archie, "I don't like to moan, and I don't like to speak ill of anyone, but this lot . . . well . . . suffice it to say that they'd probably rather run under a bus on the High Street than help out." "Isn't there anyone we can ask?" sighed Ann-Marie, "I mean, assuming people will vote us on . . ." "That might be a problem," said Archie, "Carol and her friends might make things a bit difficult."

"Leave Carol to me," said Ann-Marie with a tight little smile, "I've just had a glance at the books while you were folding your laundry, and there are a couple of receipts that shouldn't have gone through. As far as I know, refreshments are not supposed to include alcohol." "That's right!" said Archie, "We're not supposed to charge drinks for meetings to the residents' association, unless it's tea and coffee. Are you sure? Carol never said . . ." "Yes, one hundred per cent," his friend replied, "And I know just how to handle it. Meanwhile, why don't you try your friends who help out in the garden? I know not everyone wants to sit on a committee, but you never know. They'd probably do it out of loyalty to you, and they certainly care about this place." "My only worry is putting too much on them," said Archie thoughtfully, "But I'll give it a try."

Two weeks later, with Banton and Viktor both on-board, thanks to the intervention of Archie, the special meeting took place, and the tenants found themselves with an enthusiastic four-person committee in place. Ann-Marie had had a quiet word with Carol in the laundry-room on the subject of 'inappropriate spending', and Archie's nemesis was absent from the meeting, as were Veronica and Mandy. Interestingly enough, Evie turned up, and seconded Archie as Chair. "Well," he said after the meeting, "I didn't expect that!" Banton smiled knowingly: "She locked herself out of the building yesterday. She was hanging around outside with a couple of big shopping bags looking dog-tired. Once she'd got over the shock of a black man talking to her, she was OK. I let her in, and then we found the lift had broken down, so I carried her bags upstairs for her. She made me a cup of tea. I guess I'm in her good books!" he said. "Wonders never cease!" said Archie. "The timing's amazing, isn't it? Must be angels on our side!" said Ann-Marie.

The new committee sat down for their first official meeting. There was a pot of tea on the table, and a coffee for Archie. He armed himself with his usual cup of coffee, and Ann-Marie got out a spiral notebook to take the minutes. "So," said Archie, "I guess there are a couple of things to clear up. Ann-Marie: are there any procedural points?" "Yes," she said, a copy of the constitution on the table in front of her. We probably should get the accounts audited as soon as we can. That way, we distance ourselves from what's gone on before. There's a chap from the council who does that, and I'll email him this evening. Should take about a fortnight. Also, we should set a date for the AGM." "What, already?" protested Viktor. "Yes," said Ann-Marie, "I think what we should do is put on a few activities, show people what we can achieve, then have the AGM in, say, three months' time." "Makes sense," agreed Banton, "That way the other tenants won't have had a chance to get sick of us!" "OK," said Archie, "So what do we want to do?"

Ann-Marie smiled broadly: "Well, I've been chatting to a few people already, and got some ideas. That way we can say the ideas came from other people, rather than just us. I've written them down. Here's the list: a garden party, tai chi, a weekly coffee morning and a film show." The film show wasn't going to happen until a projector could be borrowed or bought, so that went down on the list of possible purchases once the books came back. Archie knew a place down the road where there were tai chi sessions, and promised to contact the organiser to see whether someone could come along and do some taster sessions. Ann-Marie offered to start the coffee mornings going: "I can just keep the receipts for the drinks and biscuits and pass them to Banton. Archie: have you passed the petty cash to our new treasurer yet?" "Got it here, and the petty cash book," said Archie, passing them across to Banton.

The garden party idea caught their imagination, and they set a date for a day in May. Ann-Marie, who had a printer, was detailed to produce posters, and the men volunteered to get the garden up to scratch and clean the outdoor furniture before the event. "Have we got any bunting?" asked Archie. Ann-Marie said the chap from the council was the best source for that kind of thing, and she would ask him when she emailed.

"Anything else?" asked Archie, sitting back in his chair, looking remarkably chilled out. "How about an evening party?" asked Viktor,

"I was thinking, maybe we could have a karaoke night. My cousin Prokop has a karaoke machine and I know he'd let us borrow it. He might even come along and do the whole thing for us." "That's great, man!" said Banton, "Nothing like a sing-song to bring people together!" And so it was proposed and unanimously accepted that there would be a karaoke night right after the garden party. And if it rained, the party could just be moved indoors straight away. "We could make it a bring and share buffet for the evening," proposed Ann-Marie, "I think people would like that. Gives everyone the chance to contribute. There are a few of the ladies I've met who say they're good cooks . . ."

By the end of the meeting, everyone was pleased with what they'd achieved. "I'll type up the minutes this evening," said Ann-Marie, flipping her notebook shut and standing up, "And print off copies for the notice boards. Then I'll get going with the posters." "That's great," said Archie, "I'll walk you home." Viktor and Banton winked at each other. Archie blushed: "Well, it's getting a bit dark, isn't it?" he said. "Thank you, Archie," said Ann-Marie sweetly, trying to look like a woman who was too afraid to walk a few yards alone at twilight. Viktor got up to go as well, but Banton stopped him: "Hey, Viktor! Stick around for a bit, would you?" he said. It was obvious he was trying to think of a reason to stop Viktor following Archie and Ann-Marie. "Um, I wanted to ask you about . . . something . . ." "OK," grinned Viktor, catching his drift, "You go on," he said to Ann-Marie and Archie, "I'll see you tomorrow."

As soon as Archie and Ann-Marie got outside, they looked at each other, puzzled. "Have you said anything to anybody?" asked Archie. "About what?" replied Ann-Marie. "About, well . . . us?" said Archie. "Us?" asked Ann-Marie, giving him a bashful smile. There was silence until they got into the lift.

Almost as soon as they were in, and the doors had shut, a strange feeling came over Archie. His palms began to sweat, and he felt his knees going from under him. Ann-Marie looked at him, and slowly a radiant smile spread across her face, which was almost as flushed as

Archie's. She moved closer and, putting her hands on his shoulders, she pressed her lips to his. Archie groaned and his arms shot out, as if of their own accord, and round her waist. Their bodies moved together as if by magnetism, and they began to kiss with an abandon that would probably have surprised their neighbours. By the time they got to Ann-Marie's floor, Archie was having palpitations, and had to pull away. "Should we be doing this?" he asked his friend, sounding worried. "I can't think of any reason why not," replied a breathless Ann-Marie, "But then, I don't seem to be able to think at all, when you kiss me."

Archie stepped out into the hallway. Ann-Marie took out her keys and fitted them into the lock. As Archie turned away to catch the lift before the doors closed, she caught his hand and pulled it gently. Archie let the lift go on up, and followed her into her flat. Whether the minutes and posters were done that night will never be known. What did happen has not been written down. Suffice it to say that, next morning, Big John and Big Frank met in the middle of the car park, and an animated progress report was passed from one to the other. By tea-time the following day, everyone on the scheme who had talked to anyone knew that Archie Prescott and Ann-Marie Osborne were an item.

Chapter Twenty-Eight

GLADSTONE

"Wake up, sleepyhead!" called Zooie, knocking on Tim's door. His mother and sister had been up for an hour, helping clean out the parrots' cage and top up their food and water. Tim threw on a dressing-gown he found hanging on the back of his bedroom door and went along to the kitchen, still rubbing his eyes. When he walked in, everyone burst out laughing. "Nice dressing-gown, Timmo!" said Elspeth. Tim looked down at himself, and smiled ruefully. The dressing-gown in question was purple, quilted nylon with floral braid on the collar and pockets. "I think that was my mother's," laughed Zooie, "Never mind, Tim: I know you love family heirlooms!" "Yes," said Tim, sitting down and reaching for the coffee-pot, "Just showing respect for Kiwi antiquity," he said, yawning fit to break his jaw, "So, where are we going? How's the weather looking?"

The previous night's discussion had resulted in a decision to wait and see what the weather forecast promised. The outlook, Christine reported, was dry and sunny, though the wind might be a little brisk: "The venturi effect, it's called," she had explained, "The wind gets squeezed through a gap at Cook Strait, so it can come on a bit strong, but you won't get blown off your feet." "How about that vineyard tour, then?" suggested Elspeth, "The one with the restaurant?" "I'm all for that!" agreed Zooie. Marjory sat smiling and listening. She felt better than she had in years, and was happy to go along with what the others decided.

So, the vineyard it was: Gladstone Vineyard, to be exact. Its *pinot noir* had won awards, not only in New Zealand but in the UK, and Marjory had enjoyed many a glass with her husband Percy over dinner, after her sister had recommended it. "I'm looking forward to the wine-tasting," Zooie told her partner, as they went out to check on the collection of borrowed bicycles they'd assembled from neighbours for the occasion. "Do you think they know we don't have a car, Zoo?" asked Christine, "Do you think they'll object to these?" She patted the one she was working on, which was a bit rusty. "Yes, they know. Ach, it'll do them good," said Zooie, giving her partner a pat on the knee, which left a big smudge of oil. Christine yelped, and smeared her oily hand across her partner's face. "Hey, sorry!" said Tim, who had come out to see if he could help, "Didn't mean to interrupt." "That's OK, Timmo," said Zooie, "We were getting side-tracked. Could you help your Aunty finish these off while I get a shower?" "No problem," said Tim, and squatted down beside Christine, "What needs doing? Do Mummy and Elso know we're riding these?" "Not yet," answered his Aunt, "But your Mum knows we don't have a car, so maybe she's already figured it out." "I doubt it," said Tim, "She's probably expecting a taxi or something. Never mind, if I know Mummy, she won't say a word. As long as she doesn't have to get up on horseback, she'll be fine."

An hour later, the bicycles were ready, and everyone had assembled in the kitchen. Marjory came in last, having had some trouble deciding what to wear. She had settled on a knee-length tweed skirt, a sweater and boots. Christine looked her up and down. "Er, Sis, you might want to rethink the outfit," she said carefully. "It's a question of transport . . ." ventured Tim. "Bikes," said Zooie, making it plain, "Push-bikes. Sorry. But it's only about eight kilometres to Carterton . . ." Christine put an arm round her sister's shoulders. "It's OK," she said, "Come with me." Ten minutes later they reappeared, and this time Marjory was wearing a pair of her sister's jeans and trainers. Elspeth laughed, but not unpleasantly: "Mother, you look ten years younger!" she exclaimed, giving her a kiss on the cheek, "That look really suits you." "Let's go, folks!" said Zooie, picking up her shoulder bag from the counter.

Tim had been right about his mother: she didn't say a word as
she straddled the brand new Chinese Flying Pigeon she'd been given.
She was fortunate: it was the newest of the bikes and the one in the
best state by far. Tim handed his sister the second best of the bunch:
a mountain bike, the twin of the one he was sitting on, but a couple
of years more recent. Christine and Zooie took their tricycles. It was
immediately clear, as the party set off, that they were used to heavy
bikes, their calf and thigh muscles standing out impressively as they led
the way along the main highway. Marjory was thankful that the road
was not as up and down as she had feared, and the tarmac surface was
well-maintained. She admired the neat commercial buildings and the
bungalows with their pretty gardens as she rode along in the sunshine,
as well as the stretches of open countryside with their tall trees and
wide fields.

They stopped in Carterton itself to browse the shops, and Elspeth
bought a shoulder bag for her mother, who was struggling with her
handbag on the bars of her bike. "Here you are, Mummy," she said
as she handed it over, "It's big enough to put your handbag in. And if
it rains, you can easily wear it under your mac." The bag was from a
retro and antiques shop on the main street, and reminded Marjory of
the handbag she had carried around Oxford when she was a student
in the 1970s: suede with beads and fringes. "Thank you, darling,"
Marjory said to Elspeth, giving her a kiss on the cheek, "It goes with
my outfit a lot better than the Smythson. Silly: I could have had the
shoulder bag, but Daddy said it wasn't the thing . . ." "We're going to
have to think practical while we're here, Mummy," said Elspeth, "Rain,
hail, howling gales: we need to dress for the weather, not the paparazzi
or the neighbours! What a relief, though . . ." Marjory agreed: "It is
nice to be normal. Now, where's this vineyard?"

The party turned off the main highway and kept on until they
found Gladstone Road and the entrance to the vineyard. The sun was
beaming down, and the air was fresh and delicious. Christine had
phoned in advance and booked them in on the guided tour, which
included wine-tasting, but that wasn't until three o'clock, so they had

time to enjoy a leisurely lunch in the restaurant—Marjory's treat. The tables were out of doors under huge, colourful umbrellas, surrounded by greenery. The women chose Thai salads and pasta, while Tim who, according to Elspeth, had "hollow legs" made short work of an enormous surf and turf.

"I don't know about you, Marjory," said Christine, "But I don't think I can wait for the wine-tasting. I'm really tempted to try a glass from what they're calling their Jealous Sisters range. How about you?" Marjory laughed: "I hope that doesn't mean two angry women are going to jump on us if we drink it!" she said, feeling a bit embarrassed at her weak attempt at a joke. "Let's see, shall we?" said Christine, "Fancy a glass, Zoo?" Zooie said she thought they could run to a bottle, so they ordered the 2012 Pinot Gris and five glasses. The first bottle disappeared too quickly, so they ordered a second. "Hey, Aunty!" said Tim, "I hope you can't be arrested for being drunk in charge of a bicycle over here!" "Oh yeah," laughed his Aunt, "The coppers lurk in wait as you come out of the main gates! And they're hardest on the Brits. Didn't you know that?"

After a fascinating tour of the winery, and more wine, everyone was feeling very merry. Fortunately, Zooie had packed a couple of bottles of water, so they all sat by the lake and drank it before setting off. It was Elspeth who, once they were on the main highway once more, burst into song, and it wasn't long before the others joined in. "Ten green bottles hanging on the wall!" soon turned into "Ten green parrots sitting on a perch". Their voices rang out across the fields, scattering the birds from the trees.

Sitting on her bicycle, her backside feeling rather numb, Marjory counted her blessings. The only worry she had was how Percy was coping without her. She was at the back of the line, so she sped up until she overtook her sister. "You won't mind if I give Percy a quick ring when we get back, will you?" she asked. "Lord, no!" replied her sister, "Just don't tell him how much we've all had to drink!"

When they reached the cottage, everyone flopped down on the sofas except for Zooie, who went to put the kettle on and check on Captain Birdseye and his feathered friends. By consensus, they switched on the television and watched a popular show called 'The Great Food Race', which they thoroughly enjoyed, especially when Christine took Tim out to the kitchen to copy a beetroot and goat's cheese arancini recipe that had had their mouths watering. "I'm sure I've got nearly all those ingredients," said Christine, opening the fridge with one hand and a cupboard door with the other, "Now, Timmo— no idea whether you know a frying-pan from a whisk, but could you please melt some butter and olive oil in that pan over there and fry the arborio rice for me?" Tim followed his Aunt's instructions so carefully that she granted him the honour of carrying in the tray of risotto balls and bowl of salad himself. Marjory, Elspeth and Zooie cheered when he walked in, red in the face and looking proud of himself.

"Save some for me," said Marjory, as she got up to make her phone call. "Take it in your bedroom," said her sister, "Nobody's going to listen in. Send him our love." Marjory nodded and went into her room. Ten minutes later she was back. "How's the Pater?" asked Tim, handing his mother a plate of arancini and salad, "Fine, darling, fine . . . Tired, missing us. He sends his love. I wish he were here," she said wistfully, "Though we'd have to have those wretched security guards around the place if he were. And I, for one, don't miss *them* one bit."

Chapter Twenty-Nine

IN THE MEADOW

Roger loved the meadow more than any other member of the family, and almost as much as Andrew Billett, who often strolled there after work, carefully avoiding stepping on the fritillaries and other rare wild flowers which flourished there.

Roger had no idea about avoiding anything in the meadow, but it didn't matter, as the summer flowers sprang back easily enough when his light, doggy feet had passed by. He always ran as fast as he could until he was put back on the lead. He loved the sensation of the wind in his ears. The meadow wasn't nearly as interesting to a dog in winter-time, though. The grass was too short, and there were no insects or rabbits to pester. But the area was full of strange smells, and much easier to run around on, so he made the most of it. He would not be content until he had inspected every tree, so he took off for the north-east corner of the meadow at full tilt.

Percy was happy enough to allow Roger free rein on that day, with its faint promise of spring. He was keen to try out the smoking pipe he had picked up from the wheelbarrow, to see if it actually worked. He walked a few yards down the path that went in a straight line down the east side of the meadow, and sat down on the bench his mother had had installed there, for her water-colour painting sessions. Lady Sylvia had spent whole days in the meadow. In fact, she had spent most of her time, either out of doors, walking, sketching or painting, or in the conservatory, where she had her collection of succulents. Her collection of wild flower paintings had once been exhibited at a local gallery, and one of them had been sent as a gift to the Palace on the occasion of a royal wedding.

Percy got out his tobacco pouch and the tiny pipe. He put a small plug of tobacco into the bowl, tamped it down with his little finger and lit it. It worked perfectly. Roger was disappearing into the distance, headed for a group of three oak trees where occasional squirrels were seen. "Daft dog!" said Percy, affectionately, "Always forget you can't climb until you get there, don't you, old chap?" He puffed away on the pipe. Somehow the quality of the wood from which it was carved enhanced the flavour of the tobacco. There was a rustling in the hedgerow behind him that went on for several minutes, but he did not turn round. Security had declared the area safe, so he assumed the noises were being made by foxes. Wildlife was of little interest to Percy unless he could eat it, and fox had never been on the Brandston menu, even during the war, when there had been rationing.

Had he bothered to turn round, he would have seen the same person peeping out of the hedge at him as he had glimpsed in the vegetable garden, beside the shed: a little person with a green, pointy hat, a green jacket and a pair of green trousers with a tear in one knee—one of the Brandston gnomes, in fact. Little did he know that there were nearly one hundred of them living on the estate he thought of as belonging to *his* family. But the gnomes had been there for over a thousand years. And the pipe on which he was puffing away belonged to this small, angry person. And this small, angry person was an Oak, which meant trouble. The pipe was a family heirloom, and went everywhere with him. Gnomes have very few personal possessions: clothing of course, a walking-stick, a pouch and a sack for hunting and gathering, a clan badge, a drinking cup and a pipe. The loss of one of these possessions is therefore a deeply upsetting event.

"How *dare* he?!" Gabriel Oak, the gnome in question, whispered to the other six gnomes who were standing behind him, glaring at Percy, "How *daaaaare* he?!" "He takes, does not give back, and does not know the value of the precious object," said a smaller gnome—a Willow—his fists on his hips. "One gnome lose, all gnomes lose!" said a thin, sinewy whip of a gnome, also dressed in green, who was pacing up and down and shaking his head. "Yew speaks true!" chorused the band of gnomes. "Does the human know? Or have human laws changed?" asked the Willow, puzzled. "Human thieves are punished when caught," answered the Yew, in a sorrowful voice. "This one has thieved many times. He has not been punished," said Gabriel Oak. "Then gnomes must," replied the Yew, hanging his head to hide his tears, "Too much, too much . . ."

Percy Brandston had, by this time, finished his pipeful of tobacco, and he knocked it out, turned and flung it into the hedge. "Useless thing," he said, "Too small." If his ears had been sharper, they would have picked up a chorus of howls from the angry gnomes, who were now talking in furious whispers a few yards behind him. "We have it back!" said Willow. "It is tainted," wept Uriel Oak. "We shall wash it seven times in the stream and cleanse it," said Willow, putting a small, brown hand on the shoulder of his *Ibni* in an attempt to console him. "Come," said Yew, "We shall go with you. A gnome in grief is never alone." Within seconds, they were gone.

Percy smoked on, oblivious. Roger was barking at a squirrel, which was screeching at him from the top of an oak tree. He was being warned to take his master back to the house immediately, and told why. "Danger! Danger!" shrieked the grey squirrel, running up and down the tree trunk, "Angry gnomes! Keep away!" Roger, who had had his nose smacked more times than he could remember, and once been locked out in the snow, and whose relationship with the gnomes was one of deep mutual respect, barked back: "Don't care! Don't care!" and ran rings round the three oak trees to show his lack of interest. The squirrel eventually gave up and sat still until Roger had set off back across the meadow. Then it ran down the trunk, hopped into the hedgerow on the west side of the meadow, and kept going until it reached the ash tree by the stream. It wasn't about to miss any of the action.

A few minutes later, just as Percy Brandston was about to get up from the bench to continue his walk, Roger now by his side, his ears perked up as high as it's possible for a Labrador's ears to get, Andrew

Billett came walking down the path. He stopped when he saw his employer, but Percy waved him over. "Still a chance of sleet?" he asked the young gardener. Andrew looked up at the sky, and along the horizon to the north and east. "Less likely than earlier, Sir," he answered. Percy had the chance now to mention the pipe and the mittens, but he did not. Had he done so, a family tragedy might possibly have been avoided, for Andrew Billett's mind was now, more than ever, open to the possibilities that strange things could happen on the Brandston estate: a dog could make his thoughts known, and from there to little people living in the hedges was a relatively short hop. He would probably have suggested they return to the vegetable garden together to investigate further, but Andrew never got the chance.

Percy turned to his employee and said, "My mother used to sit here and paint, did you know that?" Andrew was surprised to find Mr. Brandston so chatty. "Yes, Sir—I believe my father used to bring her fresh pots of water." "Quite so," said Percy, "I never had any talent for it. Never had any artistic talent at all, if the truth be told. A bit of a duffer at school. Dreadful disappointment to Mother and Father . . ." Andrew Billett said nothing: what could he say? Not that he normally felt uncomfortable when people confided in him—which happened a lot—but in this situation he felt completely out of his depth. He bent down and scratched under Roger's chin. "OK, old fellow?" he asked the dog. Roger looked up at him and gave him a doggy grin that was— if Andrew had been asked to describe it—rather enigmatic. As if he knew something—something he was not about to share. "Yes, well . . ." sighed Percy, "Best be getting on, then. Getting a bit chilly. Good day to you!" "Good day to you, Sir," returned Andrew. He had been about to have a walk himself, but he didn't want to invade his employer's privacy, so he waited until Percy was halfway to the tree line that marked the location of the stream and went in the opposite direction, back to his glasshouse. He never saw Percy Brandston alive again.

When MI5 interviewed Andrew Billett at one o'clock the following morning, he said that the last time he had seen his employer, Mr. Brandston had been in a somewhat melancholy mood. He was asked whether his first thought had been that the Lord of the Manor had committed suicide, and he replied in the affirmative. "He could have had a gun with him—a small one, in his jacket pocket—I suppose. I didn't hear a shot but, then, I did have the radio on in the glasshouse. What time did it happen?" The officer did not reply: "Carry on," he said.

Andrew took a sip of water from the plastic cup on the table. "He was talking about his parents being disappointed in him," he said, wiping tears from his eyes, "And—without giving too much away—I know how that feels." When details of how Percy had died came through to the officer interviewing the staff, he let Andrew go, along with the others. The only member of staff he held for further questioning was the unfortunate gamekeeper, Adam Stonebridge, who kept several ferrets. Those terrible, tiny bite marks had to be explained somehow, and as quickly as possible.

Chapter Thirty

STOPPED IN THEIR TRACKS

Detective Sergeant Jim 'Brillo' Jackson and Detective Constable Farisi Kayatta continued their search for clues to the mystery of the disappearing dog. As they walked along first a stretch of footpath, then one of churned up bridleway, they tried—with, it must be said, more than a little amusement—to put themselves in Roger's place.

"Say he ran off before the fatal biting," said Jim, "I don't know . . . After a rabbit or something, wouldn't he eventually come back to the Manor?" "I wonder whether all those strangers milling around, and maybe the smell of blood, would attract him, or make him stay away?" said Farisi, "I should have thought, being—as everyone says—a friendly dog, he'd be more likely to come back to see what was up, wouldn't you?" "Yes—especially if he heard all those voices, and the sirens," agreed Jim, "Friendliness, and the instinct to protect, would kick in, and he'd be back like a shot. Do you think he's been stolen, maybe?" "No—I don't think so, Sarge. I think it's more likely he ran out into the road and got run over, and somebody's buried him quick, so as not to get into trouble. If I ran over a dog belonging to somebody famous, I think I'd be scared of being sued, and expensive lawyers, and all that. I don't think I'd tell a soul," Farisi answered honestly.

"So, that's a definite possibility, then," said Jim, decidedly. "Other options? What about the idea that he was just fed up of being here and made a bid for freedom?" "That would assume he wasn't happy with the Brandstons, Sir," said his partner, "And I don't think anyone's going to admit it to us if that's true, do you? But if that's the case, and he's wandering around looking for a new home, then we stand at least a chance of finding him alive." The two officers wiped half an inch of thick mud from the soles of their boots and carried on, scouring the surroundings for further clues.

They were bending over a curious object caught in some brambles to the estate side of the path when they found themselves suddenly surrounded by six men in dark suits and expensive-looking, knee-high, black, wet-look, leather, lace-up boots who had appeared silently, as if they had materialised out of thin air. Farisi had to choke back a laugh when she saw the boots. "Good afternoon, officers," said one of the men, "Found anything interesting?" His tone was arrogant, and mocking. Jim and Farisi stood up and prepared to meet the Men in Black.

Jim squared his shoulders and looked their leader straight in the eye. He was glad of his height, for the man was two inches shorter than he was. "And whom am I addressing?" he asked, turning to scan the faces of the six agents, "This is a police investigation. And you . . ." here, he pointed at one of the men, who had trodden down one of the yellow markers placed carefully beside the brambles, " . . . are treading on the evidence." "You know who we are," retorted the leader, "Is that your Lotus in the car park? Only some kids were getting a bit interested in it when we came past, and you'd be well advised to go back and check it's still got its hub caps . . ."

Jim knew this was tantamount to an order to leave, but he wanted to wind the agents up, just a little bit. "I take it you're looking for the perpetrator or perpetrators of Mr. Brandston's murder," he said, pulling the evidence bags out of his case, "We picked these up, back there where you'll see the first set of markers. You can have them once we've got back to the office and had them processed." He turned to Farisi. "Shall we take this gentleman's advice and go and check on the car, Detective Constable?" he asked. She nodded, too annoyed to risk speaking, too amused by the boots to risk even opening her mouth.

The eyes of the Men in Black were fixed on the evidence bags as Jim Jackson and Farisi Kayatta went back the way they'd come, trying not to give away any of the emotions they were feeling. Once they were out of earshot, Farisi collapsed with merriment onto the log where they'd sat earlier in the day. Jim joined her. "So, what exactly have we found?" he said, pulling another evidence bag out of his pocket, where he'd quickly shoved it out of sight. The two officers held up the evidence bag to the light. Fascinating. Intriguing. Puzzling. The object contained in the bag was none other than a miniature set of false teeth, chiselled with attention to detail and perfect craftsmanship from two pieces of wood. "Well, I'll be damned!" exclaimed Jim Jackson. "I've heard they're still questioning the gamekeeper, but I don't suppose for a moment that these would fit him, though I suppose they might fit a ferret!"

He meant it as a joke, but the reddish brown stains on the teeth looked too much like blood for it to be funny. "Home, Sarge?" asked Farisi, sighing. Jackson nodded and they stood up. "This time we're stopping at the Happy Chef," he said firmly, "If I don't get some solid food inside me—and I mean something greasy with a lot of calories—I'm in danger of losing my grip on reality." "Me too," agreed his colleague.

The Lotus still had all its hub caps. In fact, the car was completely intact, but Jim couldn't help peering underneath to check for bugs and bombs. "You never know, DC Kayatta," he said as he sat in the passenger seat to pull off his wellingtons. "Are you going to let me drive, Sarge?" asked Kayatta, going round to the other side of the car to remove her own boots. She already knew the answer: "Yes, Farisi, I am," came the reply, "I'm still seething from that encounter. Just as we were getting somewhere. Typical! I'll take over the driving once I've got some hot food inside me and come back down to earth." Kayatta tiptoed round to the boot of the car with her boots. "Understood loud and clear, Sarge," she said as she slid the boots into a black bin bag, slipped on her shoes, picked up Jackson's shoes and went round to swap them for his muddy boots.

It was night-fall before the officers got back to base. Chief Inspector Masters was waiting for them in the open-plan space—a whole floor of the building, more or less,—where they worked, side by side. "Welcome back," he said, an inscrutable smile on his face, "Come into my office." Jim and Farisi followed. He closed the door behind them, and motioned to them to sit. "Get anything?" he asked.

Jackson pulled out the full set of evidence bags and handed them over. "We wanted to give these to you in person, Sir," he said, "We haven't booked them in. Given the . . . sensitive nature of the, er, investigation, and the number of agencies involved . . ." "Say no more, Detective Sergeant Jackson," said his boss, "We've already heard what happened, and why you're back so quick. Bad luck there. Any sign of the dog?" "Just a few tracks, Sir," said Jackson, "But we've come up with a couple of theories we'd like to run by you."

"Well done, Jim, Farisi," said Masters, holding one of the bags up to his desk lamp, "What the blazes is this?!" Jim looked at Farisi, and raised his eyebrows, which meant he wanted her to speak. "False teeth, Sir. With what appear to be bloodstains on them, top and bottom. And the others are small headgear, Sir. Balaclavas. With extra holes for ears. We don't have any theories for those, Sir. Sorry, Sir . . ." Masters looked up, a magnifying glass in his hand: "I'm not surprised, Detective Constable Kayatta!" he exclaimed, "You did right to bring them to me. I don't mind telling you, the powers-that-be know you've got something that relates to the murder, and they want this lot off us as soon as. The Chief has been instructed, no more officers out there, searching for the missing dog. Of course, they're claiming he's still a suspect, but I don't buy that. Something's up, and it's *big*."

Kayatta and Jackson looked at each other. "Now, you two," said Masters, with one of his signature tired smiles, "Off down the pub, and put all of this out of your minds. I'm not displeased—don't think that for a second—but, for your own good, forget everything you've seen today. I promise the Chief and I won't let this rest, OK?" His two junior colleagues nodded, and smiled back. They rose, and left the room. "Well," breathed the Detective Inspector, peering into the evidence bag he was still holding up to the light, "Well, I never." Before he left his office that night, he scanned all the evidence bags and took photos. He also made a careful note of the contents in a small notebook, which he locked inside a desk drawer. Then he went up the stairs to leave them in the night safe outside the door of Detective Chief Inspector Baird's office. And there they stayed, until the DCI arrived for work at five, the following morning. He was not alone. Behind him, marching along the corridor on silent feet, came two MI5 agents.

They examined every square inch of his office, but found nothing. They did not think to check the night safe, because it was a feature Baird had introduced quite recently, and he had had it disguised as a junction box. They went away angry, frustrated—and empty-handed. Before the evidence bags were passed over to MI5 later that day, every one of the detectives in the office downstairs had seen their contents. They were sworn to secrecy, but were under orders to keep their eyes, ears and minds open. "There may be further developments, sometime in the future," said Masters, as he briefed them before lunch, "And if there are, I want all of you to be ready." "Ready for what?" he asked himself as he left for the canteen, but he had to confess he hadn't a clue as to what the 'what' might be.

Chapter Thirty-One

ARCHIE GETS A SPRING-CLEAN

Over the next few weeks, as the warmer weather finally arrived, Archie and Ann-Marie began to be more intimately acquainted, and their increasing closeness only served to foster the love growing between them. For example, Archie learnt that Ann-Marie could get herself ready for a date in half an hour flat, and Ann-Marie learnt that Archie's eyes watered at emotional scenes in films, and that he was not ashamed to let her see it. But one thing remained: for Archie to invite his beloved upstairs to his own flat.

For a while, it was a matter of Ann-Marie's being quicker to reach from the lift, when they came indoors from an activity in the common-room, or gardening, or an outing. Then it became more about how quickly they became a natural 'nesting pair'. Her flat was already beginning to feel like home to Archie, and more like a home to Ann-Marie with Archie in it. But one day, Archie asked if he could borrow some sugar, and Ann-Marie, as she was handing over a spare packet, said suddenly: "My goodness me! It hadn't crossed my mind that you might be running short of things, Archie! We've been here whenever we're together, haven't we? I'm so sorry, I never thought!" Archie looked a bit serious, but didn't speak. "What is it, love?" asked Ann-Marie, gazing into his eyes, worried. Archie appeared to be searching for the right words: "I . . . er . . . Well, to tell you the truth, it's a bit of a tip. I wouldn't want you to see it the way it is. The fact is I'd be embarrassed if you saw it."

The upshot of the discussion that followed was that Archie agreed he would invite Ann-Marie in a week's time, for dinner and a film. And so, the following day, after many hugs and kisses, Archie disappeared upstairs to do his spring-cleaning. Fortunately, he knew exactly what he was doing, having learnt from his mother, and having spent years as a single parent, with no other choice but to work *and* do all the housework and decorating, *and* create a cosy atmosphere. He went from room to room with a pen and the back of an old cereal packet, making notes: jobs to do, items he needed to buy.

It came as no surprise to Archie Prescott when, the following morning, he found the gnomes waiting for him in his living-room. He had now made considerable progress with his lessons, and had learnt twenty phrases of Gnomish, as well as a great deal about their culture, just as he had been learning about Ann-Marie. For example, he now knew that wizards wore pointy hats because they had learnt their skills from gnomes, who had adopted their style of headwear many thousands of years before their first interaction with humans. And why did gnomes wear pointy hats? It was the most fascinating fact he had learnt about the little people: it was because of the way they procreated.

It was already known, thanks to folklore, that magical dwarves looked exactly the same, whether male or female, due to their beards, but Archie had assumed that the same would be true of gnome females—to whom he expected to be introduced at any moment. This was far from the truth.

There were no female gnomes, he learnt to his great surprise, nor was there any form of mating involved between gnomes. The mating took place between a gnome and his sacred tree. The gnome would sit in a hole under the tree's roots and wait until the tree linked one of its roots to the gnome, via the belly-button. There would be an exchange of energy, which Ned described as "like lightning, but more gentle" and the gnome would become, to all intents and purposes, pregnant. The Gnomeling—or occasionally twin Gnomelings—grew out of the top of his head, and resembled the shoot of the same tree, except that it was covered in gnome fur. Eventually, a bud would form, and the Gnomeling would develop inside it, bursting at the right moment, which was usually when the father gnome was asleep. Gnomelings, when born, would be safe and snug under the hat until their parent awoke. And in due course, the father gnome would suckle his offspring in exactly the same way as human females did. This, Archie worked out, made sense, and explained why human males had residual nipples. It was all falling into place.

There was a further fact he learnt about gnome multiplication that made him feel very sad: there had been no Gnomelings for fifty years. "But why?" he had asked Alevin, an expression of shock on his kind face. "Because the Great Mother is sick," said Alevin, in a voice as grave as a cold morning in January, "This world. Humans are making her sick. They have forgotten the wisdom we taught. They have forgotten . . ." Archie had paced up and down the room after the lesson, horrified and feeling impotent. Was it too late? Was there anything he could do? He could not wait for the next lesson, when he would get the chance to ask advice. Already, he had been learning what plants to grow in the garden to help pollinators such as bees, and how to avoid using pesticides, but he felt it was not enough.

On spring-cleaning day, however, he was proud of himself. As the gnomes went through the cleaning materials he had prepared, they were nodding their heads up and down and saying "Good! Yes! Yes! Mun-tili manni!" and "Bne orla!" which Archie had learnt meant "It's all OK!" "Archie Prescott, Friend of Gnomes, you are also a Friend of the Great Mother," said Norman, bowing to Archie as soon as he stopped pacing up and down. "The materials you have prepared for cleaning are suitable." Archie had bought only products labelled 'eco-friendly'. "So, gnomes will help!" added Norman, looking around at his brothers, who all nodded and smiled.

And so it was that Archie became the first tenant in Eden Tower ever to have his carpets swept, his bath scrubbed, and his kitchen de-greased by gnomes. As the gnomes scuttled around, impeded from time to time by Cholmondeley and Hugo, who would insist on putting the sofa cushions on the floor and bouncing up and down on them, creating clouds of dust for the other gnomes to sweep up, Archie wondered what he should be doing, but Norman soon solved the question for him. "Mun-tili manni," he said, planting himself squarely in front of Archie, which the latter knew was a sign to listen especially carefully, "You must take care of the things which are for your woman. Go! Out! Bring flowers, and cakes, and scents for your burrow!"

Archie was glad to be let off the cleaning. The dust the gnomes were raising between them was giving him a nasty tickle in the nose. He picked up his wallet from the table, put on his light jacket and let himself out of the flat. Before getting into the lift, he knocked on the door of Enid, his next-door neighbour, and picked up a short list from her. He also stopped on the first floor to see if Robert wanted anything, and added a third list to the two already in his pocket. He was disappointed when the lift passed by the fifth floor and Ann-Marie was nowhere in sight, but it was a lovely day, and he was looking forward to choosing fragrant candles and other decorative items. He hoped he would not bump into her on the way back, as the candles would make a smell in the lift and give the game away.

Once on the High Street, Archie nipped into the supermarket and chemist's for the food and medical items needed by Enid and Robert, and then slowed down. Up and down he went, comparing prices and sniffing everything, which finally made him sneeze. "Oh, dear!" exclaimed a shop assistant, as Archie put his handkerchief to his nose, "Early hay fever?" "Something like that," said Archie, blowing his nose as quietly as possible, "Could you please recommend a nice bubble-bath? Preferably something that smells like roses?" "You're asking for trouble, aren't you?" remarked the shop assistant, laughing, "Are you sure you wouldn't prefer something with minerals that won't make you sneeze?" "It's all right," replied Archie, "I've just bought some antihistamines." "Good thinking," said the shop assistant, leading him to a display in the far corner of the store, "You might like this," and she pointed to a collection of items on the top shelf, "Our newest range: Summer Roses. I only put it up this morning. It smells lovely. Would you like to try the tester?" Archie shook his head, "I'll take your word for it!"

The shop assistant picked up a bubble-bath in a pink bottle, decorated with red and gold roses, and put it into Archie's basket. "Thank you," said Archie, still with his handkerchief to his nose. "Don't mention it. Enjoy!" said the shop assistant, and she walked away, leaving Archie to look for an empty till.

The final item on Archie's list was flowers. He had a nice vase he'd won at Bingo. It wasn't crystal, but looked almost as good. He walked back up the High Street and, after checking that the man on the corner with the flower barrow still had plenty of stock, sat down on a bench in the churchyard, and tried to breathe without sneezing. Just then, who should come past but Carol, arm in arm with Veronica. He looked up at the sky, and down at his feet, hoping they wouldn't notice him, but a moment later, he heard Carol's voice: "Well, if it isn't old Archie! Had to stop for a rest, have you?" she boomed. Archie was quick with his answer, having had plenty of practice: "No, Carol, just trying to avoid you. Why aren't you in the pub? It's been open an hour. You're wasting drinking time!" Veronica chuckled, taking Archie's comments as a joke, but Carol looked annoyed. Several passers-by were looking at her.

Carol dragged Veronica towards the bench until they were three feet away from Archie. "You've always thought too much of yourself, Archie Prescott," she hissed, "And now you're Chair, you're getting way too big for your boots." Archie couldn't let that go. "It makes a change," he retorted, "I spent enough time being made to feel small by certain people. Anyway, things are changing for the better, now we've got some decent people on the committee. Even you should have noticed the difference by now." Veronica bent down until her face was six inches from Archie's. "It won't last," she hissed, "You'll see! It will all come to nothing!"

The two women left it at that, and walked away, their noses in the air. Archie could have kicked himself as soon as they were gone. What had Ann-Marie said to him? "Let it go, Archie, please. There's a reason why Carol's the way she is. Please try to be nice when you next see her. For me?" He had said he would, but there was too much water under the bridge, and he still felt overwhelmingly negative towards Carol. Evie had come around, he could tell. She said hello whenever she saw him, and had actually come and sat in the garden when the men were planting the other day, and said how nice the place looked. Why couldn't Carol do the same?

"I've let Ann-Marie down today, as well as myself," thought Archie ruefully, "If I were a gnome, I'd be a lot better behaved." He got up from the bench and went over to the man with the flower barrow. He was a young man with a bald head and an outrageous bright yellow tracksuit. "Hello there," said the flower man, "What can I get you? Some nice bouquets in today . . ." Archie, whose nose was now behaving itself, stooped and sniffed. "Irises," he said, "Two bunches please, and one of those pots of hyacinths. Pink." The man nodded, approving his choice, and wrapped up Archie's purchases.

Archie managed to get all the way home without getting into trouble of any kind, and without bumping into Ann-Marie who, as it happened, was in town buying a new top for her date with him. It was just as well she did, and that she stopped to get her hair done, for at 6pm her mobile phone rang, and it was Archie. "Missed me?" said his voice, a chuckle in it, "Don't answer that. You'll never believe this, but I've finished the cleaning. You doing anything tonight? Seven-ish?" Ann-Marie thanked her lucky stars that she'd been quick off the mark and accepted his invitation. As soon as they had finished on the phone—which mostly involved blowing kisses to each other—she ran for the bathroom. Archie Prescott was in for a treat.

Chapter Thirty-Two

DINNER AND A MOVIE

Given Ann-Marie's speediness when engaged in beautifying herself, Archie had expected to see his beloved half an hour later, but it was an hour before Ann-Marie turned up on his doorstep, ready for their romantic evening together. Archie's face was pink and glowing when he opened the door, and it was evident he couldn't wait to show her round the flat. "There's been something of a transformation," he said, stepping back to let her in. He was just about to say "But I can't take all the credit . . ." when he remembered that she was not yet *au fait* with the gnome phenomenon, so instead he said, "The layout's exactly the same as yours, of course: bedroom on the left, bathroom on the right, living-room straight ahead and the kitchen at the far end." Archie had left all the doors propped open so Ann-Marie would know it was 'access all areas'.

Ann-Marie looked into the bedroom and turned to look at Archie, her face radiant. "It's lovely!" she exclaimed, "I don't understand why you were ever shy about me coming here!" and she kissed him swiftly on the lips. Then she peeped into the bathroom, which was softly lit by scented candles along the shelf, from which Archie had shovelled all his manly gear and stashed it in a cupboard. "Oh!" breathed Ann-Marie, "You did all this for me?" "Who else?" said Archie, gallantly. The living-room glowed with colour and smelled deliciously of hyacinths. "Would Madam care to sit?" asked Archie. "Madam would love to sit," answered Ann-Marie, and settled herself on the sofa.

Archie smiled. He was remembering how the gnomes had beaten the dust out of the cushions, and wondered what his girlfriend would think if she had walked in while Cholmondeley and Hugo were up to their antics. He stood looking down at Ann-Marie, who seemed already so at ease it was as though she had always been sitting on his sofa. He had thought it rather ugly before, with its green, leaf-patterned nylon covers, but now it seemed almost elegant. Ann-Marie, in her floaty, buttermilk-coloured tunic and white skirt looked like a fairy—albeit a rather plump one—nestling in a tree.

"Would Madam care for a cocktail?" asked Archie, who had on his black trousers and a white shirt he'd bleached to near-extinction, so he could look like a waiter. He knew a lot of women liked that kind of thing. "Oh! Well! That would be lovely!" said Ann-Marie. She didn't ask if there was a choice. She knew enough about Archie's budget to be tactful. Archie went to the kitchen and came back with a fruit cocktail he'd made using juices and ginger ale. He'd dug out some tiny paper umbrellas from a back drawer—souvenirs of his days on the island. Ann-Marie sipped her drink and pronounced it to be delicious. "Now, just you relax," said Archie, "Dinner will be served in five minutes. You can see the kitchen later, but for now, stay where you are. I want to surprise you." "Archie," said Ann-Marie, "Every moment with you is a nice surprise."

Ann-Marie relaxed, closed her eyes and breathed in the scent of hyacinths and food preparation, thanking her lucky stars once more that she'd met Archie Prescott. Five minutes later, Archie placed a tray on her knees. "I hope you like it," he said, "I know you're not one for fussy food, so I made something I know you like." Ann-Marie looked down and laughed delightedly: Archie had made roast chicken with all the trimmings. "I made my own stuffing," he said proudly, "It's so much tastier than from the supermarket."

The chicken was followed by home-made cherry trifle. Archie had even made his own sponge fingers. "You're going to tell me you made the 'hundreds and thousands' next, aren't you?" said Ann-Marie, digging into her dessert with enjoyment. "Ah, there I draw the line!" laughed Archie.

After dinner, Ann-Marie insisted on helping with the washing-up, and declared Archie's kitchen to be pristine. "I'm having a great time," she said, "And I totally love your flat. Thank you for inviting me, and for going to so much trouble."

Archie had been given certain instructions by Norman and Nick before they had left. "Show great love towards your woman," he was told, "But prepare for visitors when the moon reaches the top of the ash tree!" The gnomes' intention was to make themselves known to Ann-Marie that very evening, once she had eaten and had a chance to relax. He had been about to say that, in his opinion, it was still early days in their courtship, and that the idea made him very nervous, but he thought better of it. The gnomes had, so far, shown their judgement to be faultless, and who was he to question thousands of years of wisdom? And in any case, if Ann-Marie had hysterics and ran when she saw the gnomes, wouldn't that be a sticking-point, given his own growing attachment to the little fellows? Archie hoped he would not have to choose between Ann-Marie and the gnomes.

"You're very welcome, my love," he said, handing his friend a fresh towel for her hands, "Now, let's pick a film. I've got a few I think you haven't seen, that you might like. Lady's choice, of course." They settled, after some discussion, on "The Impossible"—a film about a family trying to find each other after a tsunami in Thailand. Not a romantic choice, but they both preferred something real and courageous, where love and determination conquered all, and it promised to fit all the criteria.

Five minutes into the film, Ann-Marie cuddled up to Archie. "I think we're going to need tissues," she said, passing one over from her handbag. They did, in fact they had to pause the film several times in order to pull themselves together. At last, it was over and Ann-Marie gave a huge sigh of relief. It was then that Archie noticed the gnomes, perched on top of his tall bookcase, looking down at them. "Erm, there's something I've been meaning to tell you," he said to Ann-Marie, "Nothing bad—I don't want you to worry—just some special friends of mine I'd like you to meet."

Ann-Marie was dabbing at her mascara and looking into a small hand mirror. "Oh, I wondered when you'd get around to that," she said, an ironic tone in her voice, "You couldn't possibly mean the gnomes, could you? It's just that one of them has been waving to you from the top of that bookcase for the past half hour . . ." Archie burst out laughing. "You know?" he exclaimed, "You KNOW! How come?" Ann-Marie was losing her battle with the mascara, as she was now laughing so hard, she was crying again. "I was forewarned," she said, "By the appearance of the one on the right, who I believe is called Syd, turning up in my bathroom while I was in the shower. He was standing on the sink when I came out. He was looking the other way, so I did manage to cover myself up in time. I got the shock of my life, though!" Archie looked very serious, and frowned up at the gnomes, most of whom were giggling and digging each other in the ribs. Even grave Alevin Yew and sarcastic Nigel Blackthorn were grinning.

"Gentlemen," said Archie, keeping his eye on the gnomes, "I think you should come down, don't you?" One by one, his friends hopped down from the bookcase to the desk, and piled into the armchair opposite the sofa. They began to look a little shamefaced, but Ann-Marie got up and put the dish of miniature chocolates Archie had given her in front of them. "I'm not sure they deserve those," said Archie, still holding out, "A lady deserves privacy in her own bathroom!" The gnomes, falling over each other, they were so squashed together, somehow all stood up and bowed deeply. "Sincere sorries," said little Syd, looking remorseful, "We are not so used to females. Our encounters with humans have most often been with males, although we have had some good female friends: my own favourite was Miss Virginia Woolf, who used to carry me about her garden in a wheelbarrow and feed me raspberries in season."

Ann-Marie now fell about, laughing. "You knew Virginia Woolf?!" she exclaimed, "Who else?" "Norman went about the pocket of Mr. Will Shaksper, and taught him all the names of wild flowers," said Nigel, puffing out his chest, "And I travelled to the Galapagos Isles with Mr. Darwin. There I ate turtle, which did not agree with me." Ann-Marie's eyes were shining with amusement: "What about you, Nick?" she asked the third of the Blackthorn brothers. Nick pulled a solemn face: "The Reverend Charles Dodgson was my friend for a while, but his garden had a terrible infestation of wasps in summer-time, and I was forced to leave. He would eat jam in the garden. Professor Tolkien made a great favourite of me, but he was inclined to spend too much time indoors, at his writing. He forgot me, and so I came here to be with my brothers. Travel is harder these days. Roads are dangerous for gnomes." Ned had been itching to speak, and now it was his turn: "Writers make interesting companions for gnomes," he said, "Often they believe where others will not. Writing opens the head, I believe. There is also a royal personage of whom I am fond, but I am rarely able to visit him."

"Well then, I must seem quite boring to you," remarked Archie, "I'm as common as muck, and I've never written anything in my whole life!" Terry, the Mushroom-gathering Gnome, spoke up—thing which did not happen very often—"Muck, as you call it, is what we are all made of. It is the stuff of life, along with air and water. Despise it not, Archie Mun-tili! As for writers, some write with the pen and the tapping-machine. Some cannot. Perhaps it is for you to do, and for your lady to write it down . . ." Ann-Marie smiled: "It had begun to cross my mind," she said.

"Anyway," said Ann-Marie, "Now we're all here, all together, there's a question I'm longing to ask. Why, after living so secretly for so many years, have gnomes decided to make contact? And why here, why now?" "That is three questions," remarked Alevin, "But Alevin Yew shall answer in one answer." Ann-Marie sat forward on the sofa and took one of the chocolates. As if that was the proper signal, the gnomes each followed suit. They began to sniff at the sweets. Nick, who Archie had realised was by far the most widely-travelled and cross-culturally informed of the band, unwrapped his and began to nibble on a corner. The others copied him, and they were soon all happily munching away, all except Alevin, who put his in his pocket.

"Here is the answer, and it is a question: who took care of the tiny creatures in Noah's Ark?"

There was a pregnant silence in the room, until Ann-Marie exclaimed: "I understand! You were always there, and always helping. You only reveal yourselves in times of dire danger! So . . . if I may ask another question, Sir, what do we need to do, given that you've chosen us?" Alevin, who was staring at Ann-Marie with something like amazement, turned to Norman: "You were right, Ibni," he said, nodding, "They are the right humans for this time." He turned back to Ann-Marie, and this time included Archie in his stare when he spoke: "You must get the people ready. You must make more Friends of Gnomes. You must unite with Friends of the Great Mother. It is your duty to lead. Archie shall lead and Ann-Marie shall be his helper."

"Well, this is turning out to be an interesting dinner date!" said Ann-Marie, leaning over to give Archie a peck on the cheek. She turned to the gnomes. "I will help Archie to lead," she said, "I shall be Mrs. Noah, as you say."

This was all getting a bit heavy for Archie, who wanted nothing but to be alone with the woman he loved, to snuggle up and watch TV. He managed to wiggle his jaw and nose until he manufactured a yawn, got up and stretched and said, "Ooh! My goodness me! I need to move around a bit. I'm in danger of falling asleep!" Cholmondeley and Hugo had already fallen asleep on the arms of the big chair, draped across them like a pair of rainbow-coloured arm caps. Hugo was snoring like a walrus whilst Cholmondeley sounded like a whistling kettle.

"Archie Friend of Gnomes wishes aloneness with his woman," remarked Ned, quietly. "And Ann-Marie, who wishes to be a Friend of Gnomes, also wishes to be alone with her man," whispered Ann-Marie, reaching over and preventing Hugo's cap, which was sliding, from falling off his head. Hugo made a little, contented sound and scratched his chin.

Nigel, who was sitting with his arms folded, reached out a foot and kicked first Hugo and then Cholmondeley, so that they woke with a start and fell off the chair onto the floor. "Nice, clean floor," mumbled Cholmondeley. "Nice brown jam," murmured Hugo, who had fallen asleep with his chocolate in his mouth. "Come brothers!" called Alevin, hopping down from the sofa, pulling Sigmund and Sigfrid Rowan down after him. They made no protest. In fact, Archie had rarely heard them speak. He had had this explained to him during one of his lessons on the gnome clans. Rowans were considered the most magical of all trees, and protection against evil spirits. Therefore, Rowans were by nature discreet, even secretive: guardians of deep mysteries that would lose their power if revealed.

"Thank you, friends," said Archie, "Thank you for all your help with the spring-cleaning. I wish you *flabaarraay!*" He was about to turn to Ann-Marie to explain, when she whispered, "Yes, I know—farewell in Gnomish—Syd said it to me earlier," and echoed his farewell, her accent, including the long, rolled 'r' flawless. The gnomes clapped their hands in delight and, coming forward one by one, they bowed low, first to Archie, then to his lady before disappearing into the hallway. Ned, last to leave, stopped at the doorway and said, "*Muuurrriii!*" before disappearing. He strung out each letter, a sleepy smile on his face.

"That means 'thank you for your noble hospitality'," explained Archie, "They've had a good time—at least, Ned has. The more the word is drawn out like that, the more they've appreciated it." "Cute," said Ann-Marie, "Now, do you want to check they've gone, only I'm planning on being here for a while, if you have no objection, and I don't fancy the idea of them hiding under your bed!" Archie blushed furiously. "They wouldn't . . . would they? I'll just go and make sure." He returned a few minutes later. "Checked everywhere," he said, "No gnomes, bogles, boggarts or sprites! Although . . . ," "What?" asked Ann-Marie. "They do seem to be able to appear and disappear at will . . ." "Never mind about that," said Ann-Marie, "Let's see what's on TV. I think we need a bit of Ordinary after all that, don't you?"

So they did. The two lovers made themselves a nest on the sofa and forgot about the planet and all its woes for an hour. "I wonder how poor Noah managed without TV when he wanted to relax," mused Ann-Marie. Archie looked at her, hesitated for a second or two, nudged her with his shoulder and said: "He probably made love to Mrs. Noah," said Archie, "And I might just take a leaf out of his book . . ."

Chapter Thirty-Three

A GARDEN PARTY

It was three days before the Community Garden Party, and Archie and Ann-Marie, along with Banton and Viktor, were in the common-room with one of the officers from the local authority. The air in the room was warm, and the officer's perfume was a little overwhelming. Archie was getting a tickle in his nose, and knew that it was only a matter of time before he sneezed. He felt in his pocket for his clean handkerchief and found it. At least that was one thing that was going his way.

"Now, about this garden party you're holding for the tenants on Sunday," said the officer, "What have you done about safeguarding?" Banton sighed: "It's just a little gathering with some sandwiches and fizzy drinks," he said, guessing what was coming. "Have you done a risk assessment?" the officer asked, smiling in what Banton thought was a rather patronizing way. The men looked at each other, but Ann-Marie was ready: "As a matter of fact, I downloaded the proforma yesterday, completed it electronically and printed off two copies," she said, pulling papers from a green plastic file, "Here's yours."

The officer looked surprised, but took the stapled sheets Ann-Marie handed to her. "My assessment is that there are seven potential areas of risk," said Ann-Marie in a mock-serious tone. Archie looked at her, and saw that the corners of her mouth were twitching. "Number one, of course, is people tripping over their feet," Ann-Marie continued, "High risk, with people being so excited. Viktor went over the garden yesterday and the surface is smooth, including the paths. He has kindly removed a few small stones that could have presented a hazard. And the grass was cut yesterday. We can also warn people as they come in to be careful. Those are our strategies." "Hmm, yes, I see," said the officer, sipping her tea, "And I see you've thought about sunstroke, insect bites and people getting too near to the trees and getting poked in the eye by twigs. Well," she said, not bothering to read all the detail: Ann-Marie's risk assessment was spread over ten pages of very small font, "Everything seems to be in order."

Ann-Marie wasn't finished. "I've also informed the local police, just in case there are incursions." "Incursions?" said the officer, looking genuinely puzzled. "Yes, incursions. People from outside the estate coming into the garden while we're enjoying ourselves," explained Ann-Marie, giving the officer a tight smile, "One has to take into account every possibility. And I've spoken to the fire brigade and let them know, just in case anyone gets too close to the garden torches we're igniting in the flower-beds when it starts to get dark and sets something on fire. Such as their hair, for example . . ." "Oh, of course! Of course!" said the officer, "Well, I must get on now, so have a lovely day on Sunday, and don't forget to take some photos!"

The committee made a hasty exit from the room, and went to sit in the garden. As soon as they sat down, Archie collapsed in a heap, laughing like a hyena. "You're priceless, Ann-Marie!" he gasped out, between guffaws. "Did you see the look on her face? Heeheehee!" Banton looked confused. "Do you mean, you weren't serious?" he asked. Ann-Marie smiled sweetly: "Oh, one hundred per cent!" she said, "We're getting older, and of course our brains have fallen out of our ears!" Viktor caught on at this point, and he and Archie looked at each other and laughed until they were clutching their aching sides. "Ah! Yes! Now I see!" said Banton, and joined in.

It was good to laugh, and especially with their first big event imminent. The whole committee had been worrying about the tasks they had each undertaken: Banton had been chewing his nails over getting in the receipts and entering each small purchase—bottles of lemonade, bread and sandwich fillings—in the books. Viktor had been over the garden with a fine tooth comb, at Ann-Marie's suggestion and picked up every piece of broken glass from the bottles that passers-by had thrown over the fence. Archie had been worried that the weather would be terrible and nobody would come, whereas Ann-Marie, who was in charge of publicity, had redesigned the poster at least a dozen times. It was so hard to persuade people to come and mingle.

They needn't have worried, for the day dawned, bright and promising to be warm in the afternoon. Archie woke up to the sound of bird song, and of gnomes snoring. They had taken to sleeping on his sofa on Saturday nights, when it was most likely someone would throw a beer bottle a little too far, and hit one of them. Archie woke the gnomes, and they left to take up their positions in the gnome garden before anyone noticed they weren't there. As soon as they were gone, Archie went out onto his balcony and looked down at the garden. All was calm. No litter blowing about.

Half an hour later, he noticed that Ann-Marie was down there already, attaching bunting to the fences. He jumped into a pair of jeans and a sweatshirt and took two cups of coffee down to the bench seat just next to the gnome garden, where their little friends were standing looking as if they had never moved in their lives.

Ann-Marie came over, the one remaining string of bunting draped around her neck. "Morning, Archie," she said, putting her hand on his shoulder, "Hope you got a good night's sleep." "I've had better!" he replied cheekily. Ann-Marie rolled her eyes. "Nearly done," she said, "Then we should do the balloons and stick tickets on the raffle prizes."

An hour later, Viktor and Banton joined them, carrying a box of paper cups and a tea urn, lent by the women's group of which Banton's sister Lucy was organiser. The urn had not been mentioned in the risk assessment, but Ann-Marie dashed up to her flat and made a sign saying "Tea urn! Hot water and metal! Watch out!" in big red letters and took a photo, just in case. Tables and chairs were set up, and by eleven o'clock everything was ready. "What do we do now?" asked Viktor, "There's still an hour till the start. The sandwiches have all been done: June sent Big Frank down with them just now. All that's left is to get the lemonade out of the fridge." "I've got that covered," said Ann-Marie and, going to the shed, she took out a picnic basket. "I figured we'd probably be too busy this afternoon to get much to eat," she said, "So I've made us this. There's cheese-and-onion or ham-and-pickle sandwiches, chicken drumsticks and a chocolate cake. Help yourselves!"

The immediate result of the committee sitting down to their picnic in the sunshine was that a trickle of people starting to come along and ask if the party had started yet. And since they hadn't the heart to say no, by noon there were already fifteen tenants in the garden. One or two brought their own fold-up chairs with them, and most brought food and drink to add to what was already there.

By two o'clock, half the tenants had turned up, some of the older and frailer ones leaning on each other for support. Banton and Archie fetched extra chairs, and Viktor nipped to the corner shop for more lemonade. Ann-Marie made cups of tea and took sandwiches to those who looked too comfortable to get up.

Everyone was enjoying the refreshments and a friendly chat when suddenly Carol, Veronica and Mandy appeared at the garden gate. There was a hush as people turned to see what would happen next. Evie was already at the party, and had been chatting to Big Frank's sister June, who had managed to join her neighbours: the first time she had been out of the building for nearly a year. The three women at the gate were whispering to each other. It was Banton who took the bull by the horns, and went over to ask if they were coming in. "Not much of a party, is it? Where's the music?" remarked Carol, her face a stony mask. Banton gave her his most charming smile and said, with a presence of mind that astonished Archie, who was standing near the gate himself, "It will be, now you're here, lady. As a matter of fact, I was just going to get my ghetto-blaster."

Carol seemed lost for words. She didn't smile back, but she walked slowly into the garden, followed by her cronies. Ann-Marie went over immediately with a plate of sandwiches, and showed them where the drinks were. Viktor gave up his seat to Veronica, who seemed flattered. Gradually, the conversation returned to its previous pitch. And when Banton reappeared with his ghetto-blaster and a stack of CDs, a cheer went round.

It was seven o'clock and getting rather chilly when the party moved into the common-room, which had been decorated with balloons and streamers. Some people left and others arrived, a few bringing friends and family members. Nearly everyone joined in with the karaoke, and Ronald Greeley, who was passing by on his way home from the pub, and was more or less dragged inside by two of the ladies, was pronounced to have the best voice of the night.

By ten o'clock, Ann-Marie was looking exhausted, so Archie had a word with Viktor and Banton, and they were excused. The party was due to finish at eleven, and several people had already offered to help clear up. As Archie walked Ann-Marie back to their building, he put his arm about her waist. "Thank you for today," he said, once they were in the lift, "What with you and the gnomes, I hardly recognize this place. It's come alive. And I've come alive with it." Ann-Marie gave him a tired little smile: "I'm happy you feel that way, my dear," she replied, "It's all because of you. You were the one who started it all. And you kept going, even when there was no-one else."

When the lift stopped at Ann-Marie's floor, she turned to Archie. "Do you know what I'd like right now?" she asked, feeling in her bag for her keys. Archie remained silent: there were so many possibilities, he couldn't begin to guess. "I'll tell you," she said, "What I'd like most of all in this whole world is to curl up next to you in a nice, warm, cosy bed." Archie blushed with pleasure. "I think you should definitely get what you want," he responded, "Especially as it just happens to be what I want too . . ." Ten minutes later, they were both fast asleep.

Downstairs in the common-room, the party was winding down. In a corner of the dance-floor, Banton and Carol were dancing together. Viktor was wiping down tables, and Big Frank and June were washing up the plates and forks. Mandy and Veronica had left, envious of the attention Carol was getting. Ronald Greeley went outside to smoke his pipe, and looked up, just as Ann-Marie's bedroom light went out. "Lucky chap!" he said, out loud, as he struck a match, "Lucky old blighter!" There wasn't a man in the place who would have disagreed.

Chapter Thirty-Four

NATIVE WILDLIFE

After their successful outing to Gladstone Vineyard in Carterton, Christine and Zooie and their visitors couldn't wait to plan their next trip together. There were walks, of course, mainly into town to explore the antique shops and to visit the chocolate shop and the cafés. Tim and Elspeth went out alone every day, exploring the bike trails for which Greytown was famous—including the newly opened Rail Trail, which ran along five kilometres of old track. The young people very soon began to look toned, tanned and fresh-faced, so that they could almost have been mistaken for natives. Meanwhile Marjory took over the care of the parrots, to allow her sister and Zooie more time in the garden, and helped freshen up some of the paintwork around the outside of the cottage.

"I think it's a good day for Cape Palliser. What do you think, darling?" Christine asked Zooie over breakfast one day. Zooie agreed: "I think it's high time. "That's not bikeable is it, Aunty?" asked Tim, who had been poring over Google Maps while eating his toast and marmalade. "No, Timmo, but the chap down the road's offered to take us out there if we go. Lives on his own. Wife died a while back. Nice chap. And he's got an old Landrover. Likes a bit of company occasionally. I'll pop along in a bit and check, but I saw him last week and he said, any day."

"So, what's at Cape Palliser?" asked Marjory, who was learning more about parrots than beauty spots. "Well," said Christine, "There's a lighthouse, perched up on the rocks, pretty spectacular views. And there's a beach with fur seals. You can get quite close if you're careful.

There's a fishing village called Ngawi which is really picturesque. And the Putangirua Pinnacles—can't describe them, but you'll see. If we don't get there today, we'll go another day. Think 'The Lord of the Rings'. Think Dimholt Road . . . And mustn't forget to mention the Lake Ferry Hotel, which has a spectacular fish menu. Sound good?"

"Sounds fantastic," answered Marjory, "When are we leaving?"

The day turned out to be one of the best Marjory had ever spent. The chap down the road—whom the visitors were expecting to be an elderly widower—turned out to be handsome fellow in his mid-thirties called Humphrey Barton. He came knocking on back door of the cottage at ten o'clock to see if Christine needed any help carrying anything to his Landrover, which he'd parked on the drive. It was, of course, Elspeth who was alone in the kitchen at the time, and she did a double-take. "Don't panic!" said tall, athletic Humphrey, "I'm the neighbour with the car." He stretched out his hand, and Elspeth, who was trying to catch her breath, took it. "Did someone freeze-frame in here?" said Zooie, coming into the kitchen carrying rain macs, "Morning Humphrey, how's tricks?" "Everything's good," answered Humphrey, slowly withdrawing his hand, "I take it this must be the lovely niece you told me about. Pleased to meet you, Elspeth."

Elspeth stammered out a greeting and rushed off to find her mother, who was in the bedroom, putting on an extra pair of socks. She shut the door behind her, and sat down on her mother's bed. Her mother took one look at her and exclaimed: "Elspeth! You're all red in the face! Whatever is the matter?" "There's a Maurie look-alike in the kitchen, Mummy! I think Aunty's trying to set us up! I don't want to go!"

Marjory knew it was useless to argue with her daughter when she was in a state, so she went along to the kitchen and introduced herself to Humphrey. Five minutes later she returned. Elspeth was putting on mascara and lipstick, and had changed from her t-shirt into a blue check shirt that matched her eyes. Marjory hid her smile. "He's nothing like Maurie, darling!" she said, gently stroking her daughter's back, "He's tall and fit—sporty, I mean—and he smiles a lot, but there the resemblance ends. Please don't be put off! It wouldn't be the same without you, you know . . ."

At half-past ten, the party piled into Humphrey's Landrover and set off for Cape Palliser. On the way, Humphrey pointed out places where the Big Storm of June 2013 had caused damage, particularly to the coast road with its spectacular views of rugged coastline. The weather was fairly calm, but when they walked along part of the beach, a fine sea spray hung in the air constantly. "You should see this in winter," he said to Elspeth, who had got over her initial reactions to him and calmed down, "The waves are sky high, and the wind could knock you off your feet." "I think I've already been knocked off my feet, and not by the wind," thought Elspeth, shaking her head at her own foolishness. "Don't you believe me?" asked Humphrey, noticing her shake of the head, "In that case, stay on till August!" Elspeth stopped and turned her face to the wind, so that her hair blew back from her face. Humphrey waited for her reply, his eyes glued to her face. "Actually, Humphrey, you might be able to give me a bit of advice," she said, looking around to check they were alone. The others had gone off to look for rock pools. "I *have* actually been thinking of staying on in New Zealand, though I haven't said anything to Mummy or Tim yet. You see, I do love it here . . ." she paused, basking in the sunlight, eyelids closed, "And I'm pretty useless at a lot of things, but I do know a lot about antiques, and there's a job going in one of the Greytown shops. I might not get a visa, so I'm not counting my chickens just yet, but I've pretty much made up my mind to try."

Humphrey looked pleased. "So, what exactly do you need my advice about?" he asked, bending down to pick up a sea shell. "I want to get to know some more people in town," said Elspeth, looking at what he had on the palm of his hand, "I don't want to just be a tourist, going in and buying things. I want to know about the lifestyle." "Good on you," said Humphrey, "Course I'll help." Elspeth thanked him, and asked, "What have you found?" "It's a violet sea snail," answered her friend, "Fascinating creature—though this one is just an empty shell, otherwise I would have put him somewhere safe. They float upside-down and their bodies are transparent, like a blob of clear glue, or a string of bubbles."

Elspeth took the beautiful, violet-coloured spiral shell from Humphrey's hand and examined it. "Keep it," he said, "Souvenir of New Zealand. There are actually over three thousand six hundred species of mollusc in the seas around our islands," Humphrey told her, "Though you've probably only been aware of one, and that's the paua." "Oh yes," said Elspeth, fishing under the neck of her shirt and pulling out a pendant on a silver chain, "I have a paua shell necklace. Aunty Chris sent it over for my eighteenth. It's my favourite, even though I've got more expensive jewellery—including some truly hideous family heirlooms—than I know what to do with!" Humphrey touched the necklace that Elspeth was holding between thumb and finger. "I guessed it would be this one," he said. Elspeth looked up enquiringly, their faces inches apart, and her gaze rested on Humphrey's lips as he explained: "That's called a *hei matau*. It's the Maori lucky fish hook. Aunty Chris was trying to make sure everything goes right for you. And I hope it does, from here on in."

Elspeth, feeling her knees give a little, broke away, though it was obvious to them both that they had just acknowledged an attraction between them. She tucked the necklace back inside her shirt and smiled at Humphrey: "Race you to the rocks!" she said, gathering up her hair in one hand. She took off in the direction of where her mother and brother were standing, talking to the two aunts—possibly about her and Humphrey. The young man laughed out loud, gave her a head start and ran after her. He overtook her two yards away from the others. "Couple of big kids!" said Christine, but she looked pleased with herself.

Humphrey walked back to the Landrover with Tim, to give Elspeth breathing space. He wasn't the pushy type. "So, Tim . . ." he said, "What do you think of our fine country? Your sister seems to like it here . . ." Tim grinned. "There's only one thing missing!" he said with feeling, "And that's a good night out on the town. What's the Wellington night life like?" Humphrey frowned, "That's not my style,

I'm afraid, Tim. But my kid brother Richie goes most Friday nights. I could have a word, if you like." Tim's face lit up. "Thanks, Humph," he said, "That would be wicked."

At the top of the two hundred and fifty-eight steps that led up the cliff to the Cape Palliser lighthouse, everyone turned to admire the view. The lighthouse door was locked, but they were already high enough up to drink in the glory of the sea, the sky, the long sweep of beach, and the towering cliffs, jagged cones that reminded one of sharks' teeth, though they were dark grey and black in colour. Tim was fascinated by the basking seals, and asked his aunts whether it was possible to get closer. "Not here, Timmo," said Zooie, "You should have been here when there was an oil spill a couple of years ago, up north. Everyone was up there, working with the seals and birds. Even folks from Oz. Are you interested in wildlife?" "Not really had much chance," answered Tim, looking rather ashamed of himself, "Been a bit of an indoors wimp, to be honest. But I was reading something in one of your magazines the other day. How easy is it to do volunteering here—I mean, for someone like me?"

Zooie looked at Tim thoughtfully. "Humphrey!" she called, having to shout to be heard above the wind, even though he was only a few feet away, "Are you still involved in that conservation group? You know, the Friends of Maungawhau?" "Yes!" shouted Humphrey, "Very much so! Why?" Zooie looked interested: "You know, I've been thinking we should take these guys up to Auckland—do the whole guided tour, maybe even stay for a couple of days," said Christine, who was listening in, "There's Tom and Betty up there who'd put us up, no problem. Friends of ours with a six-berth caravan in their garden," she explained to the visitors, "You can't come all this way without seeing the best of what New Zealand has to offer."

Humphrey chipped in: "And since I'm already volunteering up there one day a week, I can show you what we're trying to do," he offered, "I bet you'd like to see a volcano or two, wouldn't you, Elspeth?" Elspeth was delighted. "Absolutely!" she said. "If it's no trouble," added Marjory. So it was settled that Tim would have his night out on the town with Richie Barton and his mates the following Friday, and on Sunday they would all head north together, if the caravan was free.

Tim lay in bed that night reading all he could find about the people who were trying to get their work of saving the volcanic cones of North Island—which needed urgent attention—recognized and funded by government. Too many feet had trampled the tops of the famous volcanoes. Weeds had taken over, and an extensive programme of cleaning up and re-vegetation was needed. Humphrey had been involved with the Friends for years, having met his Maori wife, Airini, at the top of volcano, where she was pulling up hawkweed and 'old man's beard' which, she informed him, was a type of clematis that could run up anything and choke it to death. "It'll run up your leg if you stand still long enough," she'd told him. His Aunt Christine had told them Humphrey's wife had died in a helicopter crash in bad weather. "He took it well," she said, "The nicest thing he said was that he'd been a lucky man ever to meet her, and he had to be grateful for that. Impressive chap, if you ask me."

Tim Brandston was tired of being useless. He'd seen enough of first Maurie and now Humphrey, to make comparisons that made his self-esteem, manufactured for too long out of the status he'd been born with, the social connections that had brought with it, and the possessions he owned. He'd picked up from conversations with his sister how she felt about the country, and was wondering whether there might not be a way for them both to stay, possibly sharing a flat somewhere. They were getting on so well now that he was sure she wouldn't balk at the idea. Mummy loved it too, and with both of them there, wouldn't she have the best possible excuse for visiting regularly? He determined to speak to his sister on the trip up north, and to speak to Humphrey and his brother when he went round to their house on Friday night.

By the time the party reached the hotel, famed for its fish and chips, they were all feeling the need for a comfortable seat and a hot meal indoors. The floor-length windows allowed them an uninterrupted view of sky and water. "We can always have a wander outside when we've eaten," said Christine, passing round the menus. Humphrey made a helpful suggestion: "Why don't we all choose different dishes? Then we could all get a taste of six different ones?" "Great idea!" said Tim, and the others agreed. Half an hour later, all six attractive plates of food arrived on the table, along with a heap of fresh lemon slices and a herb mayonnaise: a creamy clam chowder, a classic battered fish and chips with a side salad, a bowl of *moules marinières* with crusty bread and butter, a dish of *paua* fritters, a pan-fried flounder in a coating of chives and hot sauce, and a heap of whitebait fried in breadcrumbs. Everyone set to, and pronounced every dish delicious. They ate in silence, too tired and too absorbed to do more than pass the food round and sip their wine and mineral water.

"We really should move soon," said Christine at last, lounging back in her chair, looking not at all like someone who wants to move. "Yeah, I do need to get back shortly," said Humphrey, "Richie calls the cops if I'm out after his bed time!" Elspeth laughed: "I'm looking forward to meeting this brother of yours!" she exclaimed, "He sounds interesting." "Yeah, but he's not as good-looking as me!" replied Humphrey, "Or half as intelligent. But don't tell him I said so—he thinks he's going to get all the best girls."

There was no singing on the journey home, but in the front seat, where Tim sat with Humphrey, there was a conversation in hushed whispers, so as not to disturb the women in the back seats, who were nodding off. "Hey, Tim, is your sister attached?" asked Humphrey as quietly as possible. "Not at the mo," replied Tim, leaning in, "But can I give you a tip about Els? Make friends. That's what she needs right now. Someone to talk to, to laugh with. To forget that life tends to become over-complicated. If you can do that for her, and you can manage not to make her cry, you have my blessing." Humphrey nodded. "Understood. Thanks. Come round tomorrow evening for a bit and I'll introduce you to Richie, and we can talk some more."

Back at Huruhuru, Tim and Humphrey unloaded the raincoats from the back of the Landrover, and gently woke the women. "Thanks for your safe driving," said Elspeth as she shook hands with the young man, trying to hide a yawn. "See you all soon," he replied, and drove his car the few yards along the Rongotai Road that separated the two cottages. As he turned the key in the lock, he heard Richie, singing raucously the other side of the door a pop song he recognized (barely) as 'Someone to Be Around' by Six60. "Not much chance singing that badly!" he said as he rushed in, surprising his brother who was standing on his head trying to juggle four oranges. "Ach, you're just tone deaf!" said his brother—a shorter, blonder, but no less athletic version of himself—as he turned himself the right way up. They high-fived each other, bro-hugged and clapped one another on the back. They spent the rest of the evening playing pool on the back verandah. Just down the road, at Feathers, everyone was already fast asleep.

Chapter Thirty-Five

ARCHIE RECEIVES ORDERS

For a while, Archie was so caught up in the progress of his romance with Ann-Marie that the small matter of his role as leader of the human race was placed in the background. He and Ann-Marie were discovering the delights of love in older age. They romped like puppies, careless of what was happening in the outside world, beyond the sanctuary of the bedroom, the home, the housing scheme, their small urban community, their city.

It was a time in history when humankind was at a place that was not even a crossroads: there was but once choice, which was to shape up, learn respect, be humble or perish. At his next meeting with the gnomes, Archie was like someone who had been doped up, his brain full of serotonin, his body vibrating from the unaccustomed touch of a tender lover.

"Archibald Prescott, your head is not here!" Alevin admonished him, wagging a finger, "Bring your head! Gnomes are not here to play!" Archie hung his head in the appropriate gesture for contrition: "Archibald says sorries!" he said, "Love is taking his head away!" "Gnomes understand," said Ned in a conciliatory tone, "But gnomes cannot let time run away like ants from fire!" "Gnomes are always right," said Archie, "My head has returned and I am listening."

Norman, who had been polishing his belt buckle on a small handkerchief, began: "Today you must learn why gnomes are angry. For thousands of years, gnomes have lived beside humans. There have been times of anger, yes, and times of sorrow, but the days of now are of a new anger that may carry us far." There was silence. Even Cholmondeley and Hugo were not smiling. Terry the Mushroom-gathering Gnome was dripping tears down the front of his jacket. "I am sorry," said Archie, "For all the badness of humans. Truly sorry. My hands are also soiled. I have been wasteful and done damage. My guilt is on me always." Archie was doing well, for Norman ventured a small, grim smile. They were now speaking in Gnomish, and Archie had not even noticed the changeover. Very good.

"Archibald, you know that Gnomes have no council of elders, no government over all gnomes . . ." Archie nodded. Norman continued: "So each gnome belongs to a Band." "Except for those who travel alone," chipped in Sigfrid, "The travelling healers." "Yes, except for them," agreed Norman, "A traditional Band has eleven, such as we: one gnome for each of the Sacred Nine—an Oak, a Willow, and so on—with a Blackthorn and a Rowan." "The Blackthorn for diplomacy and the Rowan for survival," added Archie. "Yes, Mun-tili, you have learnt your lesson well," agreed Norman, "In these days of the Scattering of Gnomes, and the roads that kill, it is hard to send messages between Bands. Some have not been heard of for many years, and some have broken away."

Archie believed he could guess what was coming, and he shivered. Norman was weeping and could not continue. Ned, gentle Ned who was so honest about his feelings that he could handle them better than anyone Archie had ever met, took up the narrative: "Archie, Friend of Gnomes, you must understand that gnomes are good. No gnome has ever departed from the Code of Honour. It is impossible. Tree energy feeds us in our souls, and no tree is evil, therefore we cannot perform evil . . ." Ned paused, leaning over to lend his handkerchief to Terry, who was crying fit to break his heart: "Messages are sent and received, but there is no reply. These Bands have been filled with a new anger." "A right anger!" said Alevin, "I have seen it in the Yew Bands I have visited. They have been making bows and arrows. And the Rowans have been setting traps for humans."

This was something of a shock to Archie, who had assumed that, since gnomes were peaceable, they would never turn to violence. But he understood: throughout human history war had seemed necessary in one place or another, and on occasion vast tracts of the planet had been overrun by armies. "Ibni, I understand," he said meekly, "And I am so sad, my words stick in my mouth. What can a mun-tili do? My hands are hanging idle, like a pair of empty mittens, and I feel ashamed." Norman rose from his seat on the sofa at this, and crossed the floor. For the first time, he touched Archie, a soft pat on the knee. Archie felt a rush of energy through his body, like cool water. "You have given me a great gift!" he exclaimed, "I have the strength to do what I must."

When Archie arrived later at Ann-Marie's door, he was a soberer man than when he had left her the night before. She took one look at his face, and put the kettle on for coffee. "We have been given our first task," he said, as he sat down on a kitchen chair, "We have to go and rescue someone who's in danger." Ann-Marie nodded: "From the gnomes?" she asked, already knowing the answer. "Yes!" sighed Archie, "A Yew Band has formed in a village in the south-east of England, and they are about to commit an assassination. I don't know how we're going to do it, but we have to try and stop them, even though the chosen victim is not someone I'd normally stir out of doors for . . ."

Gold coins appeared on Archie's bedside table the following night, with a tiny note instructing him to 'sell and pay for travel', which he did. The man in the jeweller's looked at him strangely, but weighed the gold and gave him several hundred pounds in return. It was enough for train tickets and taxis, and a couple of nights' bed and breakfast. "Where are we headed?" asked Ann-Marie, carrying a small rucksack into Archie's flat, where they were to share breakfast before setting off. "Best not to say," said Archie, "I've been sworn to secrecy, just in case."

Chapter Thirty-Six

BRANDSTON

The train journey took the couple from the Midlands down to London, which they crossed from Euston to Charing Cross Station via the underground. At Charing Cross, they bought tickets to Hastings, in the county of East Sussex. "Norman's instructions," explained Archie, "We're getting off a few stops earlier than that." Where they got off is top secret, but enough to say that they arrived in a market town of considerable size, and went for a walk until they found a bed and breakfast in a narrow, winding, side street that seemed quiet. They checked in as Mr. and Mrs. A. Birch, and paid with cash. They made a great show of asking for tourist brochures and directions for the Tourist Information Office and a nice restaurant.

The landlady thought them charming, especially when she saw they were holding hands. "A lovely older couple," she told her husband when they had gone up to their room, "And so nicely spoken, even though they're from Birmingham." "Don't be fooled," answered her husband, "They're all savages north of Watford Gap." He returned to his newspaper while his wife went to check that they had mushrooms for breakfast. She always went to extra trouble for guests who were well-behaved.

Once they had freshened up and changed into walking gear, Ann-Marie and Archie left their lodgings and went to look for a bus to the nearby village of Brandston. They were in luck: a bus was at the stop, and the driver had nipped into the tobacconist's for a bar of chocolate and a can of pop. "Yes, this is the Brandston bus," he confirmed, "Takes about forty minutes. Tourists?" "Yes," said

Ann-Marie, giving him a charming smile, "We've heard the church is worth a visit." "Don't know," said the driver, "Never visited. The wife's been there—got family in farming. Half-decent pub, by all accounts: The Headless Man. Hahaha!"

Ann-Marie and Archie sat on the bus, enjoying the view of a part of the country so different from what they were used to. "It's pretty down here," said she. "Couldn't bear to live here, though," said he, "Too out-in-the-sticks." "Too green?" said Ann-Marie, with a little laugh, "Maybe one day it'll all be like this again, and with a lot more trees and less concrete and tarmac!" "Heaven help us!" Archie laughed back, "Making our own clothes out of bark and living on fish!" "We'd be cold most of the time, too," added Ann-Marie, "Have to cuddle up even more!"

After they had been travelling for about half an hour, the conversation dried up, and they both began to feel very nervous. They held hands tightly. Archie had no idea how he was going to get them into Brandston Manor, or even if he could. Or, failing that, whether they would be able to make contact with the Yew Band. None of his gnome friends had any idea how a Band composed entirely of Yews would operate, and were worried about the mood they might be in when Archie and Ann-Marie approached them. He had Alevin's clan badge as a *laissez-passer* but it was small, and he would have to get quite close before the Yews would be able to see it.

Archie sighed deeply. Ann-Marie reached over and rubbed both his hands, which were icy cold. "It'll be OK, love," she said into his ear, "We'll find a way somehow. And if we can't, we'll have given it a damn good try." Archie said a little prayer to the Great Mother that Ned had taught him, under his breath. Ann-Marie heard him, and joined in. There was nothing more they could do to prepare. If Alevin and Norman, who were probably the best teachers in the entire world, had missed anything out, it was because there were so many unknowns involved in this mission. All that could have been done had been done.

Ten minutes later they stepped down from the bus into a picturesque village that ran along a river in either direction. "We can't ask for directions," explained Archie, "It would give the game away. But the church has a footpath running along the back that skirts the estate. That's what we're heading for. In one direction, you get to the Manor gates, and in the other you can walk round the boundary wall. Footpaths and bridleways most of the way, and not visible from the road because of trees and bushes. We should be OK. But first, I think a visit to the pub is in order, don't you? If there should be . . . any comeback . . . and the bus driver remembers us, and that he recommended the pub, we'll have an alibi." Ann-Marie looked alarmed: "An alibi?" she repeated, her eyes wide, "It's not going to come to that, is it, darling?" Archie blushed at first: it was the first time Ann-Marie had called him that. Then he returned to serious mode. "Probably not, but we don't have a choice, do we?"

At the bar of The Headless Man, Archie ordered two double whiskies with ginger ale, and the pair went to sit at a table near a window looking out over the main road which ran through the village. There were very few people about—mainly churchgoers, it looked like—and cars were passing through without stopping. The church bells were ringing out a cheerful peal that cut through the clear, icy air. "We should probably eat, darling," said Archie, pushing a menu towards his beloved, "It's going to be a while before we get our dinner, and it's a bit nippy. We need hot food inside us." They ordered fish and chips with mushy peas, and sat back, sipping their drinks. Thankfully, the meal arrived quickly. They were early for lunch, and there were only a few tables occupied, mostly with lone men and women. They ate quickly and left.

They found the footpath behind the church, and headed west in the direction of Brandston Manor's main gates. Half an hour later, they spotted the first security guard, a short man with the figure of a bullock, leaning on the wall and talking into a walkie-talkie. They approached cautiously, going at a pace they thought appropriate to an older couple out for a Sunday ramble. As soon as the guard caught sight of them, his hand went to his hip. Alevin had warned the couple that the guards would be armed, so they simply smiled and said good afternoon. "Could you cross the road, please, Sir, Madam?" asked the guard, adding: "Mind the traffic!" Archie took a deep breath and said, "We will, but could we have a word?"

The guard spoke into his walkie-talkie and two more guards appeared from a sentry-box the other side of the gates. They stood in front of the gates, and the first guard crossed over the road with Archie and Ann-Marie. "What's up?" he asked, in a friendly-enough voice. He seemed to be expecting them to ask for directions. His hand was off his hip and scratching his head under his cap instead. "We'd like to see Mr. Percy Brandston, please," said Ann-Marie, "We have an urgent message concerning his personal safety." At this, the guard, whose name (according to his badge) was H. Posnic, did a double-take. "You've got to be kidding!" he exclaimed, "Nobody gets to see Mr. Brandston on the fly! Best advice I can give you is to write a letter." "That won't do," insisted Ann-Marie, "You see, it's like in the film, it's Clear and Present Danger. Like, today!"

The guard's expression became a lot more serious, and he called over one of his colleagues, a thin, tired-looking, red-haired man whose badge read 'D. Grey'. "Hey, Damien. The lady and gentleman say there's a threat to Mr. Brandston's personal security. What do we do? Call the police and have them questioned, or what?" "No idea," answered Mr. Grey, "Get a bit more info?" "There's not much we can tell you," said Archie, trying to stay relaxed and as unthreatening-looking as possible, "Could you maybe get a message to him to tell him to stay indoors, or make sure he's guarded by a couple of people wherever he goes?" "What are you?" asked Mr. Posnic in a mocking tone, "Psychics?" But his colleague laid a hand on his arm. "Good idea," said Damien Grey, "We'll pass that onto the boss. Now, off you go and stay clear, please. If the boss sees you, he'll take this a lot more seriously than we have, and you don't want to get yourselves locked up, now, do you?"

"You *will* make sure he's warned, won't you?" asked Archie, giving the guards a wan smile. The guards nodded, but said nothing. "Come on," said Archie to Ann-Marie, "There's nothing more we can do here." Disappointed, they turned back towards the footpath. They looked back once, just before disappearing from view, and saw that the guards were all watching them. And they were clearly enjoying a joke.

Chapter Thirty-Seven

SISTER AND BROTHER

The day after the trip to Cape Palliser, the household at Feathers woke up rather late, and it was ten o'clock before Elspeth and Tim fetched their bikes from the shed and set off for their morning ride. They took off down Rongotai Road, a fine rain and a light wind refreshing their faces. They had not planned where they would go, but had agreed they would stop in Greytown town centre for a coffee on the way back.

Tim went first, enjoying the feel of the muscles in his calves working and the steady rhythm of his breathing. He was beginning to feel like a new man, even though he had been in New Zealand less than two weeks. There was a kind of freedom here that changed a person. Looking back at his old life, he realised why he had been so irritable and unhappy for so long: it was a combination of always doing what was expected, of dirty air and sticky atmosphere, of wearing a suit with a stiff collar and tie, and of being constantly jostled by the bodies of other people—in the street, in the tube, in shops. He saw it now: the craziness of his old life, and how it broke a person down, little by little, from the inside out, and from the outside in. He breathed deeply and free-wheeled down the next incline, his feet stuck out. Behind him, he heard his sister chuckle.

Elspeth felt the healing in her heart more than in her body. Healing from years of worrying about being dressed appropriately, of looking exactly right, of running in high heels with the balls of her feet on fire whilst smiling and appearing to love it. And of being discarded by Maurie. She had wondered for a long time why they had ever married, when they could have simply lived together. She no longer saw anything sinister in Maurie's behaviour, and had come to the conclusion that they had both simply got carried away. It was OK now: she could wish Maurie well, let him go and think about her future. "I know it's a cliché, darling, but you're still very young and you have your whole life ahead of you," Mummy had said as they stood on the steps on the lighthouse looking out to sea, "It will all work out just fine."

Tonight was the night when Tim was due round at Humphrey and Richie's, to meet the person who was going to show him the nightlife of Wellington. Elspeth hadn't been invited, but she was going to learn how to make the famous New Zealand lolly cake this afternoon, and she intended to take one round to the brothers, just to say hi. She could always excuse herself, if it looked as though a blokey evening had been planned. The truth of it was, of course, that she wanted to see Humphrey again. She hadn't been able to erase his image from her mind, and she had tried hard to do so. She had a feeling that things, once started, would go fast, and that scared her. It had crossed her mind more than once that there was a type of woman that men found it easy to leave, and that she was that type. Whoever came along, however well they got on, it would happen again until she was old and living somewhere alone with a couple of cats.

Christine and Zooie's relationship made her totally envious, and she had been watching them carefully to see if there was a magic formula for happiness with a significant other. She thought she had worked it out: something built on mutual respect and shared interests. The love of your life would be someone who was a best friend: that much was obvious. The chemistry went far beyond wanting to share a bed: it worked like yeast through dough—all the way through, from waking up to going to sleep. That was what Elspeth yearned for, but she was enough of a realist now to understand that it was chance—or fate—that determined whether you met such a person, and that there was a good chance that either might mess it up.

Tim was not thinking beyond a squeeze on the dance-floor and a good night kiss. He could have had any number of one-night stands, but the idea repulsed him. On the other hand, romance and settling down was—to his mind—for older people, or for people who did not have a sense of adventure, and now, more than ever, he was enjoying being single, exploring who he could be in a different context, a different environment. There had been women in his life, flitting in and out like butterflies. The moment a woman wanted to find out anything about him beyond his name, his favourite tipple and what he did for a living, he backed off.

Cycling was the perfect way to blow away cobwebs and clear the mind of worries. Tim and Elspeth made the most of the opportunity. They had been going longer distances each time they went out, and could now cycle comfortably for two hours without getting out of breath or suffering with cramp in the legs the following day. It wasn't much, but it was a start. "Soon be time to turn round, Tim!" Elspeth called to her brother as they crested a hill. Tim signalled her to pull over and they stopped on the hilltop to admire the view of grey-blue sea, greenery, and the picturesque patchwork of fields and buildings. It seemed everything in New Zealand was laid out in neat squares. Perhaps it was the proximity of the sea that made the natives want to keep their landscape as tidy and symmetrical as possible: the sea, which constantly broke itself against the cliffs, rocks and beaches, ever-changing, ever unpredictable. The relationship between sea and human geography made a powerful contrast, and it made you want to set clear parameters for your life, but live as free and authentically-you a life as possible.

"Race you to the café!" yelled Tim. "The Jack and Jill or the Eden?" yelled back Elspeth as she took off after her brother. Tim's happy voice floated back to her, clear and strong: "Jack and Jill went up the hill to fetch a pail of water; Jack fell down and broke his crown, and Jill came tumbling after!" "No tumbling!" shouted Elspeth. Too late: Tim slid on a patch of gravel, his front wheel wobbled and he flew off the road and into a ditch, where he lay, tangled up in his bicycle.

Elspeth screamed and screeched to a halt. She dropped her bike on the roadside and scrambled down to where her brother lay, not moving. She knelt down and leant over. Tim was upside-down and there was no way she would be able to move him on her own. He was groaning, which was probably a good sign. The crash had not been that serious, and the landing had been soft, but there was always the possibility of a neck or spine injury.

Tim's phone was sticking out of his pocket, and Elspeth knew he had Humphrey's number, so she searched his contacts until she found 'Hump', which made her smile as she pressed the call button. Humphrey answered after two rings: "Timmo!" he shouted enthusiastically, "How's it hanging?" Elspeth spluttered: "No, it's me—Elspeth. And as for how it's hanging, the answer is upside-down. Tim's come off his bike into a ditch, near the top of the hill the other side of town. Can you come? Please?" She heard Humphrey relay her message to his brother and a door slam. "Richie's getting the Rover out of the garage as I speak. Don't panic. We'll be there in a few minutes. And Elso?" "Yes?" came her voice, much less worried than before, "Don't try to move him. Richie's a physiotherapist, so just hang on." "All right," replied Elspeth, "See you soon."

By the time the Landrover pulled up and Humphrey and Richie jumped out, Tim had managed to wriggle free of his bike and was crawling out of the ditch. Elspeth had told him several times to lie still, but Tim seemed too dazed to hear her. She suspected a concussion: his helmet had slipped. He probably hadn't done up the chin strap tightly enough. "Hey Elso," said Richie, putting an arm round her shoulders, "Are you OK? Listen: you go and sit in the car with Humphrey while I take a look at your daft brother. You're shivering a bit—probably shock."

Elspeth did as she was told. Humphrey opened the passenger door for her and helped her in. "I probably shouldn't have bothered you . . ." she said, zipping up her rain mac. Now that she was in the car, she felt even more shivery. "Yes! You should have!" said Humphrey emphatically. "The way he landed, upside-down, he could have had a serious injury. Let's wait and see what Richie says, but my guess is he's probably going to call out the ambulance to get your brother properly checked out. Do you want to call your Aunt?" Humphrey took out his phone and passed it to Elspeth. The number's on there under Feathers." Elspeth rang the cottage. It was Zooie who answered. Elspeth brought her up to speed. "Tell Mummy everything's OK. Humphrey and Richie are here. If an ambulance is needed, which it probably will be, Richie's in charge. They're looking after both of us, so please tell her not to worry."

Richie tapped on the car window ten minutes later and said he'd called the ambulance service, as he wanted Tim to get a proper check. He'd evidently had quite a bump on the head and was saying he felt sick. "Listen," said Richie, "You guys head on home. I'll wait here for the ambulance. I'll call you when we have news and you can meet us at the hospital if he's taken there, which I'm guessing is pretty certain." "Can I just have a word with Tim?" asked Elspeth. "Of course!" replied Richie, "Just don't expect him to be all there." "He never is!" smiled Elspeth, but she wasn't smiling. She got out of the car and went to kneel down beside her brother, who was now lying flat on his back, having resisted Richie's instructions to keep still. "I can see the sky!" murmured Tim, "Elso! Peth! I can see the sky!" "Jolly good," said Elspeth, "Just keep counting clouds and when you get to a million, you can stop." "OK!" said Tim, looking up through half-closed eyes. Elspeth bent to give him a swift kiss on the cheek, and turned to go. There were tears in her eyes.

"OK, hon?" asked Humphrey as he turned the key in the ignition. Elspeth nodded. "Well done for keeping your cool." "You didn't hear me scream when it first happened," Elspeth answered, but she was smiling. Somehow the sight of Humphrey's strong hands on the steering wheel made her feel utterly secure. "Everyone's allowed a scream once in a while. If it means anything, I think you handled that like a professional. Let's go!" he said.

Marjory, Christine and Zooie were waiting in the kitchen when they arrived at Huruhuru. "I'll make some tea," said Zooie. They all sat down and waited. It was an hour before Humphrey's phone rang. He put it on speaker phone so everyone could hear. It was Richie, letting them know that Tim was in hospital, but that he was about to be seen, so they should just wait on and see. "He may be discharged in an hour's time," said Richie, "It depends how long the wait for x-rays is going to be. Either way I'll keep you informed. Don't worry! I'm hopeful it's nothing serious. He just told me to tell Elspeth he's counted two and a half million clouds and can she please find him something to do that's not as boring! Oh, and he's chatting up two nurses . . ."

The women laughed with relief, and Marjory wiped her eyes. "Trust him!" she said. Christine passed her sister a clean tissue: "With the two of you there, I should think every nurse in the hospital's buzzing round! Tell them to behave, or they'll have me to answer to." "D'you mean us or the nurses?" quipped Richie, "Hold on . . . Doc's here, gotta go. Talk later. Bye!" and he was gone.

Nobody felt much like eating, so Christine made a plate of sandwiches and heated up some home-made carrot and coriander soup. The smell was enough to tempt Humphrey, and he managed to prevail on the women to join him. "I'd feel bad eating alone," he gave as his excuse. It was mid-afternoon before they heard a car draw up outside. It was a taxi, and it contained Tim, his head wrapped up in a spectacular bandage, and Richie. The bike, which had survived the crash, but for a bent front wheel, was on the roof rack. Tim apologised to everyone immediately, and hugged his sister, wincing from the bruises on his ribs. "Elso-Peth was a star!" he announced, his arm still round her neck, "What a clot I am. I've ruined everybody's day and I'm really sorry." Marjory was next in line for a hug. "We're just relieved you're all right, darling," she said. She tried to break away from the hug, but Tim held on, rocking his mother from side to side until she laughed and relaxed. "I'm starving!" he announced, "What's in the fridge for a wounded soldier?" "Wounded soldier my arse!" said Christine, but she patted Tim's cheek, "How about an artery-clogging fry-up?"

Humphrey and Richie were, of course, included in the invitation to a late lunch. Then somehow the conversation was flowing along so comfortably that it was six o'clock in the evening before anyone thought of making a move. "I take it there'll be no clubbing tomorrow night, then?" Zooie asked the men. "More like card games and a movie," answered Humphrey, "You'll come along, won't you Elspeth?" She turned to him and smiled: "Of course!" she answered, pleased to be included, "I'd love to." Elspeth and Humphrey gazed at each other for a while, until Elspeth noticed her aunts nudging each other out of the corner of her eye and broke contact.

"And what'll us old ladies find to do while the youngsters are doing their thing?" asked Christine. Zooie grinned: "Maybe we should go clubbing in their place," she said, "Someone's got to prop up the economy!" Marjory knew she was joking. "I've got a better idea, and one that doesn't involve going out," said Zooie. "Sounds good," remarked Marjory, "To be truthful, I don't care what we do as long as it involves sitting on a comfy sofa and thanking God my son is alive and well . . ." "You'll be able to do that, sweetheart," Zooie reassured her. "Beauty treatments!" said Tim, "If I know anything about women. You'll be lying around with mud-packs on your faces and doing each other's nails." "None of your business!" retorted Zooie, "Off you go to bed now, Timmo. Talking of beauty, your bruises are coming out a treat, and if anyone needs beauty sleep, it's you!" Tim was too tired to argue. All he wanted now was his painkillers and to sleep the clock round.

Chapter Thirty-Eight

THE YEW BAND

"So, what now?" asked Ann-Marie, when they were safely out of sight of the guards. "Back in the other direction and see if we can spot any gnome activity, or a place where it looks like we could leave a message. Alevin said there's a place where there are a couple of yew trees, where there was once a family cemetery, on the south-west corner of the estate. It's not too far." The couple kept walking, feeling rather dejected, stopping occasionally to wipe the thick mud from their shoes with a stick. Eventually they saw the yew trees, which overhung the wall by a good few feet, on the corner where the south side of the wall met the west side.

On the other side of the path grew thick shrubs, choked with wild clematis, affording the pair some protection from view. Open fields lay on the south side of the estate. They stopped and examined the area closely. There was a stone missing from the bottom of the wall, and the hole had been covered up—they guessed, by gnomes—by means of a heap of small twigs and leaves. "I take it we're not about to try climbing over the wall," said Ann-Marie, seeing Archie look upwards. "No! There might be cameras, and we mustn't draw attention to the area, if we can help it," he answered. "Let's sit down, so as to look natural, and have a think."

It was so cold by now, that their toes had gone numb. Archie removed Ann-Marie's shoes and massaged her feet. Then she reciprocated. They spotted two men in black uniforms patrolling the fields with an Alsatian which, thankfully, was on the lead. The couple ducked down until they had gone past. "This is tricky," said

Archie in a hushed whisper, "But I think I'm going to try something." Ann-Marie did not say 'be careful'—she knew he would. Archie went into a crouch and up to the hole in the wall. "Kuvinah lek fre Ibni Alevin!" he said, his face against the stonework, "Breganti ash! I ver mun-tili manni. Turit! Turit! A mi!" There was silence. Ann-Marie was impressed: her beloved had a good grip on his Gnomish. She understood "I'm a safe man" and "Beware!" and "Come to me!" and hoped this would work.

After a few seconds, there was a scuffling, and a sound of small voices arguing on the other side of the wall. Archie turned round. "I think they're discussing whether to answer," he said, "One of them just said 'It might be a trap' and another one said 'What if it's not?'" The heap of leaf litter at the bottom of the wall began to move, and a tall, yew-green hat pushed its way out, followed by a head with snowy white hair and a slender body. A pair of stout boots came out last. The gnome stood up and shook bits of dead leaf off himself. He looked up at Archie, who had sat down so as to make himself as short as possible. "I'm sorry," said Archie, in Gnomish, using the words Alevin and Norman had taught him, "A human called Archie Prescott and his lady, Ann-Marie Osborne, will be forgiven for crossing the line when gnomes hear his message."

The gnome stood with his head on one side. He was an ancient Yew, and seemed used to the idea of good humans for he had no weapon in his hand, though he was frowning and had his fists on his hips. "I come from Alevin Yew and his Band. Greetings from Blackthorns, Rowan, Birch, Willow and Alder of Brummagem. May I have respectful words with noble Yew Band of Brandston Manor?"

The gnome gave a low whistle, and four more gnomes, all dressed in dark green, but wearing black hats (which Archie had never seen before), popped out of the hole in quick succession. They formed a semi-circle behind their leader, who was pulling on his snowy beard. At last he spoke, in English with an accent that sounded a little like Cockney: "The good man speaks fair. My name is Derwin Yew, and these are my brothers: Constant, Myshin, Albo and Bernal." As he

pronounced their names, each black-hatted gnome nodded, first to
Archie, then to Ann-Marie, who had joined the group and was now
sitting next to Archie in the mud. The gnome went on: "It is rare for
humans to humble their back quarters on our good earth here. Most
walk in hard shoes or ride their metal carriages and feel no reverence.
It is many years since I heard news of my brother Alevin and his Band.
Is Alevin using humans as messengers? The world is indeed changing.
Speak and fear not. Gnomes will listen."

Archie bowed as low as he could get, and continued: "Alevin says
to his brothers of Brandston that the anger of gnomes everywhere has
grown into a fire. He understands the anger of the Yews of Brandston.
He feels this deep in his soul. Mistake him not. He will know why
your brothers have put on their hats of black." Derwin Yew pulled
himself up to his full height (just over one foot) and squared his
shoulders. "If Alevin sends a message to keep peace, the Yew Band
will not listen!" he said, in the nearest thing to a shout Archie and
Ann-Marie had ever heard coming from a gnome, "Alevin does not
know our story of recent days!" Archie sighed and asked: "Will Ibni
Derwin tell me so that I may carry the story to Ibni Alevin?" Derwin
seemed to hesitate, then he turned and went into a huddle with his
brothers. "This is the moment," thought Archie, and he pulled out a
flask of birch wine from each of his jacket pockets. "I have brought
a peace gift!" he said, "Will you not sit down with us and celebrate
friendship?"

This strategy worked like magic. "This is the strangest picnic
I ever was at!" thought Ann-Marie to herself, as they sat down on
the footpath, two large and five small behinds getting very muddy.
The birch wine was uncorked and went the rounds, and Archie and
Ann-Marie listened to the Yew Band's tale of suffering. They heard
of the disappearance of precious gnome possessions into the pockets
of Percy Brandston, of the ancient and valued smoking pipe tossed
carelessly into a hedge, of the trampling of flowers, of the stealing
of birds' eggs, and of the shooting of a family of red squirrels during
the winter. And they heard how one of the Yews, a fellow over two

thousand years old, had been rescued—too late—from a rat-trap, his little body crushed and bleeding. They heard of the cutting down of ancient trees to make room for two extra car parking spaces, and of the polluting of the stream that ran along the south side, the other side of the wall, which had killed wildlife on which the gnomes depended for many things, including food.

"Gnomes of the Yew Band are at the end of patience," said Constant Yew, a rather calm and steady-looking fellow who rose and paced up and down as he spoke, his arms folded, "Do not speak to us of it, I beg. Gnomes know when the end of patience has come." "I am sorry," said Archie once more. Ann-Marie felt sadder than she had ever felt in her life, but she wanted to speak: "I am sorry too," she said, "More than words can say. Alevin will hear. He will understand. His heart will crack when he hears, but it will not break." Ann-Marie was getting the hang of speaking to gnomes. Her academic background had served her well. "Gnomes are strong, as they are slow to come to the end of patience. I wish you well in your battles."

The gnomes looked at one another in surprise. It was Bernal, the youngest, who responded by shuffling around on his bottom until he could reach out and put a hand on Ann-Marie's knee. He had the ghost of a small smile on his face as he looked up at her and said: "The man Archie Prescott, Friend of Gnomes, should make the *husbond* with Ann-Marie Osborne, Friend of Gnomes. She is . . ." he hunted for the right words, "She is a *blessing*!" Ann-Marie touched the gnome's hand with a finger-tip and smiled, "I thank you, Bernal Yew," she answered, "Your kind words are like honey into my stomach."

Archie was about to say that he took this advice seriously when the picnic was interrupted. Just then, there was a sound of voices, a little way off to the west, and the gnomes jumped to their feet. "Turit! Naff manni—bad men—are coming!" warned Constant. "Flabaaaray!" called the gnomes in farewell, as one by one they squeezed back through the hole in the wall. "Flabaaaray! Good bye!" whispered Archie and Ann-Marie into the stonework as the last pair of boots vanished. They bent and replaced the heap of leaves and twigs, crossed the path and walked as quickly as they could, back the way they had come.

Unfortunately, they did not notice that the gnomes had left behind their collection of valuable, home-knitted, balaclava masks in their haste, or they would certainly have dropped them over the wall. The bag, which Constant had been carrying over his shoulder, had tipped upside-down, scattering the masks among the leaves. It was only when he got back to the burrow that he noticed the bag was empty, and by then it was too late to return. All hell had broken loose, and the gnomes were dealing with other issues.

Ann-Marie and Archie, to allay possible suspicion, made a point of talking loudly about a pair of magpies they had seen, and how nice it would be to have a pint in the Headless Man. It's just as well they were quick, because the people coming up the path were the same two security guards they had met at the gates of the Manor earlier: Damien Grey and Harry Posnic. "Nice walk?" asked Harry, as the security guards passed them, their mouths twitching with suppressed laughter at the couple, who they had decided were probably eccentric tourists with a large colony of bats in their belfry. "Yes! Lovely thanks!" called out Ann-Marie.

Back in the pub at last, the intrepid pair were grateful for a cappuccino with a brandy chaser. They downed their drinks quickly and caught the bus back to town, where they had hot showers, rested on their bed for an hour and went out to find somewhere modestly priced for supper. Archie was anxious to make best use of the gnomes' gold. He guessed that this was only the first of many trips he and Ann-Marie would find themselves being sent on. They decided against a sit-down meal and instead bought jumbo spring rolls from a Thai takeaway, and took them back to the bed and breakfast. Then they collapsed into bed, hugging one another tightly before falling into a troubled sleep, in which they both saw the same thing: an army of gnomes marching through a moonlit forest, their teeth bared in terrifying rage.

The following morning, they were relieved to find the sun was shining brightly. The smell of 'full English' was drifting into the room, and they were happy to be going home. "I can't bear to think what the Yew Band are up to right now," said Ann-Marie as she dressed. "Nor can I," agreed Archie, "Or what's going to happen to Mr. Percy Brandston. Or what Alevin and the others are going to say . . ."

Archie pulled on a clean pair of socks and his shoes, which Ann-Marie had managed to clean, having put them to dry, along with her own, under the radiator. He stood up, and put his arms round Ann-Marie, who was brushing her hair at the dressing-table. "I do love you so much," he said. Ann-Marie looked up in surprise and delight. "I love you loads too, Archie," she responded, "Waited all my life for you, I think. You know I'm *with* you, don't you? All the way?" Archie kissed her warm neck, which smelt of roses, "Thank you for that," he breathed, "I've never met a woman like you."

Ann-Marie got up and kissed Archie tenderly on the lips. "Breakfast?" she said. She was halfway to the door when Archie caught hold of her hand. "Stop a sec," he said, his voice shaking a little. Ann-Marie stopped and turned. Archie hitched up his trousers, got down on one knee with a small "Ouf!" of discomfort and said in a rush: "Ann-Marie Osborne, would you do me the very great honour of becoming my wife?" Ann-Marie bent down, covering him with her arms: "Of course I will!" she said, her voice shaking as much as his, "You darling, darling man!"

It was hard to eat a 'full English' whilst holding hands, but somehow Archie and Ann-Marie managed it. The landlady got out an eight-slice toast rack for the couple as she remarked to her husband: "I always said the bed in Room Six was a bit magical. Mr. and Mrs. Birch are in there, behaving like a couple of love-struck teenagers!" Her husband harrumphed as he poured himself a cup of tea and turned to the sports pages of his paper. "Lunatics!" he pronounced, "Lunatics and savages, these northerners!" "Oh, shut up, Wilf!" said his wife, "I wished you looked at me the way he looks at her!" "Ditto. When do they leave?" asked her husband, and went back to his paper.

Chapter Thirty-Nine

The Fate of Roger

Having been frustrated in his pursuit of the squirrel, Roger had become somewhat over-excited. He was not in the mood to come to heel, or to stay at heel, especially as Percy was a slow stroller and made such frequent stops to sit down. Roger did not understand why humans spent so much of their time being still, when there was so much to explore, to sniff, to dig around in, and to chase and bark at.

It wasn't long before Percy gave Roger another smack on the nose and called him a 'bad dog' for jumping around on the end of his lead, causing his master to almost trip over his brogues. Now Labradors have short memories in some situations. For example, they forget where they have buried a bone. But they do not forget unjust punishments. Roger—like the gnomes, with whom he had a nodding acquaintance—had had enough, though he only showed it by straining at his lead and whining softly. "Oh, for goodness sake, Roger!" sighed his owner, "If you can't behave, I'll . . ." He actually didn't know what he would do, but Roger understood the threat. No more walks, or to be given away to a member of staff (possibly one he didn't like very much) and replaced, or to be left chained up in the yard (possibly overnight in the cold): he was not about to allow any of these scenarios to happen to him.

So, Roger did what he had never done in his life before: he turned his head and bit Percy Brandston on the hand—the hand that smacked. Now, Percy always walked with a riding crop in his other hand, ready to deal with any nettles or brambles that had strayed across his path. He had never used it on Roger before, but he was so shocked—and, if truth be told, so frightened, suddenly, as people are when a dog they consider to be tame turns on them—that he didn't think as he brought the riding crop down on Roger's back with a hard *whack!* that made Roger yelp with pain.

Roger's back was already stiff and sore, for Labradors often develop arthritis in their hind quarters, and the pain was quite severe. The looped end of his lead was in Percy's hand, rather than about his wrist, so it was easy for the dog to tear himself away. He turned once to growl at Percy, showing all his teeth and rolling his eyes in a warning that Percy took for aggression, and ran off down the path in the direction of the stream, and the south side of the estate.

Percy was far more concerned about his hand than about his dog, but when he examined the wound, Roger's teeth had not broken the skin. Still, he was very angry. How dare his dog bite him? Hadn't he always made sure he had food and water, and regular trips to the vet for check-ups? "Ungrateful hound!" exclaimed Percy. He wasn't about to let the matter drop. He followed the dog down the path, meaning to give him a proper whipping and teach him manners. He would soon find him, and then Roger would see who was master.

The sun was already starting to dip below the tops of the tallest trees that lay between the meadow and the stream, but Percy was on a mission. Men had trembled before him, and so—occasionally—had women. He expected nothing less than obedience from all those who served him, or who worked for him. In Percy's mind, there was a clear hierarchy with God at the top, the rich and powerful below Him, then a thousand lower ranks, each with its station in life, which was to serve the rich and powerful, and—in serving them—to serve God Himself. A dog was somewhere near the bottom, especially as they could not be classed as 'wealth-creating' unless they happened to be greyhounds, pedigrees for breeding purposes, or show dogs.

Roger, meanwhile, had stopped on the far side of the first tree he came to, and was giving himself a good shake, which he found therapeutic in most situations. Then he had a good sniff around the base of the tree, where he detected a delightful cocktail of aromas of rabbit, squirrel, gnome, and his own scent, from where he had cocked his leg up the trunk a thousand times. The scent of the stream reached his nostrils too. It was running high from winter flooding, and was a stimulating blend of rotten leaf and that steely smell that comes from rain. "I'm not going back!" said Roger to himself, and thoroughly meant it. Not that he knew what an alternative lifestyle might be like: he just knew he was in big trouble with his master, and that bad things would happen if ever they met again, which meant that he would rather have run wild and risked starvation than return to the Manor.

Fortunately for Roger, help was at hand, for two sentry gnomes had seen what had passed between the dog and his master: Myshin and Albo had been on patrol nearby. Myshin was, as we already know, of a choleric disposition, and quicker to anger than most gnomes. Let us say that if another gnome would have taken three hundred years to lose his temper over something, it would have taken Myshin two hundred and eighty. Albo, on the other hand, was melancholic: he was the kind of gnome who would say "It's going to get dark soon!" at four o'clock in the afternoon in August, when everyone else was basking in the sun.

With Derwin around for wisdom, Constant for stability and 'young' Bernal for gentleness, they made a successful partnership which was all about dialogue and balanced views. Back at the burrow, there were six other gnomes: Yews, but of a clan remnant who had come over on a ferry from the Netherlands, bound for an Easter display at a local garden centre. They had only recently joined Derwin and his brothers, having escaped, thanks to a young volunteer on a work placement, who had loved them and rescued them from a tatty cardboard box at the back of a dark stock-room, once she was sure they would not be missed. She had been rather upset when, on arriving home from work, she had found that she had left the bag containing the gnomes at the bus-stop. Nobody had noticed the bag, set down behind a bench, and the Dutch Yews had managed to open the zip from the inside and take off across the fields undetected.

Myshin and Albo followed Roger down to the tree and waited for him under a part of the stream's bank which had an overhang where they could sit hidden from all but the water rats and voles, who paid them no heed. Roger was pleased, and unsurprised when, going down to the stream for a drink, he found himself face to face with gnomes whom he recognized immediately as friends of his. Myshin and Albo were the gnomes who had sat with him, the night he had been chained up outside, who had sung songs to him in Gnomish and called him a *neesh awund*, which he understood meant 'good dog'. He smiled a doggy smile, and was about to lick their faces when he remembered it had knocked them off their feet the last time he had tried it.

"Roger is sad and in pain," said Albo, bowing to his canine friend, "His master does not understand the joy of a dog!" Roger nodded. Both gnomes bowed. "Gnomes understand both joy and sadness, and for dogs and gnomes the feeling in the soul is the same. Does Roger wish to come with us?" asked Myshin. Roger bounded backwards at this, which is fortunate as a forward bound would have knocked both gnomes into the rushing stream and who knows what might have then befallen them? He had the presence of mind not to bark his delight and instead wagged his tail, stuck his tongue out and panted loudly. "Come, then!" said Albo, pleased at Roger's reaction, "There is rabbit for supper, and a place for you at our fireside can be made."

The gnomes' burrow was under the aforementioned ancient ash tree which was the queen of all the trees in the area. There were three entrances and four exits, which were used at different times of the year, depending on how high the vegetation grew around the roots of the tree. Inside was a veritable maze of passages which went uphill and downhill as well as round corners. The gnomes had tunnelled down through layers of sandstone and clay over the years, taking their time, and there was one entrance, ten yards from the tree, on the far side of the stream, big enough for Roger to wriggle inside. The entrance looked like a small cave where a fox might spend the night, but the back wall, which was solid, was set back further than it looked, and the opening into the gnome tunnel at the back went sideways, so that anyone who put his head into the cave could not see it.

"Come, Roger!" said Myshin, leading the way, "Good dog!" Roger sniffed, and could smell the warm, woolly smell of gnomes, and of rabbit stew. He left any fear he might have felt at the cave entrance and went in, following his nose. Albo waited a few seconds, scanning the outside to make sure they had not been observed, and followed Roger in.

It was a very special feast that awaited Roger, and one he never forgot, even in the terrible hours that followed his supper, when Percy caught up with him, and the gnomes caught up with Percy. He tore into his delicious leg of rabbit with such enthusiasm that the gnomes laughed, and Derwin exclaimed to the whole company: "What a day this has been! A day of anger and of celebration! A day for both black hats and yellow! Brothers, I am one with you!" and he drank a toast to the Yew Band in birch wine.

Chapter Forty

FURTHER ENLIGHTENMENT

Andrew Billett had not finished work in the Old Glasshouse. He was rather enjoying his potting up, and watching the changing light with its grey-blues and its lemon-yellows, through the windows of ancient glass that made the sky look like a moving ocean. He was also thinking about his employer, and how he had always assumed that Percy had a perfect life, and was happy. Being a thoughtful young man, Andrew was pondering the weirdness of life: not Nature, who had her own logic, but human life, the way the world was set up, what made sense and what didn't.

He often listened to his father and brother talking, and his mother chipping in, and it always seemed to be about how to make more money, and make the future of the family more secure. He also watched F5 patrolling the Brandston estate, their pistols on their hips, and had knocked many a nail into a fence or greenhouse in his time. All of this was to make people feel safer, and more in control. But Andrew didn't believe in security, nor did he believe in control. His best friend Carl, who was the safest motorcyclist in the world, had died in a head-on collision, killed by a driver who wasn't 'thinking bike' a few months before, and he'd seen hundred-year-old trees felled by a gale, and whole crops of vegetables ruined by infestations.

Andrew was reaching out for a different kind of reality: the kind that would really make sense; a roadmap that would help him find his place in the scheme of things. He was sure that it mattered a great deal what people did with their lives, and desperately wanted to get his right. It helped Andrew enormously when, shortly after he had begun his potting up, he received a visit from Pieter and Hans Ijf, two of the six Dutch cousins of the Brandston Yews. When he looked up from his pots to grab another handful of compost, there they were, sitting on an upturned bucket, their green trouser-clad legs dangling, watching him.

Bearing in mind that Andrew had now learnt about a dog's ability to communicate—if only on a basic level—with humans, it was perfect timing for the gnomes to reveal themselves to the young gardener. It was a knack they had, to pick the right moment. "Greetings!" said Pieter Ijf, and his brother Hans bowed. Andrew immediately said "Hi!" and bowed back. He wiped his earthy hands on his trousers while he waited for his heartbeat to slow down a little. He wasn't frightened, only surprised. He gazed fascinated at the gnomes, and noticed that Pieter's trousers had a tear, and a hole right over one knee. "I think I have something that belongs to you, Mr. Gnome," he said, taking the piece of green cloth he had found in the hedge from the shelf next to him and handing it over.

Pieter bowed: "Pieter Ijf and my brother Hans. We are of the Yew clan of the Gnome people; our burrow is not far. Thank you, Andrew Gardener," he said. Andrew was interested to hear a gnome speak, and with an accent he recognized as European, having been on cycling holidays in the Netherlands and southern Scandinavia. "So, they're not only real, but they do foreign travel. And there are more . . ." he said to himself. Out loud, he said, "You're welcome. Is there anything else I can do for you? A cup of herb tea?" The gnomes accepted his offer. Andrew picked up his thermos flask and suddenly realised he had no cups small enough for his guests. What should he do? He cast about him, scratching his head. "You seek suitable vessels?" asked Hans Ijf, "We carry our own. Make your cup, and gnomes will share."

Andrew made himself a cup of chamomile tea. The gnomes smelt it, and stretched their noses in his direction, making an "Aaammm!" sound. He set it down on the wooden crate he used as a table. The gnomes unclipped cups, which were made of a metal that looked like pewter, from their belts. They all waited for three minutes in silence. Then Pieter and Hans reached over and dipped their cups into the tea and took a sip. "Is it OK?" asked Andrew. "Andrew Gardener's tea is good!" pronounced Hans, while his brother nodded. Again, there was silence as the three enjoyed their tea.

Hans and Pieter put down their cups and looked up at Andrew expectantly. He too put down his cup, and sat leaning forward, to listen carefully to what his small visitors had to say. "You seek wisdom . . ." stated Pieter Ijf, and his brother added: " . . . although you are very young. When the young seek wisdom, there is hope for all." Andrew knew better than to ask what there might be hope *for*: he had been working it out himself. "Can you teach me to be wise?" he asked. "We can teach you. A man weaves his own wisdom out of knowledge and of the stumblings on his path," replied Hans. Andrew laughed out loud at the truth of this. The gnomes appeared to understand why he was laughing, for they smiled at each other.

It was almost dark when Pieter and Hans Ijf bowed and bid farewell to Andrew Billett, and a good half hour after they had left that he finally got up from his seat and went home. They had given him much to reflect on, as they had helped him pot up broad beans and sweet peas, as well as the more unusual seeds from his collection. He had not seen Percy Brandston come past on his return from his walk, but that was not unusual: there was more than one path on the Brandston estate; more than one way back from the meadow.

When Andrew Billett heard that his employer was dead the following night, he made no connection between the death and his visit from the Dutch gnome brothers, for the simple reason that the details of the murder were kept secret, and continued to be so. Estate staff were interviewed at length—some more than once—but no-one was arrested. The case was eventually put down to terrorism and all paperwork and evidence (apart from that which had been secreted by Chief Inspector Baird) put under lock and key in a maximum security vault.

By the time Andrew's daughter Branwen was thirty years old, the same age Andrew had been on the day of Percy's demise—and therefore of an age to be introduced to, and instructed by, the

Brandston gnomes herself—Andrew had built too close a relationship with the small people ever to feel able to tell her the truth.

It was Derwin Yew, by now a battle-scarred warrior with many a tale to tell around the camp-fire, who told Andrew the truth on his sixtieth birthday, while he rubbed calendula balm into the gardener's arthritic hands with incredible gentleness. "Sometimes people go too far," he said, a look of sorrow on his little, sunburnt face, "Gnomes and humans. We are learning never to do a thing that cannot be taken back, concerning life and death. Percy Brandston could have been instructed. His heart was not made of stone. In time, he might have received wisdom . . ."

Andrew could only agree with Derwin: "Sometimes, Brother Gnome, it is only by destroying that we learn to hold a thing as precious. Sometimes it is only by seeing the darkness in ourselves that we begin to realise how determinedly it must be fought and overcome. Percy had his life handed to him on a plate, like a good meal, and therefore never knew what it is to plough, to plant, to tend, to weed and water, to harvest and to cook. We gardeners are indeed fortunate, for we learn the value of every pea and raspberry we put into our mouths."

It was Branwen Billett who, at the age of thirty-three, first persuaded gnomes to begin procreating once more, after the terrible waters of the Third Great Flood of 2045 had subsided, and who set up the first Gnomeling nursery ever to be run by humans. Her father Andrew died in the flood, drowned as he attempted to save a colony of stranded gnomes near Canterbury, and a memorial was erected in the topiary garden of Brandston Manor to honour him.

Chapter Forty-One

Shopping Bags and Bathers

In the morning Tim was still groggy, and asked to be excused whatever it was his mother, sister and aunts had planned. Humphrey arrived at breakfast-time and offered to baby-sit the invalid. "Are you sure, Tim?" asked Marjory, "I can stay behind if you want me to." Tim grinned: "I'm sure Humphrey's more than capable of taking care of me," he said. Humphrey clapped him on the back: "I'll make sure you stay out of trouble, old chap!" he said. "In that case," said Elspeth, "You'll need a pair of handcuffs to attach him to this chair!"

"Where do you plan on going?" Tim asked. His Aunt Christine, busy wrapping sandwiches, replied: "We're off to the big city before the trip up north next week. My friend Maisie's going, and has offered us a lift. We're pretty much knee-deep in open air markets in Wellington at this time of year. There are the pop-up shops on Taranaki Wharf. They're exhibitions by local designers. And the Summer Market, which has stalls and crafts and stuff. They used to do them separately, but now they've combined them for people who can't manage weekdays. So it's girly shopping, maybe a museum, lunch, a wander round. We'll be back quite late."

Tim and Humphrey looked at each other. "I think photos will be enough," he said, "Doesn't sound like my kind of day. What are we doing, Humph?" "Oh, nothing much," replied his friend, being deliberately vague, "Bit of TV, maybe a little drive if you're up to it . . ." "Am I being suspicious, or are you two up to something?" said

Marjory. "Nothing we can't tell you about later, Mrs. Brandston," said Humphrey, "Trust me. Tim won't come to any harm with me around."

The women left for the short walk to Maisie's flat in town, and Humphrey walked Tim slowly round to his house, where they switched on Humphrey's desktop and began to research all the information Tim needed for immigration to New Zealand. Humphrey had made Tim promise to tell his mother his plan, if it turned out to be feasible. With Tim's skills in business, finance and IT, things certainly seemed promising. The two men downloaded and printed off pages of information. "I think, if I were you, I'd go for the temporary visa," said Humphrey, "Visiting and setting up permanently are two very different things. You don't want to lock yourself into something you might regret." Tim agreed: "And if I don't want to upset the family, it's a better approach too. Elspeth's already told me she wants me to do the research for both of us, but Mummy and Daddy are a different kettle of fish. We're the only offspring, remember . . ."

"It helps to have family already here," Humphrey pointed out, putting two cups of coffee and a tin of biscuits on a side table, "Time for a break, Tim, before you get crossed eyes." After coffee, Humphrey made sandwiches and pulled cold drinks from the fridge. "Right, Timmo," he said, "We're getting out of here!" He took Tim round to where the Landrover was parked. "Where are we going?" asked Tim. "I'm taking you to a place called Morrison's Bush," answered Humphrey, "It's a picnic place by the Ruamahanga River. If you're up for it, you can swim. It's a great spot to sit and think. Or not think, just look. Do us both good."

Meanwhile, the women had arrived in Wellington and parked near the quayside where the market was taking place. Elspeth wandered round on her own with a map, trying to get a feel for Wellington. The city already attracted her. It was neat, clean and fresh, but not 'dressed up'—she could tell that it had a rich cultural heritage and a love of the arts. "Perfect!" she said out loud, as her mother caught up with her, two shopping bags already in her hand.

"What's that, darling?" asked Marjory, leaning over the display that had caught her daughter's attention. "It's this blouse," said Elspeth, holding up a garment, "They've combined antique lace with paua shell buttons and silk embroidery, look!" "It's exquisite," agreed Marjory, "Your size?" "Oh, Mummy—I was just admiring—I wasn't dropping hints!" said Elspeth, mortified. "I so love the handbag you bought for me, darling! And I've been meaning to reciprocate. I've been looking for something beautiful enough for my little girl all morning," smiled Marjory, "And now I've found it!" Elspeth took one look at her mother's happy face and threw her arms round her: "Oh Mummy, I do love you!" she exclaimed. "Well, what a lovely sight!" exclaimed Christine, who had arrived on the scene.

Marjory paid for the blouse and had it wrapped in tissue paper. Zooie and Maisie had gone to get a table for drinks and snacks in an outdoor café nearby, and the women sat for an hour, showing their purchases to each other and talking about where they might go in the afternoon. There were museums nearby, but in the end they all agreed that the shops were so much fun they would carry on for an hour or two longer, and then head back up the road to Greytown to finish up in the antique and retro clothing shops before going for tapas at a popular restaurant called the Bar Salute, a favourite with Maisie.

Elspeth made sure she kept close to her mother as they continued their shopping. As soon as the others were out of earshot, she caught hold of her by the elbow and said, "Mummy, I want to talk to you. I've got something on my mind . . ." Marjory turned, pleased that her daughter wanted to confide in her. "Let me guess," she said, looking at Elspeth's face, which was glowing from the sun and wind, "You're about to tell me you want to stay on in New Zealand?" Elspeth blushed guiltily: "Mummy . . ." Marjory patted her daughter's arm. "It's all right, darling—really. I think, if I were in your shoes, that's exactly what I'd be thinking, too." Elspeth leaned close to her mother. "Thank you for being so understanding," she said.

Meanwhile, Humphrey and Tim had arrived at Morrison's Bush, where they parked and walked towards the river. It was a place of lush grass and ancient trees, with a wide, gravel beach and a smoothly flowing river. Trees on one side and hill slopes on the other made it a sheltered spot. A few families were picnicking on the beach, and Tim and Humphrey found a spot where fallen tree trunks lay by the water and spread out a blanket and their picnic. Tim leaned back against a trunk and breathed deeply. "Good call, old man," he said to Humphrey. "Eat!" said Humphrey, passing him a sandwich, "Then you're going for a swim. See if we can wash the nonsense out of you." "Yes sir!" said Tim, giving a mock salute, "As long as you can guarantee there are no crocodiles." "Idiot!" laughed Humphrey, passing him a can of fruit soda, "If you want to see crocs, you're in the wrong country!" "Just checking," said Tim, getting up, crossing the beach to the water and peering into the shallows.

The two parties arrived back at Feathers at exactly the same time: the women with their heaps of shopping bags, the men looking tousled and tanned. "Had a good day?" Humphrey asked Elspeth. "Very!" she replied, looking up at him with a relaxed smile, "How about you?" "Great!" said Humphrey, returning her smile, "I'm off to tidy up the house a bit, ready for you and Tim later. Take your time. I'm making whitebait fritters. They'll be ready at about eight." "Sounds wonderful!" said Elspeth with real enthusiasm and less self-conscientiousness than the last time they'd met, "See you shortly!"

Over Humphrey's delicious whitebait fritters, bread and butter, and Richie's colourful cocktails, which Tim was forced to consume without the addition of alcohol, despite his protests, the young people got to know one another better, and discussed Tim and Elspeth's plans to immigrate. It was decided that on the following day, which was the day they had all earmarked for laundry and packing for the trip up to Auckland, they would make time to sit down with Marjory and bring her up to speed. With their mother on their side, they would only have their father to deal with. And that, they knew, would be far from easy.

"Don't worry, Elsopeth," said Tim as he hugged his sister good night, "At least we'll be out from under his feet. Maybe he'll just think it's a brilliant idea." "I wouldn't be so sure, Tim," said Elspeth, shaking her head, "You know Daddy . . ."

Chapter Forty-Two

PERCY GETS A FRIGHT

The Lord of Brandston Manor trudged along, grumbling to himself as he followed the trail of Roger the Labrador. His brogues were beginning to take up the damp, and his toes were turning to ice. He was hungry and wanting his dinner. When his stomach rumbled, he almost turned back to the house, but stubbornness won over hunger and he continued until the soft earth and sprinkled gravel gave way to tree roots and leaf litter.

Percy knew this part of his estate well. As a boy, he had come here with his elder brother Henry, who had died as a result of a fall from a tree at the age of twelve, leaving Percy to carry the weight of the family's expectations alone. The tree in question had been cut down, its roots dug out and the hole filled in. Undergrowth had covered the spot, but Percy still felt a shiver up his spine whenever he was passing it. It was to his right. Images of Henry, lying pale and still, his neck twisted, his head at an unnatural angle, his arms flung outwards, flashed across his inner eye. He slashed at some brambles with his riding crop and stomped towards the stream, looking right and left for signs of his dog.

There were Roger's footprints, clearly visible in the soft, wet mud at the stream's edge. Percy bent to examine them. It seemed Roger had come here for a drink of water and then turned east. Percy followed the tracks. Other tracks were also there: those of small feet in boots. Percy suddenly remembered the little old man in the hedge, whose appearance he had dismissed as impossible. "Midgets?" he said out loud, then "Impossible!" again.

Just then, he heard the sound of voices whispering, to his left, some yards off. There was no-one to be seen. "Damn it!" said Percy loudly, "This is a waste of my time! Roger, you useless animal, come home now or you can rot, for all I care!" The whispering stopped suddenly. Now Percy was beginning to feel spooked. He was experiencing what the ancients called 'panic'—the presence of the supernatural in a wild place, an unseen power, an unseen threat. He harrumphed, hesitated, and finally turned on his heels and began to walk fast—an almost-run—back to the house.

But that was by no means the end of it for Percy. The watching gnomes—two Ijfs—went smartly back to the burrow and reported that the *naaaffff manni* (very bad man) had gone, but that they feared he would return later, possibly with reinforcements. They were correct as to the first, but incorrect as to the second, for Percy kept his intentions to himself when he spoke to his household staff on his return. He took a hot shower, dressed in one of his Harris tweed suits, a warm shirt, an Arran sweater, thick socks and a fresh pair of brogues, and sat down to his dinner.

He was an hour late, which caused the household staff no small degree of surprise, for their master loved his food and had always been in the dining-room in good time to lift each dish cover and have what the butler and footman called 'a good stir and sniff' before sitting down. When, the following day, investigating agents asked the staff if Percy had behaved any differently on the day of his murder, they cited this observation, along with several others: he had stormed into the house in an angry state, muttering curses under his breath; he had dressed, after his shower, in warm outdoor clothing instead of his usual Sunday evening attire of slacks, polo shirt, jacket and loafers; and he had forgotten to telephone his wife and children, who were holidaying with relatives in New Zealand.

He had suddenly got up from the table and gone to the library telephone to make a call during the first course, but the call had been to Marcus Pripson, the man in charge of security. Was that unusual? Not really. Mr. Brandston often rang the man, just to check F5 were doing their job. None of the staff had heard what was said: the doors were too thick when closed. "The dog's missing," said one of the housemaids, who was rather fond of Roger. "That's unusual. Mr. Brandston always came back to the house via the back kitchen door and dropped Roger off to have a rub down and his supper."

Percy finished his dinner with unaccustomed haste, which the staff put down to his late start. He went into the library, took a cigar and let himself out of the French windows, which gave onto the terrace. In ten minutes he was through the topiary garden and the vegetable garden. He saw two security guards and waved to them as if nothing was the matter. He had of course told Marcus Pripson he was going out for a stroll after dinner: "Nothing the matter," he had told his security chief, "Just fancy a bit more exercise." When MI5 questioned Pripson, he told them he knew nothing about a lost dog, and couldn't tell them whether his employer had gone out looking for Roger. "None of my business what the gentry do after dark," he said, his face a mask of inscrutability, "I'm just here to make sure they're safe while they do what they do."

Percy crossed the meadow and went under the trees to begin his search at the stream, where he had found the footprints. They had gone. "That's odd!" he remarked. The gnomes had, of course, been back to cover their tracks, but Percy remembered the direction in which the prints had led, and turned east, shining a torch along the path and to either side. To his left was the line of tall trees, to his right the stream, which flowed along a wide ditch, beyond which ran the estate's boundary wall. The ditch was at least twelve feet wide in places with, here and there, a kind of beach, where he and Henry had sat and fished for tiddlers, and caught newts in small fishing-nets.

All was quiet, except for the sighing of the wind, the rattling of twigs, and the soft, sweeping sound of dry leaves carried along. It was the dark of the moon, and without a torch, Percy would not have found his way without tripping. His feeling of panic returned, bringing acid into his mouth. He stopped and spat on the ground, something his father had told him gentlemen never do, and which he enjoyed when he was alone, as a small act of disobedience. "Roger! Here, dog!" he shouted, but there was no response: no sudden bark, no sound of panting. He suddenly felt incredibly tired. He was now at a bend in the stream, where it ran on the far side of the ditch. On his side of the ditch, there was a gentle slope down to a fallen log. He stepped off the path, half slid down the slope and went to sit on the log.

He would have turned and run for home if he had known what now awaited him. He put his torch beside him on the log and reached into his pocket for his cigar. As soon as he had lit his cigar and taken a puff, there was a rustling sound all around him, and the sound of breathing in his ears. Percy picked up his torch and shone it around in terror, expecting to see khaki-clad, dreadlock-headed anarchists, or sword-wielding ninjas in Spandex and head-bands surrounding him. The sight that met his eyes left him dumb-struck. To his right, to his left, behind him and in front of him were what looked like garden gnomes, except that they were moving. They breathed, they shifted from foot to foot, and they glared at him. And instead of the usual variety of clothing worn by garden gnomes, they were all dressed in dark green and wore black hats. Every single one had a weapon in his hand: an axe, a sword, a spear. Those furthest away carried bows and arrows. His first reaction, once he had managed to take a breath, was to laugh. It was a loud, hysterical laugh that went on and on . . .

Chapter Forty-Three

WEDDING PLANS

"We should consult the gnomes, I think, don't you? A register office wedding is fine, but I think we want something more," Ann-Marie said to her fiancé, as they sat at Archie's kitchen table with a brand new notebook between them. The notebook was white with silver lettering: Wedding Planner, the cover read. It was patterned all over with tiny silver hearts and horseshoes.

The happy couple had already begun to make a list of things to do. The planner was helpful. It was divided into sections: One Year to Go, Six Months to Go, and so on, right up to On Your Big Day. The wedding was nowhere near as far ahead as a year, but the sections were useful. Each had a list of suggestions: order flowers and stationery, book hair appointments, manicure. A separate section at the back was entitled After the Event and had a list of reminders for items such as writing to thank guests and those who had sent gifts. Although nine out of ten items seemed to apply to the bride, it all looked frighteningly complicated to Archie. He was relieved when Ann-Marie suggested talking to Alevin and the others.

"You and me, we're neither of us fussy or ostentatious," continued Ann-Marie, taking Archie's hand across the table, "At the end of the day, it's all about you and me, and love, and our family and friends. Not making a big splash. But it should be somehow unique." "Just what I was thinking, my darling," replied Archie, smiling, "I was actually thinking, what about having the reception right here? There are quite a few of our neighbours who can't go far—not even to the shops—but they could come along for a cup of tea and a slice of cake if we had it in the common-room." "Oh, Archie," exclaimed Ann-Marie, "What a great idea! It's been on my mind for days, how to make people feel comfortable. There are so many we know who are scratching around for money to cover electricity and gas and food. If we keep it simple, we can save them a whole load of embarrassment." "I like your thinking," said Archie, "So how about asking our guests to give a plant for the garden, instead of the usual stuff. We've got two of everything, like toasters and furniture. It's not like we're going to need anything for the home . . ."

The only big decision the pair had had to make was in which flat they would live, once they were married. After some discussion, they had settled on Ann-Marie's, simply because it was lower down the building, and easier if—as frequently happened—the lift broke down. They had already informed the local authority of their decision, and Archie had begun to sort out the items he would take with him from the items he would not need. Ann-Marie had begun to put her unwanted items into boxes too. The committee had planned a Bring and Buy sale a fortnight before the wedding, so that nothing would go to waste.

The visit to the Register Office had taken place, paperwork had passed inspection, the fees had been paid and the date booked. They had carefully calculated how much money they had in the wedding budget. Ann-Marie had managed to find a hotel nearby that was offering a special deal: three nights for two with full board, for what seemed a ridiculously low price, and she had enough in her savings to cover it, as well as taxis to and from the hotel, so "Book Your Honeymoon" was already ticked off the list.

The wedding was due to take place in June, four months away, the month of both Ann-Marie's and Archie's birthdays. This would mean the garden could be used, as well as the indoor space, for the reception. "The gnomes will take care of the weather," said Archie, "Syd Willow knows good weather spells." "Yes," agreed Ann-Marie, "And the Rowans will make sure the garden gets a sprinkle of gnome dust so it looks perfect. I always wondered why it looks so alive compared to other gardens around, until they explained to me how they do it. Now, about your stag party . . ."

It was on the following evening that Alevin, Ned and Syd came visiting. "Gnomes are in conference tonight," said Alevin, pulling on his beard so hard, they feared he would soon have no whiskers left, "We must not tarry. There has been a Dire Event at Brandston, and anger has been unleashed." "I'm so sorry," whispered Ann-Marie, making a space on the sofa beside her for Syd, who liked to sit close to her, "I wish we could have prevented it . . ." Alevin stretched out a hand towards her, palm facing her: "Have no regrets!" he said gravely, "Past is past. We must speak of the future. We must reach out with the eyes of our minds and see the possible paths of its unfolding. And we must seek the counsel of the Sacred Nine, so that each may see his own path ahead. One step at a time is enough."

"I understand," answered Archie, "When you are at liberty, we wish only to ask for your counsel regarding our wedding. We wish a wedding that has . . . ," Archie searched carefully for the right words: "That has . . . both simplicity and great depth. Like our love." "Gnomes understand," said Syd, "Look to the ancients of our land, and you will find the answers you need." "Of course!" exclaimed Ann-Marie, "You are so clever!" Archie looked at her, a little puzzled. "It's all right, darling, I'll explain later," she said.

Archie stood and bowed to Alevin: "Alevin Yew and his ibni are wise," he said, pulling on his own chin, which was however clean-shaven, "Ann-Marie and I will bend our prayers in your direction. My heart tells me you will know what to do." "Gnomes thank you!" said Ned, hopping down from the armchair, along with his fellow gnomes, and lining up for the farewell bow: "Flabbbbaaarrray! May the Great Mother line your pockets with joy!" The gnomes stretched out their word of farewell more than they had ever done before. Ann-Marie's eyes filled with tears at the tenderness of it. She felt the strength of the attachment between herself and the small people like an umbilicus painfully stretched as they prepared to leave. "May the Great Mother lavish Her blessings on the Gnomish people!" she cried out. They bowed until the tips of their hats were touching the carpet, and in a flash, they were gone.

"How do they do that vanishing thing?" said Archie, scratching his head, "I wish I could do that!" "Magic, my love," answered Ann-Marie, putting her arms around her beloved, "And you have your own kind of magic, you know!" There was a long, tender kiss, and the pair went back to their wedding plans.

The clue given to the couple by Syd Willow proved to be the answer to all their questions. They powered up Ann-Marie's laptop, searched online for traditional weddings and immediately found an ancient Celtic ceremony called a hand-fasting, complete with vows, and a drinking ritual involving a two-handled cup. It was clear to both that this was indeed both simple and powerful. "Now," said Ann-Marie, as they kissed good night at her front door, "All I have to do is find a frock!" "Darling," whispered Archie, his soft breath on her flushed face, "You'd look beautiful in a bin-liner!" "Thank you for that," laughed Ann-Marie, giving his bottom a squeeze, "But I fully intend to knock you off your feet. Now run along, and leave me to do the kinds of things that brides have to do. I'll see you in the morning."

Archie opened the door and stepped out onto the landing. "I feel so happy I could burst!" were his parting words as he pressed the button to call the lift. "Me too!" said Ann-Marie, "Me too!" The lift doors opened and Archie did a double-take. Carol Manley was in the lift, swaying slightly. "Evening, Archie!" she slurred. Archie and Ann-Marie rolled their eyes at each other. "Be nice!" whispered Ann-Marie. The lift doors closed, but as it went up, she distinctly heard Archie say: "Evening, Carol. And how are you this fine evening?" "Well done, Archie," said Ann-Marie, as she locked her door for the night, "Well done!"

Chapter Forty-Four

In Which There is Overwhelming Provocation

Percy sat frozen, a cold sweat forming all over his body, and his breath coming in ragged pants interspersed with nervous giggles. "I must be going mad!" he thought to himself, and: "I'm in danger!" His hand went to his pocket and touched his mobile phone, but he drew it out again. Not much point calling security if he was having an hallucination. It was the second episode in one day. If he admitted this to anyone, he would be locked up. The Cabinet already had two ministers who experienced psychotic episodes, and the Prime Minister would certainly feel that three was one too many. His career would be down the drain, and he might never see home again.

He looked to his right. The gnome nearest to him, a skinny fellow with a grizzled beard and an axe in his hand, looked as though he was about to attack. The little chap, who was perching lower down the log so that his head was at the same height as Percy's, was on the balls of his feet and leaning towards him. Percy thought hard: what if he stuck out an elbow and knocked him down? What would happen? Would it scare them all away? Or would it make matters worse?

As he was pondering his options, there was movement on the far side of the stream and he suddenly caught sight of Roger, who had emerged from the shadows into the torch-light, and proceeded to sit between two grim-looking longbow-carrying gnomes, his tail thumping the ground. Before he could think, Percy called out:

"Roger!" and jumped to his feet. The dog opened his mouth in a wide grin, showing his teeth. Percy grabbed the torch and shone it straight at Roger. The dog's collar and lead were gone, he noticed immediately. Roger was dazzled by the light, and ducked his head. The three gnomes who stood between Percy and the stream moved to the sides as the man stepped closer to the water. "Roger! Here! To me!" shouted Percy. He could hear his own voice, and it sounded peevish. Roger did not move.

Now Percy was in the centre of a ring of gnomes, and they were all moving closer. He realised with horror that he was not hallucinating: this was really happening, and he knew this because two of the gnomes behind him were whispering to each other and scuffing their boots. He was sure that off-stage sounds such as these were not usually part of a delusion. "Roger!" he called out, one last time. Then he stepped backwards in the direction of the whispers and scuffing sounds. "I could squash one of them and make it look like an accident," he thought to himself. Sure enough, there was a sudden yelp of pain, and the sounds of a fall, and of something bumping against the log. "Albo!" cried the other gnome behind him.

Percy smiled a nasty smile and turned. He shone the torch towards the ground, and there lay one gnome, his head against the log and his little face pale with pain. He was clutching his foot, which was twisted to one side. His companion was kneeling beside him, wringing his hands. Another gnome ran up, brandishing a sword in his hand and took up the *en garde* stance, the tip of his weapon pointed at Percy's ankle: "Get back, you!" shouted Percy, and kicked out hard at the attacking gnome, managing to get a toe into his stomach, so that the gnome flew backwards and landed in a holly bush. The little fellow yelled "Ow!" as he slithered through the prickly branches and fell to the ground with a thump.

Roger howled as all hell broke loose. Percy turned this way and that, shining the torch on the bushes, the water, the log, the trees, as from every direction there came screams of rage and the sounds of rushing feet. His hand went to his pocket where it found, not his phone but his Swiss army knife, which he had not realised was still there. "Saved!" he thought, as he opened it with one swift movement and began to stab wildly in all directions. But he was stabbing too high in his panic. The gnomes closed in on him, and he felt pain in his ankles and calves as they began to bite him. "They're *biting* me!" he thought. This was something he had not expected. "Lay off!" he shouted, dropping his torch and stumbling around in the darkness, "You little bastards!"

Suddenly, Percy tripped over a part of the log that was sticking out, and down he went, full-length in the mud, gravel and leaf litter. His knife flew out of his hand as he landed. He lay there winded on his stomach, the taste of regurgitated apple pie and horseradish sauce in his mouth, his head turned to the left, so that he could see Roger still sitting calmly on the far side of the stream, still grinning, still unmoving. "Dog . . ." he mouthed, no breath in him to make a sound.

The gnomes encircled Percy, growling in their anger and hatred. There seemed to be more and more of them, from the sounds they were making. He realised he had made the classic mistake of underestimating the enemy. "Julius Caesar's warning . . ." he thought vaguely as he lay as still as he could, hoping the horrible little people would go away. He recollected it now. It wasn't 'never underestimate the enemy': it was 'never underestimate stupid people in large groups'. Well, the gnomes were far from stupid, it seemed. They had come out at him armed to the teeth and prepared to bring him down. Perhaps negotiating was still an option?

"Oops, sorry . . ." he said, his throat still tight and sore, so that he had to force his words out, "Misunderstanding . . . Panicked . . ." He lifted his head an inch or two and eyeballed the thin, grizzly-bearded gnome, who was standing by his head. The gnome bent closer until his face was six inches from Percy's. "You lie, naaaafffff manni!" he hissed. At this, hysteria returned to Percy, and he giggled and attempted to humour the gnome: "Don't know about 'naff', but you're absolutely correct about the first bit, old chap!" he said, beginning to try and get himself up on his elbows, "Made my living at it!"

Percy did not at first realise how badly he was injured, for the bites—as well as the tiny cuts from axes and swords—were small, and the pain in his chest and stomach from being winded was causing him the most obvious discomfort. He made it up onto his elbows, and began to roll slowly, hoping to get onto his side, curl, get to his knees and then stand. This, however, was not going to be allowed. The gnomes wanted him low down, where they could more easily control his movements. As he rolled onto his right hip, several pairs of arms pushed on the arm that was uppermost, and he flopped instead onto his back. He lay looking up at almost complete darkness. A few stars twinkled overhead. He turned his head to left and right, and saw dozens of pairs of eyes, glowing green, unblinking, as they looked down at him.

"Any chance of negotiating a peace treaty?" Percy asked in a feeble voice, "Only, I have a phone in my pocket that gives me a direct line to the Foreign Secretary . . ." "Foreign? Foreign?" whispered the gnomes to one another, "What is 'foreign'?" There was some muttering in a language Percy did not understand, and thought he had never heard before. "I take it you people are from overseas," remarked Percy, rubbing his bruised stomach. The grizzly-bearded gnome shook his head at Percy: "There is but one land and one sea," he said, as if speaking to a child who is slow to learn, "And all belong to the Great Mother. It is only humans who divide and make barriers. This is very stupid talk, Percy Brandston, for one who lies on his back!" Another gnome, shorter and Titian-haired, stepped forward: "He is one who *lies* on both back and front!" he said, and a hundred gnomes laughed bitterly at his joke.

"What do you want me to say?" asked Percy, creeping terror and pain now having a serious effect on his ability to think, the initial shock having worn off. "Do you not understand anything?!" exclaimed the Titian-haired gnome, who carried an axe whose blade looked so sharp, Percy thought it could probably slice through brick, "You wish us to tell you what to say. Then you will say it, but it will mean nothing, for it will not come from your heart! Naaaaffffff manni!

Wake up and bring your head!" Percy understood 'bring your head' very well. He tried to pull himself together, but he felt cold, damp and terrified, and his brain felt as if it had run out of battery power. "Give me back my dog and I will go home," pleaded Percy, "I won't tell anyone what you've done, I promise!"

There was a long pause, full of the rustling sounds of angry, small people who have many things to say, but are not saying them. At length, an imposing-looking gnome with chiselled features and a Roman nose came into the light, and stood, arms akimbo, in front of the other two. "I am Constant Yew," he said, in a voice that rumbled like an old mill wheel, "Your dog, Roger of Brandston, belongs to himself. He has chosen to stay with gnomes. Gnomes do not smack him on the nose. Gnomes do not beat him with sticks. Gnomes do not leave him out in the cold and forget him. Gnomes do not call him *naaff awund!* He is Roger, Friend of Gnomes. You will not go home. You cannot be trusted to keep mouth shut."

Fingers of ice crept into Percy Brandston's blood and froze it in his veins. He found he could not move his legs. So they were going to kill him. His voice came out faint and far away: "You can't do that to me! I have important friends, powerful friends! They'll come and root out the whole, sorry, rat's nest of you! Let me go!" "He speaks threat, and there is no peace in him," said Derwin Yew, leaning over Percy and searching his eyes for any sign of remorse, "He has hurt Roger, he has hurt gnomes, he insults rats, he kills trees, he steals the eggs of birds . . . No doubt he has hurt many of his kind. In his soul, he is a small stone. He will die easily, for he has little life in him."

There was a murmured agreement from the four or five bands of gnomes who encircled Percy's prone body. Had he been able to see them all, in full knowledge of—and respect for—their traditions, he would have understood that his evil deeds had brought about the largest gathering of gnomes that had taken place in England since the mid-twentieth century, when they had banded together to cleanse and heal, by their magic, a countryside ravaged by war. All of the Sacred Nine were represented, and a few more besides: Rowans and Alders,

Willows and Birches, Oaks and Hollies had come together. And Percy was only the first of many humans on the watch list of those they had now decided to waylay and bring to justice.

He should by now have been getting to grips with the reality that confronted him, but Percy had never really connected with the world around him. He believed—and had always believed—in the "fill the Earth and subdue it" approach, which had taught him that everyone and everything around him was there to be taken and used. Only Marjory had ever truly touched his heart, and even then, if she had not been suitable wife material, he would not have hesitated to take her and use her too. His daughter and son, for whom he felt mild affection, were a means to an end: to ensure the continuance of the bloodline of the Brandstons. Even now, lying on his back, bleeding into the ground, he thought only of himself.

"You're not fighting fair!" he whispered, as he made one last, pathetic, effort to raise himself from the ground, "You little bastards!" "What ith thith 'bar thtardth' he callth uth?" asked a blonde gnome, who was among the group who had rescued the gnome Percy had kicked into the holly bush and ministered, unseen, to his bruises and scratches. He reached into his pocket and brought out a set of wooden false teeth, which he inserted into his mouth. "What is 'bar stards'?" he asked again, climbing on Percy's chest and prodding him in the nose with a spear.

Percy looked at the spear, and saw that the head was made of beaten silver. "I bet they've got hoards of precious metals. Could have made useful allies . . ." he thought. "Bring your head and answer!" insisted the blonde gnome, prodding him this time in each earlobe, "Gnomes are waiting!"

Percy thought of making something up, but something about the way the gnomes were staring at him told him they could detect lies very easily. Perhaps they would respect him if he showed a little more courage? He rallied the last of his strength. "It means," he said, puffing out his chest—which hurt quite a bit—"People whose mother and father were not married when they made them! Stick that in your pipe and smoke it, Mr. Gnome!" A ripple of shock and anger ran round the assembled gnome army. "All gnomes are married to the Great Mother!" shouted Derwin Yew, "And our pipes are sacred! Enough of the insults of this naaaaaafffffff manni!" Silence fell and a long minute passed. Then, while a million stars and one dog looked on, a hundred small bodies hurled themselves at Percy Brandston. Seconds later, he was no more.

Chapter Forty-Five

A DAY OF LOVE

The tenants of Eden Tower and Paradise Tower awoke to sunshine and warmth. Summer had arrived in all her pristine finery. The garden was aglow with colour. The men had been working all week, planting and watering, re-staining benches, hanging solar lights from every tree and bush, and putting up gazebos for the wedding guests. The scent of roses, lavender and wallflowers reached halfway up the buildings, and most balcony doors had been left open all night.

Ann-Marie had not expected to be able to sleep, but tiredness had won over excitement, and she woke at five o'clock feeling full of energy. As she opened her eyes, she thought of Archie, her fiancé, soon to become her husband, and her heart swelled with joy and gratitude. "My Archie!" she whispered, and stretched her warm limbs under the covers, wiggling her toes. She lay, enjoying her delight, for a few minutes, then got out of bed and put on her dressing-gown. "Tea!" she said out loud.

Meanwhile, three floors above her, Archie also woke and looked around him at the few boxes and two suitcases that remained, at his wedding suit hanging on the door under its plastic cover, and at the heap of gifts, wrapped in silver, blue and white paper, lying in the corner. "Oh my darling, oh my darling, oh my daaaarling Ann-Marie!" he sang, as he unzipped his sleeping-bag and sprang up from the camp-bed he had been sleeping on. Five minutes later, he was directly above Ann-Marie, sipping his coffee. He blew a kiss through the floor, guessing she was at her kitchen table, drinking her tea.

Down in the common-room, people were already cleaning the kitchen and putting up decorations. The committee—whose number had now swelled to fifteen including regular volunteers—had been at work since four o'clock, and a local balloon company was arriving to put up arches and standing displays in pale blue and white. Carol and Evie were among the first to pick up the buckets of white roses and marguerites, blue alyssums and hydrangeas collected from a local florist and begin to arrange them in the silver vases hired for the occasion. The women had been at Ann-Marie's the previous evening, eating pizza and giving the bride last-minute beauty treatments. As they had left Ann-Marie's flat, Carol had given her a genuine hug: "See you in the morning!" she'd said, smiling warmly, "And thank you . . ." Ann-Marie had kissed her on the cheek. "For what?" she'd asked, then, seeing that Carol was blushing and searching for something to say, she'd added hastily, "It's all water under the bridge. I'm glad we're friends. Thank *you* for coming!"

Archie had had his stag party the previous weekend: a trip to the bowling alley down the road, followed by a curry. Ann-Marie had been highly amused to find him at her door at midnight, looking very merry and smelling of spices. "This is the first time I've ever had to put you to bed!" she'd remarked, as she'd pulled off his shoes, socks, trousers and shirt and covered him up. "I like it!" he'd giggled, as he'd pulled her in after him, protesting that he'd better not make a habit of it. That was the last night they'd spent together before they went off on their honeymoon. Ann-Marie had been strict about this: "I'll need a week without your snoring if I'm going to look my best!" she'd told him. Archie had been more amused than crestfallen. They both snored, and in fact found each other's snoring reassuring. They both hoped that would last.

At nine-thirty sharp, Archie, scrubbed bright pink, clean-shaven and looking dapper in his grey pinstripe, white shirt and sky-blue tie, went downstairs in the lift, patting his pockets for the umpteenth time to make sure he had the rings. Ann-Marie, who was tidying her hall, ready for the arrival of the bridesmaids, heard the lift go down, and

Archie singing 'I'm getting married in the morning' from 'Pygmalion'. She laughed. At nine thirty-eight the lift came up and stopped at Ann-Marie's floor. Out tumbled the bridesmaids, Archie's daughter Bryony and three cousins—wearing jeans, scarves tied over their hair and carrying their dresses and shoes in oversized carrier bags. Evie had delivered the bouquets upstairs and stopped for a cup of tea with Ann-Marie, and to make her some toast. She was feeling a little queasy.

Everyone in the foyer of the Register Office—staff and guests at other weddings—turned to look when the bride and bridesmaids arrived, lighting up the room with their smiles. The bride was resplendent in a three-quarter length electric blue wrap dress, patterned with silver butterflies, and silver sandals. The bridesmaids' dresses were shimmering silver sheaths. Little Katie, Bryony's daughter, carried a basket of alyssums and marguerites.

All but the receptionist, who had checked Archie and his groom's-men in, had assumed he was a father-of-the-bride, and whispers went round when Ann-Marie walked up to Archie and gave him a resounding kiss. "Ooh! Isn't that lovely?" said three old ladies, whose great-niece was getting married. "Gives you hope, don't it?" said two uncles-of-brides, who had been standing near the door, speculating as to whether they could sneak out for a quick smoke before their respective wedding parties arrived.

The ceremony went by in a flash, and at last Archie and Ann-Marie were stepping out of the taxi in front of the common-room door. "Now the real wedding begins!" whispered Archie to his bride. The nurseryman from whom guests had been ordering plants for several weeks, had made a gorgeous display of rosebushes, apple-trees, summer-flowering bulbs and perennial shrubs either side of the doorway, and the fortunate couple stopped to admire them before ducking under the balloon arch and into the room. Archie picked a white rose and tucked it behind Ann-Marie's ear.

A cheer went up from the guests, who had packed into the space and spent the morning getting to know one another. Someone pressed glasses of champagne into the hands of the guests of honour, and a deep voice from the back of the room, which Archie recognized as coming from Bill, the pleasant young man to whom Bryony had at long last given her heart, called out: "A toast to the bride and groom! I give you Mr. and Mrs. Archibald Andrew Elijah Prescott!" There were a few amused giggles, along with the response. Most of the guests had never heard Archie's surname, let alone his middle names.

Once everyone had had a chance to sample the delicious food, half of which had been prepared by the committee, and half brought along by guests, and to take photographs, Bill announced that the bride and groom would now make their wedding vows and share the wedding cup. This part of the day had not been kept secret: Archie and Ann-Marie had wanted everyone to understand why they were reviving ancient traditions. Not that they told anyone the idea had come from the gnomes—nobody else had as yet been let in on that particular secret—but it had all been explained at the stag and hen parties, and to the committee at the last meeting before the wedding.

Archie and Ann-Marie stood in a space in the centre of the room, holding hands and speaking their vows in ardent tones that sounded so unlike their usual voices, and so powerful and mysterious, that people found themselves trembling:

> "You cannot possess me for I belong to myself,
> But from this day forward, I give you that which is mine to give.
> You cannot command me for I am a free person,
> But I shall serve you in those ways you require,
> And the honeycomb will taste sweeter coming from my hand.
> I pledge to you that yours will be the name I cry aloud in the night,
> And the eyes into which I smile in the morning.
> I pledge to you the first bite of my meat
> And the first drink from my cup.
> I pledge to you my living and my dying, each equally in your care.
> I shall be a shield for your back and you for mine

I shall not slander you, nor you me: I shall honour you above all others, And when we quarrel, we shall do so in private And tell no strangers our grievances.
This is my wedding vow to you: this is the marriage of equals."

Bryony came forward with the two-handled cup or *quaich*. It was not the traditional pewter or silver: either would have been beyond their means. It was a two-handled coffee mug bought from a popular chain of coffee-houses. But it was filled to the brim not with coffee but whisky, the drink of the Celts who had first recorded the vows Archie and Ann-Marie had exchanged. Ronald Greeley had provided the whisky: a smokey, fruit-and-nutty, full-bodied Islay. Archie held the cup to Ann-Marie's lips, and she let it fill her mouth for good luck. She licked her lips slowly, looking at Archie, who blushed. A few guests saw this exchange and nudged each other. Archie passed the cup to Ann-Marie. It was his turn, and with a huge grin all round, he covered her hands with his, tipped up the cup and drained it. There were loud cheers and applause.

During the afternoon, speeches were made by at least a dozen people, and everyone came up to the microphone to sing along to Viktor's cousin Prokop's karaoke. Neighbours who had never ventured into the common-room gathered outside the door, and Ann-Marie asked Banton, who preferred to be out in the sun, to encourage people to come in for food and a drink. Some went away at first, but returned with contributions to the buffet, and joined in. Those who were too shy, or who didn't feel they had done enough to merit a place at the feast brought a drink and sat on chairs in the garden.

At ten-thirty in the evening, the newly-weds' taxi drew up in the car park. Archie went to find Ann-Marie, who had disappeared to powder her nose and check that everything was switched off in her flat. "Don't change out of that dress!" Archie had instructed her, "You look so lovely in it, you should wear it every day!" They had already been up earlier to say farewell to the gnomes. "Onnnnnea! Good luck!" the gnomes cried as they bowed to their friends. Then,

one by one, they had approached to shake hands for the very first
time. Archie and Ann-Marie had been touched by this: the first real
physical contact they had had with the gnomes. "Their little hands
are rough, but warm—almost hot to the touch!" remarked Ann-Marie
after their visitors had left. "I think maybe that's how they show love.
The warmth . . ." replied Archie, gathering his bride into an embrace
almost as warm as the gnomes' hands, once they were in the lift and on
their way back down to the party.

When the couple had left, waving and blowing kisses until they
were out of sight, the guests went inside and began to pass round cups
of tea and coffee. It had been a remarkable day. Neighbours who had
never met before stayed until midnight to get to know one another
better, and everyone helped tidy up, and take flowers, balloons, gifts
and the best of the leftover food up to Ann-Marie's, to greet the
couple on their return. No-one had a bad word to say about Archie
or Ann-Marie, or about the arrangements. "I'm going to ask them for
a copy of what they said to each other and send it to our Vicar," said
Enid, who had managed to get downstairs in a wheelchair, with Carol's
help, "They should use those words at the church."

At the hotel, Archie and Ann-Marie checked into their room,
dropped their bags and collapsed onto their huge double bed. They
lay side by side, looking up at the ceiling with its crystal chandelier
and stucco cherubs. "Well!" said Archie. Ann-Marie waited for him
to continue, but he was lost for words. Ann-Marie turned to face him
and traced the line of his cheek and jaw with her finger. "How fine you
are to me!" she said, quoting the line from the film 'Rob Roy'. Archie's
eyes misted over. "And how much finer are *you* to *me*!" he said in a
hushed voice, as he reached up to stroke her hair, which was coming
loose from its bun. He felt behind her head and began to pull out
hairpins, tossing them one by one onto the bedside table. As each pin
fell, Ann-Marie moved closer until, as the last one was gently tugged
away and her hair fell over his face, their lips touched.

And so, 'tired but happy' as the saying goes, Archie and Ann-Marie
Prescott began the first night of married life. Back in their snug

burrow, Norman and friends toasted them in birch wine, ate a rather savoury pigeon stew, smoked a pipeful or two, and intoned the ancient song that gnomes sing when they join with their sacred tree to make Gnomelings:

> *"Great Mother, I call upon you to come and bless this coupling! Great Mother, let your sacred sap flow from the heartwood! Great Mother, let me be one with you! Great Mother, let our offspring be pure!"*

That night, Archie and Ann-Marie dreamt they were sitting in a gnome burrow, surrounded by rush-lights, singing with the gnomes. And when they woke the following morning, roused by the sound of room service knocking on the door with their breakfast tray, they compared notes, and found they could still remember the words of the song . . .

Chapter Forty-Six

BAD NEWS

Marjory and her children agreed a plan for Elspeth and Tim's move from England to New Zealand towards the end of the English summer. Application papers were tucked inside suitcases. All that remained was to sit down with Percy and—having apologized for not telling him sooner—somehow persuade him that he must both approve and support his children's decision. Elspeth and Tim had sat down with a notebook and listed the positives, from their father's point of view. "Number one has to be saving money," said Tim. "Number two, less wear and tear on the old Pater's nerves!" Elspeth contributed.

In five minutes, over coffee in the kitchen at Huruhuru, they had a list of twenty arguments: all of them rational, and most of them appealing to Percy Brandston's overwhelming concern for financial security. Elspeth had received an offer of a job in one of the antique shops in Greytown. She had emailed people she knew from the trade in England to send references, and the owner of the shop had been impressed. There was a possibility of a partnership in the near future, if all went well.

Tim had three job offers to choose from. The demise of his business had not got in the way of his success, it seemed—indeed, the people who had interviewed him had commended his courage, unlike his father, who had been disappointed in him. The only downside brother and sister could see was that all the jobs were in Auckland. "Never mind," Elspeth reassured Tim, "Humphrey has lots of friends up there. You met most of them on our volcano trip, and they liked you as much as you like them . . ." "Yes," agreed her brother, "They're a pretty cool lot. I'll have to work on my 'cool', but not one of them made fun of my accent or my strange English ways, and that's pretty amazing." "Absolutely! And we'll both be able to afford decent cars, so seeing each other won't be a problem most of the year," said Elspeth, closing up the notebook and relaxing back in her chair.

"Where's Mummy?" Tim was just about to ask, when Zooie hurried into the kitchen, out of breath. "There's a limo pulled up outside!" she said, almost shouting with excitement, "A real, honest-to-God, live limo! Is Humphrey taking you on a special date, Elsopeth?" Elspeth blushed crimson. "No, that's to . . ." She clapped a hand over her mouth. Tim guffawed. "Morrow with knobs on!" he said, finishing her sentence for her. "Oh, really!" said Zooie, grinning with delight.

Marjory and Christine joined them in the kitchen, and they all waited for the knock on the door, which was heard a few moments later. It was loud, and made them all jump. Christine opened the door. Outside on the back porch stood three men in the uniforms of the New Zealand police, and a smartly-dressed woman they took to be a plain clothes officer. The policeman who had knocked stepped back, making way for another man they had not at first noticed. He wore a dark suit and overcoat, and looked grim.

Zooie said, in a voice that shook with excitement: "Oh my God, it's the Prime Minister!" She leant against the counter, collected herself and apologized. "I'm so sorry! It was a shock. Please do come in, gentlemen, lady . . ." The Prime Minister of New Zealand smiled at Zooie, his eyes searching the room until they rested on Marjory. "It's all right. No need to apologize," he said, his voice grave, "Am I correct in assuming that the person standing in front of me is Lady Brandston?" Marjory put her hand to her neck, guessing that she was in for a shock of much greater proportions. "I am she," she replied, "Though we don't call ourselves Lord and Lady Brandston. Something my husband Percy decided many years ago. It was supposed to help people accept him as a parliamentary candidate . . ." Her voice tailed off into silence. "Mummy?" said Elspeth, moving closer to her mother, and putting her arm around her waist.

Christine and Zooie discreetly left the room, but stayed in the hallway, with the door open a crack. The Prime Minister came into the kitchen and suggested that Marjory and her children might like to sit down. "I'm afraid I have some bad news for you, Mrs. Brandston, Tim, Elspeth," he said. He waited until they were seated and holding hands. The male police officers stood on guard outside, but the female officer came to join the group in the kitchen. She positioned herself near Marjory.

"It's Percy, isn't it?" enquired Marjory, her voice trembling, "I knew there was something wrong. I was ringing home all this morning. I had a bad feeling. The line was engaged the whole time. What's going on?" There was a long silence as the Prime Minister of New Zealand searched for the least painful way to tell the widow of the British Secretary of State for Work and Pensions that her husband had been violently killed and found in a ditch on the Brandston estate.

At length, he took off a black leather glove, reached across the table and patted Marjory's hand. "I'm afraid your husband is no longer with us," he said. Marjory turned pale. Tim and Elspeth's sharp intakes of breath carried to the listening aunts the other side of the hall door. "How? How?" said Marjory, "How did it happen?" The Prime Minister patted her hand once more, then folded his hands on the table. "I'm afraid that's not something you'll want to hear quite yet, Madam," he said, "It wasn't a natural death, you see . . ." "Tell me!" cried Marjory. Tim and Elspeth both said: "No, Mummy!" but she merely squeezed their hands and shushed them. "I want to hear," she insisted.

The Prime Minister turned to look at the woman police officer, who sat down opposite Marjory. "Mrs. Brandston, you will need to prepare yourself to hear the worst," she paused for a few seconds. Marjory took a deep breath and squared her shoulders, which were shaking. "Mrs. Brandston, your husband appears to have been killed."

In the half hour that followed, Marjory pressed her visitors for more and more detail of her husband's final hours. The police officers used their mobile phones to get the latest updates, and delivered to the widow and her son and daughter the terrible news that Percy Brandston had been bitten to death and found lying on his back by security men on the south side of the estate in the middle of the night. "Bitten? Bitten to death? How is that possible?!" exclaimed Marjory, "Was it an escaped zoo animal?"

One of the officers—a Commissioner, from his pips—who had just been updated by phone, answered her: "That's proving to be something of a puzzle, Madam. There have been no reports of escaped zoo animals, or stray dogs. Your husband's dog Roger is missing, but it seems the bites are smaller than dog size anyway. They've ruled out the gamekeeper's ferrets. Apparently, the wounds . . . I'm so sorry, Madam . . . the wounds contain no detectable DNA, and don't match the bite pattern of any known animal. The lab is saying they follow mostly closely that of a very small human, but that they're way too small for even the smallest child to have inflicted them. And . . ." he paused, seeing tears come coursing down Marjory's cheeks. "Go on!" she insisted, thumping her fist on the table. Elspeth grabbed hold of the fist and held it in her two hands, her knuckles white with tension. "Your husband appears to have wounded one or more of his assailants. There is blood on a log nearby, and on a piece of cloth found in a holly bush at the scene, and it is not his. Apparently, it's causing the lab the same kind of problems as the bite signatures. No detectable DNA. Not human, not animal . . ."

"But that's impossible!" blurted out Tim, rising from the table and going to get glasses of water for everyone. He desperately wanted to help, and it was all he could think of doing. Elspeth looked across at the woman detective. "Detective . . ." she began, then stopped. "I'm Detective Inspector Newry, but please call me Jill," she said. "Jill," said Elspeth, smiling faintly, "What happens next? I mean, we need to get back, don't we? As soon as possible?"

Jill Newry looked to the Prime Minister for an answer to that question. He rose from his chair and shook hands with all three Brandstons. "No need to even think about that at present," he reassured them, "You're best off here, I believe. You have your family around you, and you're a long way away from the Press and all the hoo-ha. Give it a couple of days to let the news sink in. Maybe think about how you would like to mark Mr. Brandston's passing. If necessary, we can pass on your instructions to the appropriate people. I must say, you're handling yourselves very well, but maybe the news hasn't really sunk in. Be prepared for all kinds of reactions from yourselves, and from each other. Don't let anything alarm you. I'm personally taking care of everything, and I won't stop until the last 't' is crossed." Jill Newry nodded, and added: "There'll be a discreet police presence outside the cottage. I'll leave you my number. I'll stay on now if you want me to, but I imagine you'd prefer to be by yourselves. I'll be on-call at Greytown police station, and if you need me, I can be here in five minutes. Is that OK?"

Marjory looked up from where her startled gaze rested on the hand of her daughter, which was still gripping hers tightly. "Thank you," she said, "Prime Minister. Officers. On behalf of the family, thank you. Today is Monday. We need to be in England by Friday. I don't care about the Press. We'll stay in the house and keep the TV and radio off. We'll stay away from the internet, all of us. I need to see Percy and I know the children will too." "Understood," said Inspector Newry, getting up, "You'll be on a private chartered flight and we'll pick you up on the day. Transport will be arranged at the other end. Goodbye, then. Please, don't hesitate to get in touch, even if it's just for groceries, to save you having to leave the cottage." Marjory was silent. "Thank you," said Tim, "Elspeth and I and our aunts will take care of Mummy. We appreciate the trouble you've gone to . . ." "No trouble," said the Prime Minister, his hand on the kitchen door, "We're all so very sorry." And he was gone.

As the door closed, Christine and Zooie came into the kitchen. "I'll put the kettle on," said Zooie. Elspeth's phone rang. She picked it up automatically and answered, her face blank. "Oh, Humphrey. Hello," she said, "Yes. Visitors, yes. Bad news. Can't talk now. No, don't come round. I'll come round to you later. Yes, *we're* OK. No, there's nothing you can do, but thanks. Got to go, bye." She ended the call and sat, looking at the phone. "I'll go round, Peth," said Tim. "I'll go now. There might be media people here in a bit." Elspeth looked at her brother with such love, it went straight to his heart. "OK," she said, "I trust your judgment."

Humphrey and Richie were shocked to hear Tim's news. They sat him down and asked if there was anything they could do. "Yes," said Tim straight away, "Go on the internet and tell me what they're saying in England. I need to prepare Mummy and Elspeth for how they're talking about Father. I suspect there may be . . . mixed reviews." "Good call. No worries," agreed Richie, going over to his desktop, "No politician's ever had completely rave reviews. Let's see what the media are cooking up . . ."

Chapter Forty-Seven

CELEBRATIONS

"Well, that was a great breakfast!" said Archie, leaning back against his pillows and loosening the cord of the hotel bath-robe in fluffy, white towelling which was the only thing he was wearing. "Ouf, yes!" agreed Ann-Marie, doing exactly the same. Somehow they had both been absolutely ravenous, and had consumed the fruit juice, cereal, cooked breakfast, toast and even the yoghurts and pastries. Now they could barely move.

Archie peered across at his wife of one year and twenty-four hours. He reached for his glasses and perched them on his nose: "All the better to see you with, my dear!" he said in the best imitation of a fairy-tale wolf he could manage, "You look good enough to eat!" Ann-Marie giggled and wriggled sideways until their shoulders were touching. "If I could move, I'd go over there and put the TV on," she said, yawning. Archie waved the remote control at her: "No need, my little wifey!" he said, and pressed the 'on' button. The screen sprang to life.

The couple had agreed they would stay in all day and recharge their batteries. Their legs were still aching from the previous day, when they had hardly sat down for a minute. The gnomes had sent them off on what they reckoned was their sixth assignment, and it had—as it so often did—involved tramping through mud to deliver a message.

"So, what's on the menu?" asked Ann-Marie. She caught the twinkle in her husband's eye and blushingly added, "I mean, on TV." Archie scrolled down, rejecting the soap operas, the talk shows, the endlessly-repeated comedies and old films. "Hang on a minute!" said

Archie, struggling to sit up. "What is it?" said Ann-Marie, putting on her own glasses. "There's a programme about that chap. You know . . . That one we . . ." Ann-Marie put a finger to her lips: "Say no more," she whispered, as if the room was bugged or someone was listening at the door. Archie found the channel he wanted. The programme was just about to begin.

Archie and Ann-Marie pulled the quilt over themselves and settled down to watch. The title came up: "Lord Percy Brandston: A Tribute to a Quiet Man". "I don't suppose he managed to keep very quiet when the gnomes got him," whispered Archie to his wife, "It must have been pretty bad . . ." "Best not to think about it, eh, love?" she whispered back, "And anyway, people die every day in all kinds of horrible ways, like that neighbour of yours who was there before Enid, the old man who died of hypothermia. I'm sorry to say, that kind of death bothers me a lot more. Oh, look! It's his wife Marjory. Doesn't she look lovely? And that's her daughter Elspeth. I recognize her from a magazine article. She's in the antiques business. I think that's her husband next to her. Humphrey, I think. He's in volcano conservation. They live in New Zealand."

The feature began with introductions to the family members, and brief interviews with each one. Archie was surprised to find he rather warmed to them: the son Tim in particular. He listened carefully: "Well, I was never really that successful in England," Tim was saying, reddening and looking down at his shoes. The interviewer, a famous royal correspondent, asked Tim how things were going for him in New Zealand. "Oh! He moved there too, did he?" said Ann-Marie, "I didn't know that . . ."

Tim described how he had set up his business in Auckland and how, "because of my brother-in-law's influence"—here he turned to smile at Humphrey Barton, the man who had married his sister—he had got into building websites for green companies and conservation charities. "People who are trying to save the planet—if I may put it that way—want to be out and about as much as they can. So I come along with my two colleagues and do all the digital stuff for them," he explained, "And we train them how to do online campaigns if they get stuck. Some of them have managed to get the areas they're working in—like the volcanic cones for instance—declared official heritage sites, which really helps. I love my work. It's good to feel useful."

"What a nice young man!" said Ann-Marie, "Now for Lady Marjory. I don't know that much about her, except that she was in New Zealand when her late husband died, visiting her sister, or something. She seems very serene." The camera pulled back to show Lady Marjory Brandston walking in the topiary garden of her estate. Beside her walked a very famous person indeed. "Oh, that's the Prince of Wales!" exclaimed Ann-Marie, "Now that doesn't surprise me a bit. He loves his gardens—everyone knows that. I've seen his website, and the photos are stunning. And all his gardens, and his farms, are pesticide-free and organic. People used to think he was a bit OTT, but now they're all listening. Typical."

Lady Marjory was interviewed side by side with His Royal Highness, and it was he who explained why this was such a special day for the Brandston estate: "For hundreds of years this was a private estate," he said, smiling into the camera, his blue eyes twinkling, "But from today the family are opening it to the nation. Lady Marjory and her family have been working hard to turn the whole estate into a conservation area, and I think it's splendid!"

"Well, I never!" breathed Ann-Marie, "What a marvellous thing to do!" The programme continued with a tour of the various areas of the estate: the topiary garden, which had been filled with medicinal plants, the vegetable garden, where a young gardener showed the interviewer all the unusual types of salad crops he was trying out, as well as some colourful ornamental cabbages and squashes, and the meadow, part of which had been planted with fruit trees: native species in danger of extinction.

"Mr. Andrew Billett recently won an award for his work on the estate," the interviewer told the audience, "And has been instrumental in setting up an exchange scheme, whereby young conservation volunteers from New Zealand spend two months living here at

the Manor, while local youngsters get to spend two months at the
Volcano Cone Restoration Village near Auckland. That's correct, isn't
it, Andrew?" The young gardener grinned: "Yes, that's right, Peter.
I can't begin to tell you how fantastic Lady Marjory has been. She's
even started ripping up tarmac for a bird rescue centre. We often get
birds flying into the windows here, but we've run out of space in the
kitchen . . ." "Yes, well, thank you Andrew," said the correspondent,
beating a hasty retreat, put off—no doubt—by the gardener's
passionate style of delivery.

He turned his attention to a cluster of people who were standing
in one corner of the meadow. It looked to Ann-Marie and Archie as
though a statue was about to be unveiled. Seating had been set up,
and there were lots of women in big hats and men in suits taking
their places. The Prince of Wales was sharing a small podium with
Lady Marjory, and camera people were adjusting lamps and reflectors.
The correspondent explained: "So now we move on to the big event
of the day: the unveiling of the statue of Lord Percy Brandston. This
is without doubt a very emotional moment for the family of the late
Lord Percy, especially in view of the terrible circumstances surrounding
his death in the spring of last year."

The camera zoomed in on the faces of the guests, and Archie and
his wife recognized some famous faces. "That's the Prime Minister
of New Zealand," said Archie, "I saw him on the news, arriving at
Heathrow. And that's Monty Don, the gardener. Oh, and there's the
Duchess of Cornwall, talking to Humphrey. Is that his brother next to
him? He looks a lot like him."

There was a discreet cough from the podium, where Prince
Charles was standing at ease, his hands behind his back. Lady Marjory
had put on a gorgeous broad-brimmed natural straw hat with little
green flowers and a pale green half-veil. She looked stunning. "Good
afternoon, everyone, and welcome to Brandston, on behalf of myself,
and the Brandston family," said the Prince of Wales. A butterfly—a
peacock by the look of it—flew across and settled on his lapel.
He smiled: "As you can see, we have some important guests here!"

Everyone laughed at his joke. "Isn't this a lovely occasion?" whispered Ann-Marie. "I must say I'm really enjoying this," replied Archie, snuggling closer to her, "Even though there's a western on the other side!" Ann-Marie smiled across at her husband and gave his cheek a gentle pinch. "You and your westerns!" she said fondly.

The Prince of Wales went on to commend the work done on the estate over the past year, and Andrew Billett's youth conservation exchange programme, remarking on how important it was for young people to take their environmental responsibilities more seriously than previous generations had done. Then, Lady Marjory stepped up to the microphone and paid tribute to her late husband, citing his work in politics and his family values. At last it was time for the statue to shed its covering of white silk and to be revealed to the watching world.

It was the Duchess of Cornwall, dressed in a suit of shell pink, her royal husband at her elbow, who pulled the cord that removed the three layers of silk, which came rippling down in the summer breeze, one by one. A camera homed in on the work of art, and Archie and Ann-Marie gasped. There stood Percy Brandston in white marble, depicted as the family wished to remember him, in plus-fours and a flat cap, cigar in one hand and riding-crop in the other. A dog had been placed at his side. "Roger!" exclaimed Archie, "Do you remember that picture of him in the paper? The dog that never came home? But he's there, look! I mean, in real life! That's got to be him, sitting beside that young gardener . . ." Ann-Marie peered at the TV screen. A black Labrador, with the glossiest coat she had ever seen on a dog, sat beside Andrew Billett, who was standing to one side, not far from the statue. The dog was grinning, as if in amusement, and looking up at the marble dog, which was—it was now plain to see—himself in every detail. "Well, I never!" said Archie, "It's great to know he's safe and sound, isn't it?"

But it wasn't the statue of the man that had made the couple gasp, or even the statue of Roger: it was something else. The statue was over seven feet tall, but it rested on an ornate, square plinth that raised it to a height of over twenty feet. There were the usual scrolls and oak leaves, a pattern of diamonds and spirals, and the family coat-of-arms, as well as the Brandston family motto: *familia fortis vocat.* "I think that means something like, 'the family calls you to be strong'," Ann-Marie translated for Archie's benefit. But there was something else: something nobody had expected. For on each side of the plinth, half way up, there was a jutting semi-circular shelf of black marble. And on each of the shelves visible to the camera stood a small figure: the figure of a garden gnome, leaning forward, a spear in one clenched fist and something else in the other that the camera could not quite pick out.

"What is that in his hand? Can you see?" Ann-Marie asked her husband. "No, but I can look it up online on your iPad," he said, reaching out for the iPad and switching it on. "I'll search 'Percy Brandston statue' and see what it says," he told her, flicking a finger across the screen. "It's bound to be on the web already—they're so quick these days . . ." A minute later, Archie found what he was looking for and laughed out loud. "You'll want to see this," he said, passing the iPad to Ann-Marie, who gazed at the images and writing on the screen. There, sure enough, were pictures of the statue, with a description. She scrolled down: more pictures, this time shots showing details. "I can see what it is!" she exclaimed, beginning to laugh, along with her husband, "What a peculiar choice! It looks as though someone with inside knowledge has had a hand in designing the statue, doesn't it?"

Archie got up from the bed. "Coffee?" he asked, picking up the breakfast cups to rinse them out at the sink. "Yes, please!" said Ann-Marie, peering again at the small screen in front of her face. She was looking at a perfect representation of Derwin Yew. And in his left hand he held—not a weapon, or a spade, or a fishing-rod, or any kind of useful tool a person might reasonably have expected to see in the hand of a garden gnome. What Derwin Yew held in his hand was none other than a smoking pipe. "How strange," said Ann-Marie, "Derwin with his pipe, and Percy Brandston with his cigar . . . Who would have thought they had anything in common? Perhaps they could have sat down after all, if things had turned out differently, and smoked a peace pipe together?"

Archie switched on the kettle, and began to tear open small packets of instant coffee and sugar. "That, my darling," he said, "We shall never know. Now, let's forget about all that now. Let's just drink our coffee and talk about where you'd like to go tomorrow. Norman insisted on giving me some of his gold this time, even though we're not on one of his errands, and he says I'd better not try giving any of it back, unless I want extra lessons all next week." Ann-Marie hooted with laughter: "And he means it!" she said, "Though, with the hours you've put in, I'm surprised you haven't got a PhD in Gnomology yet!"

Chapter Forty-Eight

DINNER AND A SURPRISE

Somehow, looking at brochures for heritage sites and places of outstanding natural beauty in the County of Gloucestershire, where Ann-Marie and Archie were holidaying to celebrate their wedding anniversary, made them feel very sleepy, and it was almost dinner-time when they accidentally bumped their heads together and woke up. They showered and dressed in the clothes they had worn at their wedding.

Ann-Marie took Archie's arm to descend the four steps down from the foyer to the hotel restaurant. "Are you all right, darling?" he asked, for she was leaning on him more heavily than usual. "Oh, just a twinge of arthritis," she said quietly, "Must be all that digging I've been doing." Archie frowned: "From now on, no more digging then. I'll have a word with the lads." Ann-Marie shook her head, but Archie insisted: "No, it's only right. Anyway, you've been talking about writing a book, and I'm all for that."

The staff were particularly attentive towards the couple during dinner, and the restaurant manager came to their table as they were finishing their tiramisu. "I hope you don't mind my having a word," he said, leaning over their table in a confidential whisper. Archie looked worried: "There isn't anything wrong, is there?" he asked. "Oh, no! Nothing wrong at all!" said the manager, whose lapel badge read 'Dev Dipak', "I apologise if I alarmed you, Sir!" "It's all right," said Archie, breathing out, "What can we do for you Mr. Dipak?" "Well," said the manager, "A person came into the hotel earlier and asked to see me. A person coming with a message from a very important person. A *very important person* . . . A person whose name I would be overjoyed to share with you, but I have been sworn to secrecy." Ann-Marie and Archie's eyes opened wide as they listened. This was unexpected. It couldn't be the police, or MI5, because the manager wouldn't be rubbing his hands together and looking so pleased if it was.

"Would you like to sit down for a second?" asked Ann-Marie, pulling out the chair next to her, "Only, the other guests are looking this way." "If you would be so kind as to allow . . ." said Mr. Dipak, and he sat down. He waved their waiter over. "Perhaps a cup of tea?" he suggested. "Good idea!" said Archie, anxious to hear what the manager had to say. "Tea for two!" Mr. Dipak instructed the waiter, who had been moving closer, and trying to hear what was being said. The waiter looked disappointed, but disappeared off to fetch their order.

"Now for your nice surprise!" said the manager, trying to contain his excitement by unfolding and refolding a spare napkin. "This is a very special message, with an invitation. May I take it you have nothing booked in the way of excursions tomorrow?" Archie and Ann-Marie nodded furiously. It had been their intention to visit Highgrove House, where they were both anxious to see for themselves the beautiful garden created by His Royal Highness the Prince of Wales and his team of gardeners, but that could be put off till another day. This time, they had given themselves five days of holiday.

"So, what's this about a very important person and an invitation?" asked Ann-Marie, seeing that Mr. Dipak was now carefully refolding the napkin into an impressive lotus flower. "Yes! I am spinning out this moment!" said he, pushing the napkin away from him and admiring it for a few seconds, "It is not often that we get a visit from a royal person's . . . Oops! Now I am in danger of giving the game away!" Archie and Ann-Marie did a double-take. "Royal person?" said Archie, but his wife put a hand on his arm. "He said he can't tell us, darling," she pointed out. Mr. Dipak breathed an audible sigh of relief. "I am going to give you details," he said, excitement in his voice, "Let me cut to the chase. Tomorrow morning, your breakfast will be brought to you early—at seven o'clock precisely. At eight o'clock, all being well, you will come to Reception, where you will depart via my personal exit into a waiting limousine. This limousine will take you to the famous house of this royal person . . ."

Ann-Marie squeaked: "Famous house? No, don't say it! I'm already having a hot flush . . ." "How come we've had an invitation?" was what was going through her mind. Archie was beaming, and fiddling with his own napkin at the same time. "No, no," said the manager, "No kidding. You will spend the morning taking the champagne tour as special guests, escorted by the Head Gardener, after which you will meet the . . . owner . . . and take tea. The limousine will pick you up at four p.m. precisely and bring you back to the hotel."

It was not unusual for Archie to be struck dumb, for the sight of Ann-Marie did that to him more frequently than he cared to admit, but this time he did not speak until he was undressing for bed, two hours later. "Well!" he exclaimed, "Well!" "Are you feeling all right, dearest?" asked Ann-Marie, who had been ironing her black and white tea dress and Archie's white shirt, and polishing her and Archie's dress shoes. They had been instructed to bring walking shoes with them for the garden tour. Archie said "Well!" three more times as he pulled off his socks. They both set the alarms on their mobile phones for six a.m., and rang down to Reception for a wake-up call at six-thirty, in case they went back to sleep. Nothing more was said that night, apart from their usual "Good night!" and "I love you!" They lay in the darkness, holding hands. It was quite a while before they managed to fall asleep.

Chapter Forty-Nine

GNOME SWEET GNOME

Lady Marjory Brandston held her first grand-child in her arms, and her joy was complete. Little Tui Barton, three months old, gazed up at her grandmother and reached up with her fingers outspread, trying to touch her face. Marjory's cheeks glowed pink with health, not unlike the Worcester Pearmain apples her trees were now yielding by the bucketful.

Tui had been named after the birds her mother, Elspeth, had admired in the garden of the restaurant in Wellington where she, her mother, and her brother Tim had shared their first meal in New Zealand. That day now seemed a lifetime ago to all three of them. Elspeth's husband Humphrey, who came home to their house in the suburbs of Auckland as often as the Volcanic Cone Restoration Project could spare him, called Marjory 'Granny Brandston', which amused her. He said the name sounded like a type of apple.

Elspeth and Humphrey had travelled over from New Zealand to spend a few weeks at Brandston, with Marjory—and the volunteers who seemed to have taken over most of the guest-rooms. There was now no corner of the Manor House that was not being put to good use. To the delight of 'Granny Brandston', it was Tim and his new girl-friend Heni who had taken over supervising the restoration project's office at the New Zealand end. Humphrey had been quick to introduce the indomitable Heni to Tim, when she had joined his team as Public Relations Officer. She was every bit as keen on computers as Tim was, but her love of Nature and the outdoors guaranteed he didn't spend all his time, either in front of a screen or driving. He was currently learning how to water-ski and climb mountains.

Andrew Billett was Marjory's right-hand man, and they met regularly on Monday mornings to plan the week's outdoor tasks. Marjory's job—which she had taken on voluntarily—was the care of the glasshouses, including the Old Glasshouse, where she and Andrew often sat over a cup of tea. Whether they were joined there by certain small people is unknown, for with the opening of the estate to the public, the number of visitors had increased dramatically and discretion, as well as caution, had become even more necessary than before. And so, if there were tea-parties held there in the afternoons, or celebrations accompanied by birch wine late at night by the light of the moon, Lady Marjory and Andrew kept it to themselves.

Roger the Labrador became a living icon among the visitors to the estate. His grinning face adorned several postcards and souvenirs in the gift shop, where his miniature stood side by side on the shelf with effigies of the memorial statue's four gnomes. Roger lived to sire several dozen pups, all of them with particularly sharp noses, and a way of growling at visitors to the garden who threw down their litter or tried to stub out a cigarette on a garden bench. Andrew Billett was often asked what was the secret of keeping the dog's coat so glossy and his nose so moist, but he would laugh and say: "Rabbit stew!" which no-one took seriously.

Archie and Ann-Marie returned from their holiday in Gloucestershire with exciting news to share with their gnome friends, and as soon as the front door of their flat was locked behind them, Archie went out onto the balcony and whistled: a secret whistle taught him by Ned, resembling the call of the Eastern screech owl, which most people would—he assured him—mistake for a telephone ringing in the distance. Ten minutes later, the gnomes, of whom there were now thirty-three, appeared on the sofa. Ann-Marie and Archie just had time to freshen up and to set down the tray of tiny cups of fresh apple juice and plate of mini digestive biscuits of which the gnomes were so fond, before their visitors arrived. The cups had been a lucky find online, and had been shipped from China.

"Archie and Ann-Marie Prescott of Brummagem, Friends of Gnomes, have adventures to tell!" said Syd Willow, hopping off the sofa and onto the armchair, where he sat next to Ann-Marie, while Archie perched on the arm, the other side of her. Ann-Marie reached over for a cup of apple juice and a biscuit for Syd. "Welcome home!" boomed Raphael Oak, one of the new arrivals, whom Norman and Alevin were finding a little hard to take. He was a hundred years older than either of them, and had a problem with accepting that the Eden and Paradise Band was a strict democracy.

"Thank you!" said Archie, and proceeded to tell them about the wonderful holiday they had had in Gloucestershire, and to thank them for the five days away. He was just about to surprise them with the tale of their visit to the house and garden of the royal person when the gnomes began to nudge each other. Ann-Marie noticed, but Archie seemed too caught up in his narrative. He began to describe how the hotel manager had broken to them the news of their surprise excursion. When he got to the part of the story where they were met at the back gates of the estate by the Head Gardener, Cholmondeley and Hugo began to giggle. They were quickly hushed by Sigmund and Sigfrid, who had placed themselves on either side of the Birch brothers, to keep them in order. But Ann-Marie narrowed her eyes at them, and said: "Somehow, Archie, I don't think this comes as a surprise to our friends here . . ."

She asked Alevin, who was sipping his apple juice, an innocent look on his face that did not deceive her for a moment: "Brother Alevin, tell us: did you know about this?" Alevin nodded. When he spoke, he sounded so much like Archie, that she smiled. Not only were she and her husband sounding more like gnomes these days, so that at times people gave them funny looks. It was two-way traffic, it seemed. "It was Nick and Ned who cooked it up between them," said the ancient gnome, pulling on his beard as usual, "You'd better ask them."

Ned Blackthorn smiled, showing all his sharp teeth, which made Ann-Marie shudder slightly. "You will remember that I mentioned a certain royal personage with whom I have been acquainted for some years, and with whom—if I may say this without being accused of boasting—I have a special relationship?" "Yes, yes!" said Ann-Marie and Archie, turning to give each other a look which said: "Why are we not surprised they were behind it?" Ned leaned back and stared at the ceiling. "I got in touch via a brother of the Oak Clan, a certain Gabriel, whom I believe was sent as a gift to the royal personage by a man not unlike yourself, Archie—a man who thought it a pity that the royal personage was . . . well . . . gnomeless!"

Archie and Ann-Marie laughed gaily. They had seen the gnome of whom Ned was speaking, perched all by himself on the top of a rockery in the garden of the 'royal personage' three days before. Gabriel Oak was a splendid fellow, and had risked a small bow to them as they had passed. They had bowed back, much to the amusement of a little girl who had run past them just at that moment. "Are you bowing to that gnome?" she'd asked them, flicking her long plaits over her shoulders. They had admitted that they had. "Me too!" said the little girl, "I always bow when I go past him. He's real, you know?" The little girl had run to the end of the path, where an elderly man was sitting on a bench, soaking up the sun. "Grandad! Grandad!" she'd shouted as she had jumped up onto the bench beside him, "Those nice people know about gnomes too!" The old man had smiled at them as they had passed him by, but said nothing. There was nothing that needed to be said.

Archie related the incident to the gnomes, who looked pleased. "We will leave you shortly," said Norman, "But we are one with you." "And we with you!" replied Archie and Ann-Marie, standing up and bowing. "Before I go, I have one last thing to say to you," said Norman, "You can expect many more such occasions. Matters concerning gnomes and humans are moving forward at a great pace. And I have hope." "There is always hope!" the couple responded, following the Gnomish tradition. "Yes," said Norman, nodding, "Let us say this: in England, and in other countries too, garden gnomes are . . . *enjoying something of a revival.*"

There was a moment, something like a blurring of images, and the gnomes were gone. Archie turned to Ann-Marie and smiled: "Shall I put the kettle on?" he said.

THE END

Lightning Source UK Ltd.
Milton Keynes UK
UKOW03f0625200614

233768UK00001B/113/P

THE GREAT AND
THE SMALL

To Stuart,
best wishes,

Ian ☺